TWO
LOVELY
BEASTS

and Other Stories

TWO LOVELY BEASTS

And Other Stories by
LIAM O'FLAHERTY

With Illustrations by JOHN H. DE POL

THE DEVIN-ADAIR COMPANY · NEW YORK · 1950

50-8649

Table of Contents

TWO
LOVELY
BEASTS

and Other Stories

Two Lovely Beasts

HE DERRANES were having breakfast when a neighbour called Kate Higgins came running into their kitchen. She squatted on the floor by the wall to the right of the door, threw her apron over her face and began to wail at the top of her voice in most heartrending fashion.

"God between us and harm!" said Mrs. Derrane as she came over from the table. "What happened to you?"

She put an arm about the shoulders of the wailing neighbour and added tenderly:

"Tell us what happened, so that we can share your sorrow."

Colm Derrane came over with his mouth full of food. He had a mug of tea in his hand. The six children followed him. They all stood in a half-circle about Kate Higgins, who continued to wail incontinently.

"Speak up, in God's name," Colm said, after swallowing what he had been munching. "Speak to us so that we can help you, woman."

It was some time before Kate desisted from her lamentation. Then she suddenly removed her apron from before her face and looked fiercely at Colm through wild blue eyes that showed no sign of tears. She was a skinny little woman, with a pale face that was deeply lined with worry. Her husband had died a few months previously, leaving her with a large family that she was struggling to rear on next to nothing.

"Will you buy a calf?" she said to Colm in an angry tone.

"A calf?" said Colm in surprise. "I didn't know your cow had . . ."

"She dropped it a little while ago," the woman interrupted. "Then she died herself. Lord save us, she lay down and stretched herself out flat on the grass and shook her legs and that was all there was to it. She's as dead as a door-nail. There isn't a spark left in her. It must have been poison that she dragged up out of the ground with her teeth, while she was mad with the calf sickness."

The whole Derrane family received this news in open-mouthed silence. It was a calamity that affected every household in the village. Each family had but a single cow. By traditional law, those who had milk were bound to share with those who had none. So that the death of one cow, no matter to whom she belonged, was a calamity that affected all.

"Bloody woe!" Colm said at length. "Bloody mortal woe! That's a terrible blow, and you after losing your husband only the other day. There you are now with a house full of weak children and no cow. Ah! Bloody woe!"

"No use talking, Colm," Kate Higgins said fiercely. "Buy the calf from me. I'm asking you to do it for the love of God. He must get suck quickly or else he'll die of hunger. He'll stretch out there on the grass beside his mother and die, unless he gets suck. Buy him from me."

Colm and his wife looked at one another in perplexity. Their faces were racked with pity for their neighbour.

4

"Bloody woe!" Colm kept muttering under his breath.

There was no sign of pity in the faces of the children. They moved back to the table slowly after a few moments of open-mouthed consternation. They kept glancing over their shoulders at Kate Higgins with aversion. They hated her, now that they understood her calamity threatened to diminish their milk supply.

"I'm asking you for the love of God," Kate Higgins continued in a tone that had become quite savage. "The price will help me buy a new cow. I must have a cow for the children. The doctor said they must have plenty of milk, the two youngest of them especially. They are ailing, the poor creatures. Your cow has a fine udder, God bless her. She calved only a few days ago. She won't feel my fellow at her teats in addition to her own. She'll be well able for the two of them, God bless her. She will, 'faith and she'll leave plenty of milk for yourselves into the bargain. Praise be to God, I never saw such a fine big udder as she has."

Colm was on the point of speaking when his wife interrupted him.

"You know how it is with us," Mrs. Derrane said. "We are giving milk to three houses already. Their cows aren't due to calve for more than three weeks yet. We'll have to help you as well, now that your cow is gone. So how could we feed a second calf? It would be against the law of God and of the people. We couldn't leave neighbours without milk in order to fill a calf's belly."

Kate Higgins jumped to her feet and put her clenched fists against her lean hips.

"The calf will die unless you buy him," she cried ferociously. "There is nobody else to take him but you people. Nobody else has a cow after calving. The price would help me buy another cow. I must have a cow for the children. The doctor said . . ."

5

"That's enough, woman," Colm interrupted. "I'll put him on our cow for a couple of days. In the meantime, maybe you could get someone in another village to buy him."

Kate Higgins grew calm at once on hearing this offer. Tears came into her wild blue eyes.

"God spare your health, Colm," she said gently. "I was afraid he'd die of hunger before he could get suck. That would be the end of me altogether. I'd have nothing at all left if he died on me, stretched out on the grass beside his mother. When you have a few pounds, it's easier to borrow more than if you have none at all. God spare the two of you."

Colm went with her to the field, where they were already skinning the dead cow. He took the red bull calf in his arms to the paddock where his own cow was grazing. She consented to give the stranger suck after some persuasion.

"He's lovely, sure enough," Colm said as he looked with admiration at the wine-dark hide of the sucking calf. "I thought my own calf this year looked like a champion, but he's only in the halfpenny place compared to this one."

"He'll be a champion all right," Kate Higgins said. "He has the breed in him. Why wouldn't he? Nothing would do my husband, Lord have mercy on him, but to spend ten royal shillings for the use of the Government bull. Nothing less would satisfy him, 'faith. He wasn't much to look at, poor man, but he always liked to have the best of everything."

She suddenly rushed over to Colm and put her lips close to his ear. Now her wild blue eyes were full of cunning.

"You should buy him, Colm," she whispered. "Buy him and put him with your own calf. Then you'll have the makings of the two finest yearlings that were ever raised in this townland. You'll be the richest man in the village. You'll be talked about and envied from one end of the parish to the other."

Colm turned his back to her and took off his cap. He was

6

quite young and yet his skull had already begun to go bald along the crown. He was a big awkward fellow with pigeon toes and arms that were exceptionally long, like those of an ape. He was noted in the district for his strength, his immense energy and his eagerness for work.

"Arrah! How could I buy him from you?" he said in a low voice. "How could I feed him and so many people depending on the milk?"

Then he turned towards her suddenly and raised his voice to a shout, as if he were arguing with some wild thought in his own mind.

"I have only twenty acres of land," he cried angrily. "The whole of it is practically barren. You wouldn't find more than a few inches of soil in the deepest part of it. You wouldn't find a foot of ground in all I possess where you could bury a spade to the haft. Bloody woe! Woman, I tell you that I haven't one good single half-acre. There is hardly enough grass for my cow, not to mention my unfortunate horse. You could count the bones right through my poor horse's hide. I'm hard put every year to find grass for my yearling. Woman alive, sure there isn't a man in this village that could feed two yearlings. It would be madness for me to try it."

"The English have started fighting the Germans a second time," Kate Higgins whispered. "They won't stop until they have dragged the whole world again into the war with them. The fight will last for years and years, same as it did before. There will be a big price for everything fit to eat. A man that would have two lovely beasts for sale . . ."

"Stop tempting me with your foolish talk, woman," Colm interrupted.

"Your cow could easily feed the two calves," Kate continued. "She could do it without any bother at all. She'd have plenty, besides, for yourselves and the neighbours. You needn't worry about grass, either. There's always plenty of

7

grass for rent in the village of Pusach. You'll have plenty of money to spare for buying any extra grass you'll need, because there is going to be a great price for potatoes and fish. Man alive, there will be lashings of money, same as before. During the other big war, you remember, they were even buying rotten dog-fish. I declare to my God they were. They paid famine prices for the rotten dog-fish that the storms threw up on the beach beyond there."

Colm turned away from her again and lowered his voice to a whisper.

"It would be madness for me to try it," he said. "Nobody ever tried to raise two yearlings in this village. We all have the same amount of rocky land, twenty acres a head."

"You're different from everbody else, Colm," Kate said, raising her voice and speaking very rapidly. "The others only do what they have to do. They do barely enough to keep themselves and their families alive. You go out of your way looking for work. You never turn aside from an opportunity to earn an extra shilling. You are at it night and day, whenever you get the chance. The spunk is in you. There is no end to your strength. Oh! Indeed, it's well known that there is no holding you, when there is a job of work to be done. You spit on your hands and away you go like a wild stallion. God bless you, there is the strength of ten men in your body and you're not afraid to use it. You deserve to prosper on account of your willingness. You deserve to be rich and famous. All you need is courage."

"Nobody ever tried it," Colm whispered hoarsely. "Nobody ever did. It would be madness to try it."

Kate Higgins stepped back from him and threw out her arms in a dramatic gesture.

"Let you be the first, then," she shouted. "There's nothing stopping you but a want of courage. Let you be the first. Let you show them how to do it, Colm."

8

Colm also raised his voice to a shout as he answered her fiercely.

"Stop your foolish talk, woman," he said. "He can suck on my cow for a couple of days, but I promise you no more."

Kate walked away from him hurriedly, gesticulating with both arms.

"Two lovely beasts!" she shouted back at him, when she was at a distance. "Think of that now. There's nothing standing in your way but a want of courage."

"Not another word out of you now," Colm shouted after her at the top of his voice. "What you're saying is against the law of God."

Even so, he could hardly sleep a wink that night through thinking of what the woman had said. In the morning he broached the idea of buying the calf during conversation with his wife.

"That's a lovely calf Kate Higgins has," he said. "It's a pity we can't buy it."

"Buy it?" said his wife. "Yerrah! How could we do that?"

"There is going to be a great price for beasts on account of the war," Colm continued. "With the Englsh and the Germans at it again . . ."

"Have sense, man," his wife said. "Unless you've taken leave of your gumption, you know well it's impossible for us to buy that calf. Not even if we had grass for it, which we haven't."

"All the same," Colm said, "that young fellow makes my mouth water. I never saw such a young champion."

"Yerrah! How could we leave the neighbours without milk?" his wife said.

"I'm only talking, that's all," Colm said. "There is no harm in talk."

"Well! Say no more about it," his wife said. "People might hear you and be scandalised."

9

"You never saw such a colour as that calf has," Colm said as he went out of the house. "He's so red that he's almost black."

Kate Higgins came to him again that day, while he was smashing rocks with a sledge-hammer in the corner of a little field that he was trying to make arable. She began to pester him once more with the idea of having "two lovely beasts." He threw down the sledge-hammer and ran over to the fence against which she leant.

"Why don't you leave me alone?" he shouted at her. "Go to some other village and find a buyer for him."

"I've enquired everywhere," Kate Higgins said. "It's no use, Colm. Unless you buy him, I'll have to give him to the butcher at Kilmacalla. The few shillings that I'll get for his flesh and his hide won't be much. However, they'll be better than nothing."

"I promised to let him suck for a couple of days," Colm shouted. "I can promise you no more. I can't let the neighbours go without the milk that is due to them."

"It will be a mortal sin to slaughter such a lovely young fellow," Kate said as she walked away hurriedly. "What else can I do, though? I must get a pound or two, by hook or by crook. Then I can borrow more. I have to make up the price of a new cow one way or another. The doctor said that the young ones must have plenty of milk. Otherwise they'll die. So he said. He did, 'faith."

After the woman had gone, Colm went to the paddock for another look at the young bull calf that had a wine-dark hide.

"It would be a mortal sin surely to slaughter such a lovely creature," he said aloud. "He'll be every inch a champion if he lives."

Then his heart began to beat wildly as he watched the two calves cavort together with their tails in the air. He became intoxicated by the idea of possessing them both.

10

"Two lovely beasts!" he whispered.

He went for a walk to the cliff tops instead of returning to his sledge-hammer. He stood on the brink of the highest cliff and looked down into the sea.

"Two lovely beasts!" he whispered again.

Then a frenzied look came into his pale blue eyes. He took off his cap and threw it on the ground behind him.

"Sure I have the courage," he muttered fiercely.

He spread his legs, leaned forward slightly and held out his hands in front of his hips, with the palms upturned and the fingers slightly crooked. He began to tremble.

"I have plenty of courage," he muttered.

The skin on the upper part of his forehead and on top of his baldish skull looked very pale above the brick-red colour of his bony cheeks. He had a long, narrow face, thick lips and buck teeth. His short nose had a very pointed ridge. His mouse-coloured hair stuck out in ugly little bunches above his ears and at the nape of his neck. His shoes were in tatters. His frieze trousers were covered with patches of varying colours. His grey shirt was visible through the numerous holes in his blue woollen sweater.

Yet he looked splendid and even awe-inspiring, in spite of his physical ugliness and his uncouth dress, as he stood poised that way on the brink of the tall cliff above the thundering sea, leaning forward on widespread legs, with his long arms stretched out and his fingers turned slightly inwards on his open palms, trembling with a frenzy of desire.

After a while he turned away from the sea and picked up his cap. He felt very tired as he walked homewards with downcast head. His arms swung limply by his sides. He kept glancing furtively from side to side, as if he were conscious of having committed a crime up there on the cliff top and feared pursuit as a consequence. There was a hard look in his pale blue eyes.

Again that night he could not sleep. He lay on his back thinking of the "two lovely beasts" and how he wanted to possess them. The thought gave him both pleasure and pain. The pleasure was like that derived from the anticipation of venery. The pain came from his conscience.

During the morning of the following day, Kate Higgins came to him again. She was wearing her best clothes.

"I'm on my way to the butcher at Kilmacalla," she said to him.

"All right," Colm said to her. "How much do you want for the calf?"

He was so excited by the decision at which he had arrived that he consented to the price she asked without bargaining.

"Come to the house with me," he said. "I'll hand over the money to you."

"God spare your health," Kate Higgins said. "With that money I can begin at once to look for another cow. When you have a few pounds you can always borrow more."

Mrs. Derrane got very angry when her husband came into the kitchen with Kate Higgins and asked her for the family purse.

"Is it to buy that calf?" she said.

"Hand me the purse," Colm repeated.

"Devil a bit of me," his wife said. "It would be against the law of God to put the people's milk into a calf's heathen belly. I won't give it to you."

Colm gripped the front of her bodice with his left hand and shook her.

"Hand it over, woman," he said in a low voice.

Her anger passed at once. She was a big, muscular woman, almost as strong as her husband and possessed of a stern will. Indeed, she had dominated Colm's simple nature ever since their marriage until now. Whenever he tried to rebel against her decisions, he had always been easily defeated. He had shouted, broken articles of furniture and even struck her cruel blows from time to time. She had always merely waited with folded arms and set jaws until his foolish anger had spent itself. Now it was different. He did not shout and she saw something in his pale blue eyes that frightened her.

So that she went quickly to the great chest and brought him the long cloth purse.

"What's come over you?" she said to him while he was undoing the string. "What are the neighbours going to say about this?"

Colm unrolled the purse and thrust his hand deep down into the long inner pocket. He again looked his wife straight in the eyes.

"Shut up, woman," he said quietly. "From now on don't meddle with things that don't concern you. I'm master in this house. Do you hear?"

Again she became frightened by what she saw in his eyes. She turned away from him.

"May God forgive you," she said. "I hope you have thought well about this before doing it."

"I've never in my life thought more about anything," Colm said.

Kate Higgins never uttered one word of thanks when she was given the money. She stuffed the notes into the front pocket of her skirt and rushed from the house.

"I'll go now," she cried as she hurried down the yard, "to try and get company for these few pounds. When you have money, it's always easier to borrow more. Those that have give only to those that have. To those that have not only crumbs are given, same as to a dog."

When Colm went that evening to the meeting place on the brow of the little hill that faced the village, silence fell among the men that were assembled there. He threw himself on the ground, put his back to a rock and lit his pipe.

13

The others began to discuss the weather in subdued tones after a little while. Then again there was silence.

At length a man named Andy Gorum turned to Colm and said:

"We heard you bought the calf from Kate Higgins."

"I did," said Colm.

"Is it to slaughter him you bought him?" Gorum said.

"No," said Colm.

"Do you intend to rear him?" Gorum said.

"I do," said Colm.

Gorum got to his feet slowly and clasped his hands behind the small of his back. He came over and stood in front of Colm. He was an elderly man, very small and thin, with a wrinkled face that was the colour of old parchment. His eyes were weak and they had hardly any lashes, like those of a man blind from birth. He was the village leader because of his wisdom.

"I'm sorry you are doing this, Colm," he said. "You are a good man and everybody belonging to you was good, away back through the generations. This is a bad thing you intend to do, though."

"How could it be bad to help a widow?" Colm said.

"You know well it won't help a widow if you rear that calf on the people's milk," Gorum said.

"She begged me and begged me," Colm said, raising his voice. "She kept at me the whole time. How could I refuse her? She said that she had to have the money for another cow. She said her children would die unless . . ."

"You know you are breaking the law," Gorum interrupted. "It's no use trying to talk yourself out of it."

"How could it be against the law to help a widow?" Colm shouted.

"Indeed, it isn't," Gorum said. "We'll all help her, please God, as much as we can. That's how we live here in our vil-

14

lage, by helping one another. Our land is poor and the sea is wild. It's hard to live. We only manage to live by sticking together. Otherwise we'd all die. It's too wild and barren here for any one man to stand alone. Whoever tries to stand alone and work only for his own profit becomes an enemy of all."

Colm jumped to his feet. He towered over Gorum.

"Are you calling me an enemy for helping a widow?" he shouted.

"If you put into a calf's belly," Gorum said, "the milk that you owe your neighbours, everybody will be against you."

"I'll do what I please," Colm shouted.

Thereupon he rushed from the meeting place.

"Come back, neighbour," Gorum called after him in a tone of entreaty.

"I have the courage to do what I think is right," Colm shouted.

"We are all fond of you," Gorum said. "We don't want to turn against you. Come back to us and be obedient to the law."

"I'll do what I think is right," Colm shouted as he crossed the stile into his yard. "I'll raise those two beasts if it's the last thing I'll do in this world. Let any man that dares try to stop me."

The Derranes became outcasts in the village from that day forward. Nobody spoke to them. Nobody gave them any help. Nobody entered their house. All other doors were closed against them.

Even Kate Higgins turned against her benefactors in most shameful fashion. Contrary to her expectations, the hapless woman was unable to borrow any more money, except for a solitary pound that she got from an aunt after lengthy importunities. Neither was she able to find any cow for sale, although she tramped the parish from end to end, over and over again. Her house went to rack and ruin during her continued absence. The ungoverned children burned the furniture to keep themselves warm. They grew so savage and filthy that the neighbour women removed their own children from all contact with them.

Unbalanced by her misfortunes, Kate forsook her peasant frugality and brought tidbits home to her starving brood after each fruitless day of wandering. The poor woman lacked courage to face them empty-handed. In that way she soon spent every penny of the money that she got from Colm and her aunt. There was none of it left after two months. When she had nothing more to give the little ones on her return, as they clutched at her apron with their filthy hands and whined pitifully for food, her mind began to get crazed.

She took to reviling Colm at the top of her voice in the roadway outside her house as she shuffled homeward with the fall of night.

"Colm Derrane is sold to the devil," she cried. "He put bad luck on me. I was grateful to him when he bought my calf, thinking he was doing me a favour and that I could borrow more, to put with what he gave me and make up the price of a new cow. Devil a bit of it. There was a curse on his money. People told me it was on account of the war they were unwilling to part with any of their share. They said they were bound to clutch all they had, for fear of disaster. The truth is that they would not lend to a woman that sold a calf to an enemy of the people. Here I am now without a red copper in my skirt, without a cow or a husband and my children ailing. They'll die on me, the poor little creatures, without the milk that the doctor ordered for them. I have no strength to care for them. I'm so tired every evening after my walking that I can't even pick the lice out of their hair. Ah! the poor little creatures! May God have pity on my orphans!"

Colm paid no more heed to this abuse than he did to the

16

hostility of the people. After his outburst of anger on being told he was to be treated as an outcast, he maintained strict control over his temper. He became dour and silent and indifferent, except when he was in the presence of the two young beasts that he loved. It was only then that he smiled and uttered words of tenderness.

"Oh! You lovely creatures!" he said to them as he watched them suck at the cow's teats. "Drink up now and be strong. Don't leave a drop of that milk in the udder. I want the two of you to be champions."

He was as ruthless towards his family as he was tender towards the calves. He only brought enough milk to colour the tea into the house. He let the calves swallow all the rest. Lest there might be any cheating, he forbade his wife and children to go near the cow under threat of dire punishment.

His wife came to him shortly after the calves were weaned and protested.

"I can go without butter," she said, "although the children tear the heart in me with their whinging. They keep asking when there is going to be some. It is too much, though, when I can't get enough buttermilk to make our bread rise. All I ask is enough milk for one churning."

"You can't have it," Colm said coldly. "I can't let the calves go in want, just for the sake of making our bread rise. We can eat it flat just as well. Calves must get a good foundation during the first few months, by having every hole and corner of their bellies well stuffed the whole time. That's how they get bone and muscle and balance and plenty of room. Then it's easy, when the time comes, to pile on the good hard meat. The foundation will be there to carry the load."

His wife kept looking at him in amazement while he spoke. She could not understand how a man, who had formerly been so kind and considerate of his family's needs, could suddenly become ruthless. She burst into tears after he had finished.

17

"God will punish you for being cruel," she said.

"Silence," said Colm. "Don't take liberties, woman."

Midsummer came. That was the season of abundance for the poor people of that village. The new potatoes were being dug. The young onions were succulent in the house gardens. There was plenty of milk and butter in the houses. Great baskets of pollock and rock-fish and bream and mackerel were brought each day from the sea. The hens were laying and the spare cockerels from the spring hatchings made broth for the delicate. At supper-time, the people gorged themselves on their favourite dish of mashed new potatoes, with butter and scallions and boiled fish and fresh potatoes. Then a great lump of yellow butter was pressed down into the centre of the steaming dish. The table was laid before the open door, so that they could hear the birds singing in the drowsy twilight and see the red glory of the sunset on the sea while they ate. The men waddled out afterwards to the village meeting place, sending clouds of tobacco smoke into the air from their pipes. They lay down on their backs against the rocks and listened to the bird music in raptured content. Now and again, one of them joined his voice to those of the birds and gave thanks to God for His gracious bounty.

It was then that Mrs. Derrane rose up in rebellion against her husband. She took the tongs from the hearth one evening and stood in front of him.

"I'll stand no more of this, Colm," she said fiercely. "Here we are, living on potatoes and salt, while the neighbours are feasting. Everything is put aside for the calves. My curse on the pair of them. You won't even let us eat a bit of fresh fish. By your leave, you made me salt every single fish that you brought into the house this spring, to be sold later on, so that you can have money to buy grass for your beasts. We have to scavenge along the shore, the children and myself, looking for limpets and periwinkles, same as people did during the

famine. Lord save us, the lining of our stomachs is torn into shreds from the purging that the limpets give us. We are put to shame, rummaging like sea-gulls for stinking food, while the people of our village are feasting. There has to be an end to this, or else I'll take the children and follow my face out of the house. You'll have to get rid of that calf you bought. Then we can live as we did before. We'll be outcasts no longer."

Colm got to his feet and looked at her coldly.

"I'm going to raise those two calves," he said solemnly, "even if you and the children and myself have to eat dung while I'm doing it. Let other people fill their bellies in mid-summer and remain poor. I want to rise in the world. A man can do that only by saving."

His wife raised the tongs and threatened him with them.

"I'll have none of it," she cried. "I'm telling you straight to your face. You have to give in to me or I'll split your skull with these tongs."

"Put down those tongs," Colm said quietly.

"Are you going to get rid of that calf?" said his wife.

"Put them down," said Colm.

"I'll kill you with them," shouted his wife, becoming hysterical.

She struck at him with all her force, but he jumped aside nimbly and evaded the blow. Then he closed with her and quickly locked her arms behind her back.

"I'm going to give you a lesson now," he said quietly. "I'm going to chastise you in a way that you'll remember."

He dragged her down to the hearth.

"Call the neighbours," his wife cried to the children. "Run out into the yard and call the people to come and save me from this murderer."

The children ran out into the yard and began to call for

help as Colm took down a dried sally rod that lay stretched on wooden pegs along the chimney place.

"You'll be obedient in future, my good woman," he said. "On my solemn oath you will."

He began to flog her. She tried to bite his legs. Then he put her flat on the ground and laid his foot to her back.

"I'll kill you when I get a chance," she cried. "I'll have your life while you are asleep."

Then she folded her arms beneath her face, gritted her teeth and received his blows in silence. He had to go on beating her for a long time before the sturdy creature surrendered and begged for mercy.

"All right, then," Colm said calmly when she had done so. "Do you promise to be obedient from now on and to make no more trouble about the calf?"

"I promise," his wife said.

"Get up, then, in God's name," Colm said gently, "and call in the children."

His wife looked up at him sideways in amazement. She did not rise. It puzzled her that he was so calm and spoke to her with tenderness, after having beaten her without mercy.

"Get up, woman," he continued. "Don't let us behave like this any more. It gives scandal to the children."

Then he took her tenderly in his arms and raised her to her feet. She ran out into the yard without looking at him.

"Get into the house," she said sternly to the children. "In with you."

She turned to some neighbours who had come in answer to the children's cries for help. They were standing out in the lane, in doubt as to whether they should enter the yard of a household that was outcast.

"What brought you here?" Mrs. Derrane shouted at them. "It's not for our good you came. Be off now and mind your own business."

That night in bed, she clasped Colm in her arms and put her cheek against his breast.

"I thought it was the devil got into you," she whispered as tears rolled down her cheeks. "Now I know different. You are trying to raise your family up in the world, while I'm only a hindrance to you and a dead weight around your neck. From now on, though, I'm going to help you. I will, 'faith!"

Colm took her head between his big rough hands and kissed her on the crown.

"God spare your health, darling," he said. "With your help there will be no stopping us."

Seeing their parents happily united again, the children also became imbued with enthusiasm. They willingly consented to make sacrifices for the common effort. Even the youngest boy, barely five years old, had a little job to do every day. The whole family worked like bees in a hive.

The village people soon became so impressed by this turn of events that they began to question the justice of their conduct towards the Derrane family.

"If what he is doing is bad, why does he prosper?" they said to one another. "Isn't it more likely that God is blessing his effort to rise in the world? Maybe it's us that are wicked on account of our laziness?"

At the village meeting place, Andy Gorum strove with all his skill to hold the men steadfast against Colm.

"You'll soon see him come back to us on his knees," Gorum said, "and he begging for mercy. He may seem to prosper now. His two calves are growing powerfully. His wife and children and himself are working night and day. He has a nimble hand in everything worth money. Wait till winter comes, though. Then he won't be able to find grass for his beasts. The butcher of Kilmacalla has bought a herd of black cattle, to fatten them for the fighting English. He has rented all the spare grass in the village of Pusach. Many more big people in the district have bought herds on account of the war. There won't be a single blade of grass left anywhere for a poor man to rent. The big people will have it all clutched. Colm will have to slaughter that dark-skinned calf. I declare to my God we'll be eating that dark fellow's meat when the Christmas candles are lit."

Gorum's prophecy proved false and Colm was able to find grass owing to the tragedy that again struck the Higgins family. As summer passed, the village people were no longer able to give more than the barest help to the widow and her orphans. Neither did the distraught woman put to the best use what little there was given. Indeed, she now turned on the whole village as she had formerly turned on Colm, denouncing the community at the top of her voice.

"Ah! Woe!" she cried as she marched back and forth before the houses in her bare feet. "Almighty God was cruel when he left me a widow among people that are worse than the heathen Turks. There I am, with my clutch of delicate creatures, without bite or sup from morning to night. You wouldn't see a good rush of smoke out of my chimney-top from Monday to Saturday. All I have to burn on my hearth is cow dung and a few miserable briars. There isn't a hot drop for the children's bellies. Ah! Woe! My curse on the hard hearts of my neighbours!"

There was a spell of cold weather towards the end of September and the two youngest children fell victims to it. They both died in the same week of pneumonia. The second death unhinged the mother's reason. Leaving the child unburied in the house, she wandered away at dead of night, with hardly a stitch of clothes on her starved body. They found her marching along the cliff tops on the evening of the following day and took her to the lunatic asylum. The remaining five children, finding no relatives willing to shelter them, were also lodged in a public institution. It then became apparent that the widow owed money right and left. Her creditors, who were chiefly shopkeepers of Kilmacalla, began to quarrel about disposal of the house and land. The case was brought into the district court.

"Here is my chance," Colm said to his wife. "Here is where I might be able to get grass this winter for my beasts."

On the day the case was to be tried, he put on his best clothes, took the family purse and went to the court-house at Kilmacalla. After listening to the arguments of the rival lawyers for some time, he got leave to address the magistrate.

"Your honour," he said, "it would be an injustice to the children if that farm is auctioned now, or divided up among these shopkeepers. It would be taking the bread out of the children's mouths. They have a right to do what they please later on with that land. When they grow up and come out into the world, it's for them to say if the land is to be sold, or given to one of themselves in order to raise a family on it. In the meantime, let me rent it from them, your honour. Year after year, I'll pay a good rent for it on the nail. Everybody knows me, sir. I'm a man of my word. I never went back on a pennyworth of promises in my natural life. Any man will tell you that, from the parish priest on down. The mother's debts can be paid out of the rent in no time at all. What more would these shopkeepers want, unless they are land-grabbers? In God's name, your honour, you'll be behaving like a Christian if you let me rent it, instead of letting these people slice it out among themselves. God bless you, sir!"

The magistrate finally agreed to Colm's suggestion for settling the dispute.

"Praised be God!" Colm cried on his return home. "I am secure now against the winter. Nothing can stop me from now on. In God's name, the two beasts are as good as raised."

Gorum was furious at this turn of events. He attacked Colm savagely that evening at the meeting place.

"There is a bloody heathen for you!" he cried. "The two little ones are barely dead in their graves when the blood-sucker that robbed them of their milk puts his two calves grazing on their mother's share. Ay! His two calves are lovely, sure enough. Why wouldn't they? Didn't they grow fat and strong on the milk that the little dead children should have drunk? Ah! The poor little dead creatures! It's a fine state of affairs truly, with two children dead and two beasts rolling in fat on their share of food. Mother of God! That's a cursed state of affairs for you! Beasts given rich food and children let die of hunger! Damnation has surely fallen on our village when such things are let happen here."

The men jeered at these remarks. They had lost faith in the old man.

"You are envious of Colm," they said to Gorum. "You are jealous of his success and his wisdom. You are no longer a wise man. Hatred has made a wind-bag of you."

One by one, they entered Colm's house, sat by his hearth and shared their pipes with him. Their wives brought presents to Mrs. Derrane and knitted with her on Sunday after Mass, at the women's hillock. The men came to Colm for advice, just as they had hitherto gone to Gorum. They put Colm in the place of honour at the meeting place. There was silence when he spoke.

"God is good to us," Colm said to his wife.

"He is, 'faith," Mrs. Derrane said. "Praised be His name."

Even so, it became more and more difficult for the family to make ends meet. The rent for the widow's farm put a heavy strain on their purse. The children's enthusiasm vanished during the winter in face of continual hunger. It became almost impossible to make them do a hand's turn.

Mrs. Derrane also forgot her solemn promise of co-operation and began to grumble out loud when Colm would not even allow an egg for the Christmas dinner.

25

"Great God!" she said. "There is a limit to everything. We haven't seen fish or meat since spring. You wouldn't let us buy a piece of holly or a coloured candle. We are a disgrace to the whole village, with nothing on our table but potatoes and salt for the feast of our Lord."

"Silence," Colm said. "This is no time of the year to become impudent."

To cap it all, he ordered that the cloth made from that year's wool be sold, instead of turning it into garments for the household.

"Our rags will do us well enough for another year," he said. "In any case, patched clothes are just as warm as new ones."

Everybody in the house got terribly thin and weak. Yet Colm's iron will buoyed them up to such an extent that there was no illness.

"We have only to hold on a little while," he kept saying, "and have courage. Then we'll rise in the world. We'll be rich and famous, from one end of the parish to the other."

He himself looked like a skeleton, for he practically went without food in order that the children might have as much as possible.

"You'll kill yourself," his wife said when he began to prepare the ground for the spring sowing. "You look like a sick man. For God's sake, let me take money out of the purse and buy a pig's cheek for you."

"Silence, woman," Colm said. "Not a penny must be touched. I have a plan. We'll need all we have and more to make my new plan work. It's not easy to become rich, I tell you."

The cow relieved the desperate plight of the family by having her calf a month earlier than usual, during the first week of March. The children became gay once more, for they were given plenty of the new milk to drink. There was but-

plenty of sweets and dai-dais for you when we have a shop.
There will be sweets every day and dai-dais, too. Do you hear
me? Every day in the year will be like a fair day for you."

His uncouth face, worn to the bone by privation and worry,
now glowed with the light of ecstasy, as he struggled to whee-
dle his family into co-operation with his ambition to "rise in
the world." Such was the power of the idea that possessed
him that the children stopped crying almost at once. They
listened with eagerness to his fantastic promises. Their little
faces became as radiant as his own.

His wife also became affected as she saw her dour husband
trying to win over the children by means of smiles and gaiety
and honeyed words.

"I wouldn't believe it," she said, "only for I see it with my
own two eyes."

Tears rolled down her cheeks and her upper lip trembled.

"In fifteen years," she muttered as she rubbed her eyes
with a corner of her apron, "I never once saw him dance one
of the children on his knee. No, 'faith, I never once saw him
shake a rattle in front of a whinging baby. Yet there he is
now, all of a sudden, trying to make a showman of himself.
God Almighty! Only for I see it with my own two eyes . . ."

"There will be no end to the riches we'll have when we
are shopkeepers," Colm continued. "We can have bacon for
breakfast. Yes, indeed, we can eat great big rashers of it every
morning in the year, except Fridays. The people of the village will be coming to smell the lovely food that's frying on
our pan. Oh! I'm telling you that we can have bellies on us
like tourists. We'll hardly be able to carry ourselves as we
walk the road, on account of our fat. We'll have ribbons as
well and velvet and a mirror in every room."

His wife and children were won over completely to his
side once more. So they all went to work with enthusiasm and
the shop was speedily installed. It was an immediate success.

People came specially from a long distance in order to trade with the courageous man, who was trying to raise two bullocks on twenty acres of barren rocks.

"Blood in ounce!" the people said. "He'll never be able to do it, but you have to admire his courage all the same. He'll very likely end up in the asylum with Kate Higgins, but more power to him for trying. He's a credit to the parish."

When Colm went round with his horse and cart, accompanied by one or other of the children, everybody was eager to do business with him. The people sold him whatever they had available and they forbore to drive a hard bargain. He soon had to take the house and barn that belonged to Kate Higgins, in order to store the great mass of his goods. Within a few months he was making trips to the town twice a week and getting high prices for all he had to sell.

Money kept coming into the house so quickly and in such large quantities that his wife became frightened.

"May God keep pride and arrogance out of our hearts," she used to say as she stuffed the notes into the long cloth purse. "It's dangerous to get rich so quickly."

"Have no fear, woman," Colm said to her. "We denied ourselves and we didn't lose heart when times were bad. So now God is giving us a big hansel as a reward. Be grateful, woman, and have no fear."

The promises that he had made to the children were fulfilled. There was full and plenty in the house. The little girls had ribbons to their hair and dai-dais to amuse their leisure. His wife got a velvet dress and a hat with feathers. There was bacon for breakfast.

"He must have touched the magic stone," said the astonished people of the village. "Everything he handles turns into lashings of money."

Andy Gorum alone continued to prophesy that misfortune

would fall on Colm for attempting to "stand alone and rise above the people."

"You just wait," Gorum kept shouting on the hill before the village. "God will strike him down when he least expects it. Those two beasts, that are now so lovely, will never reach the fair green alive on their four legs."

This prophecy proved to be just as false as the previous one that Gorum had made. All through the winter and the following spring, Colm and his family lavished the greatest care on the two beasts that had brought them prosperity. So that they were really champions on fair day. The bullock with the wine-dark hide was acknowledged by all to be the finest animal of his age ever seen in the district. He fetched top price.

Tears poured down Colm's cheeks as he walked back from the railway station with his wife, after parting with his beasts.

"Those two lovely beasts brought me luck," he said. "I feel lonely for them now that they are gone. Only for them, I'd never think of rising in the world. Praised be God! He works in strange ways. He strikes one down and raises up another."

"True for you," his wife said. "Praised be His holy name! Who are we, miserable sinners that we are, to question His mysterious ways?"

"Only for that cow dying on Kate Higgins," Colm continued, "we'd always be land slaves, wrestling with starvation to the end of our days and never getting the better of any bout. Look at us now, woman. We're on our way towards riches. God alone knows where we'll stop."

"Enough of that talk now," his wife said. "Don't let arrogance get hold of us. Don't let us be boastful. The people are already becoming envious of us. I can see a begrudging look in the eyes of the neighbours."

"That's true," Colm said. "That's why I'm thinking of opening a shop in the town. It might be better to take ourselves out of the sight of people that knew us poor."

"A shop in the town?" his wife said. "Don't get too big for your boots, Colm."

"No fear," Colm said. "I know what I'm doing. I'm going to hire a few men and begin buying in earnest. There's money to be picked up by the bushel all over the place. All we need is courage, woman."

"In God's name!" his wife said.

When they were hitching the mare to their new jaunting car for the journey home, Andy Gorum came along with a group of intoxicated men.

"The mills of God grind slow," Gorum shouted, "but they grind sure. The bloodsuckers are taking the food out of our country. They are giving it to the fighting foreigners, while our children die of hunger. We are barefooted and in rags, but they give our wool and our hides to the war people. They are taking all our lovely beasts across the sea to fill the bellies of pagans. The time will soon come, though, when the bloodsuckers that are robbing us will be struck down by the hand of Almighty God. They will roast in Hell for the everlasting ages."

As Colm drove away in his new green jaunting car, quite a number of people whistled after him in hostility and derision. Now that he had risen so far, he had again become an enemy.

His gaunt face looked completely unaware of their jeers. His pale blue eyes stared fixedly straight ahead, cold and resolute and ruthless.

32

The Mouse

 BLACK KITTEN was playing in the sun. He was hitting a piece of brown paper with his fore-paws and pushing it along the grass near a circular flower bed. He struck it daintily, with one paw at a time, following it in quick rushes, noiselessly, with his body crouched against the short grass. The sharp sound made by the impact of his paws against the paper amused him.

Suddenly he felt a desire for violent movement. He struck the paper with both paws and held it securely. Then he stood up on his haunches and hurled it into the air. As it came down, he thrust forth his claws and struck at it savagely. There was a tearing sound as the claws pierced it. This excited him. He pretended to be frightened and ran away as fast as he could, with his tail half raised.

He ran halfway round the flower bed. Then he pretended that there was an enemy in pursuit. He turned sharply in among the flowers. He hid himself among them and crouched. Now he felt savage and eager for a fight. The fur rose on his back. He made his body taut for a spring. He was already half-grown and developing the instincts of the hunter.

As nothing pursued him into his hiding place, he soon wearied of this game. The desire to fight gave way to a languorous pleasure in his surroundings. There was a delicious smell here. Flowers that were softer than his silken fur touched him on either side. The delicious smell and the softness of the flower petals made him want to caress something. He began to purr deeply and to push softly against the flowers. This excited him and he again felt the desire for violent movement. He rolled over, stretched himself and dragged his belly along the ground.

Suddenly he heard a cry and he sat up on his haunches. The cry was repeated. He rushed out of the flower bed in the direction of the sound and saw his mother coming down the sloping lawn from the corner of the house. She walked in a peculiar fashion, almost at a run, with her back bent and her head close to the ground. She had something in her mouth.

The kitten stared at her in surprise and mewed. She saw him and came to a halt. She dropped what she was carrying and put her fore-paw on it. Then she raised her head slightly and called him once more. It was almost a growl, the sound that she made. Her teeth were bared to the end of her jaws and her tongue was hanging out, red and shining with moisture in the sunlight, as she mewed.

The kitten became very excited. He leaped into the air and galloped to his mother with arched tail. As he approached, she tapped the thing she had dropped on the ground, several times, gently, with her paw. The kitten came to a halt and crouched, watching the thing she had dropped.

It was a little brown mouse, which she had caught nibbling a crumb of cheese under the kitchen table. He was still un-

injured, as she had not put her teeth into him; but he was
stunned by fright and by the impact of her paws when she
had pounced on him. He moved unconsciously in obedience
to the cat's tapping on his haunches. He dragged himself
along the grass for about six inches and then came to a halt
once more, unable to go farther owing to the trembling of his
body. His trembling was so minute that it was indiscernible,
except his whiskers and his pointed snout, which jerked spasmodically with each convulsive intake of breath.

Now he lay almost on his side, with his enormous tail, like
an exposed root, stretched out straight. His brown flanks and
back were moist through contact with the cat's mouth. There
the fur lay flat and indented by the pressure of the cat's teeth.

The kitten followed the mouse when the tiny animal began to move. Instead of reaching out with his curved paw
and playing with him, as he would have done in the ordinary
way, he ran around in a circle, disturbed and somewhat
intimidated by a strange emotion. Then he threw himself
sprawling on the grass and watched the long tail eagerly. It
was like a string being drawn slowly. When the mouse halted,
the kitten drew a little close, reached out with his paw and
touched the tail. The mouse crawled forward another inch
and again lay still. Again the kitten touched the tail. This
time the mouse did not move. The kitten looked at his
mother and mewed plaintively. He was at a loss to explain
this strange little animal that was pulling a familiar string
along the ground.

The mother cat had sat up on her haunches after pawing
the mouse. She pretended to have no interest either in him
or in her kitten. She began to lick her breast energetically.
When the kitten mewed, she stopped licking herself and
turned to the mouse once more. With a savage growl, she
pounced on him, caught him in her mouth and threw him
high into the air. Then she leaped into the air after him,

caught him dexterously in her paws and fell to the ground with him, rolling over. Then she dropped him and patted him roughly on the haunches.

The mouse was roused from his stupor by the fierce cries, the violent movement through the air and the rough pressure of the cat's paws. As soon as he got loose he began to run, squealing. Now his fear was released and he was struggling frantically to escape.

The cat let him run a few yards, hoping the kitten would follow and pounce on him, in imitation of herself. The kitten, however, did not yet understand the game. He still feared the strange emotion roused in him by the smell of the brown body that was pulling the string-like tail. By force of habit, he followed the tail, pawing at it and bobbing his head from side to side.

The mouse began to gather speed. The cat leaped forward once more, lest he might escape from her foolish kitten. Now she planted her fore-paw roughly on his back and crouched over him. Then she looked at her kitten, bared her jaws and growled. She took the mouse into her jaws by the head and stood up, still growling. She walked away a few paces, with the long tail dangling down her breast and the little pale naked feet beating frantically against her mouth. She crouched again, turned her head sideways and put a paw against the mouse's body, as if she were going to eat him. A cry came from the kitten. The mother dropped the mouse smartly, got to her feet and moved away, smelling the ground all round.

At last the kitten understood. His mother's gesture, as she pretended to eat the mouse, had roused the lust to kill in him. The strange smell of the brown body now made him feel savage. He felt the same desire for violent movement as when he pierced the paper with his claws and rolled himself voluptuously against the soft petals of the flowers. This passion was, however, much more violent. It made his body rigid. He moved forward slowly, in the peculiar way his mother had come down the sloping lawn, with bent back and lowered head and moist, red tongue exposed. He kept lifting his fore-paws and shaking them, to loosen the stricture of his muscles. His neck was strained stiffly forward. His tail was trailing just above the ground.

Almost smothered, the mouse again lay in a stupor. He lay on his side with his legs in the air. Except when his snout jerked spasmodically, with each convulsive intake of breath, he lay still as death. Now the kitten was standing over him, growling savagely, ready for the pounce.

Suddenly, there was a mighty roar, which made the kitten close his mouth with a snap. It was the thunderous bark of a dog. The kitten looked round and saw a large white dog with black spots coming at a headlong pace, barking as he came. The kitten at once forgot the mouse and his lust to kill. The enormous shape of the bounding dog and the thunderous recurring sounds made him convulse with terror. He fled towards the house with all his hair on end, spitting.

The mother cat also turned to flee, but she returned to secure the mouse after going a little way. Before she could reach the mouse, the dog was upon her. She threw herself on her back and put her legs in the air, with all her claws exposed. Unable to hold his rush, the dog closed with her. She scratched him on the snout and he drew away whining. In a flash, she was on her feet and in flight. He followed with equal speed and soon caught up with her once more. They fought all the way to a laurel bush, in which the cat took cover. The dog ran around the bush, barking and scratching the ground.

The noise of the barking and of the scurrying fight brought the little mouse back to consciousness. He rolled over on his belly and began to drag himself forward. He was unable to

37

support his body on his palsied legs, so he had to crawl on his belly. Little by little, however, he took courage. Finally, he managed to get on his legs and he began to run. He did not know where he was going, but he ran in the direction opposite to the barking.

Then he suddenly threw himself flat on the grass as a new terror menaced him. A woman came running across the lawn, calling to the dog. She almost trod on the mouse as she ran past. The mouse lay still for a little while, shivering, until her voice became distant. Then he ran with all his might until he came to a shed. He crawled through a hole under the door and hid himself among a heap of firewood.

The woman drove away the dog. Then the cat came forth from the bush and ran, mewing angrily, to the spot where she had left the mouse. The kitten ran from the house and joined her. Together, they smelt about on the grass, mewing angrily, with bent backs, their heads close to the ground and their tongues exposed. They could not find the scent of the fugitive.

The mouse was now fast asleep from exhaustion, safe among the heap of firewood.

The Bath

M R. CAMPBELL awoke with a splitting headache. Without opening his eyes properly, he got out of bed and groped for his dressing gown. To his surprise, his hand struck the bare wall instead of the peg on which the garment usually hung. He started, opened his eyes wide and looked around the room. "My God!" he cried. "I've done it again. Now, where am I?"

The muscular effort of opening his eyes properly, together with the fright caused by finding himself in a strange room, sent violent pains shooting across his forehead. He groaned and threw himself face downwards on the bed.

"Now, let me see," he thought. "On leaving Court, I went to the Dolphin with Dr. Reilly and we had several drinks. That would be about six o'clock. I was in a hurry, as Molly was having the McDevitts to dinner. My God! I never even

39

telephoned, or did I? Not at the Dolphin, but where did we go from there? I'm ruined this time. She'll never forgive me. The McDevitts of all people. I have it. That chap from the American Embassy joined us, when I was on the point of leaving. He was driving out to Lady What's-her-name's house near Bray, to look at an Alsatian puppy. Reilly and myself drove out there with him. We had a drink at the old lady's house and the American bought the dog. We set off back to Dublin with the dog and then . . . My God! That's it. The golf club! That damned golf club near Bray has been the ruin of me many a time before. Reilly insisted on dropping in there just for one drink. Did I telephone there? Oh! My head! My head!"

He raised himself on his elbow, opened his eyes once more and looked for a bell. There was no button, but an aged bell-rope hung down beside the bed.

"What kind of a place is this?" cried Mr. Campbell, staring at the rope. "Where on earth am I?"

He pulled at the rope angrily. Immediately, there was a devilish clanging at a distance. Then he heard a woman's shrill voice:

"Hey! Paddy, there's somebody wanting something in twenty-seven. Go on over."

"Go on over yourself," cried a man's voice. "Can't you see I'm busy?"

"Go on over and stop talking," shouted the woman.

Then Mr. Campbell heard an oath from the man and something like an iron shovel being hurled on to a hard floor.

"Good Lord!" cried Mr. Campbell, clutching his head and gritting his teeth. "This is dreadful. Where did I go from the golf club?"

Hearing heavy footsteps approach the door, he pulled the bedclothes over him. There was a knock and then the door was thrown open. A man appeared. He leaned familiarly against the door jamb, nodded towards Mr. Campbell and said with a smile:

"Good morrow, sir. Was it you pulled the bell?"

"Yes," said Mr. Campbell. "I rang. What time is it? Where am I? How did I get here?"

The man laughed heartily, slapped his thigh and strode into the room.

"By the powers! That's a good one," he cried. "And you not knowing where you are. Oh! By the holy! That must have been a fine load you carried in here last night sure enough."

He laughed again, sat down on the side of the bed, stared at Mr. Campbell and added in a serious tone:

"Don't be uneasy, man alive. You couldn't be in a better place than Short's Hotel."

"Short's Hotel?" cried Mr. Campbell. "Where is that?"

The man stared at Mr. Campbell in amazement. He pushed back his tattered hat from his forehead and then scratched his curly black hair with a very dirty hand. He had a queer face. It was bronzed and covered with wrinkles, even though he was obviously quite young; certainly not more than thirty. He had a long piece of straw dangling from his prominent yellow teeth. He chewed at the straw while he scratched his head. To judge by his clothes, he was a stable boy, as he wore an old pair of brown top boots, a pair of yellow riding breeches and a khaki shirt open at the throat.

"In S——, of course," he cried in astonishment. "Where else would it be? The most famous hotel in all Ireland. Sure, didn't Royalty stay here once? In the old days, that is. Do you mean to tell me, sir, that you never heard of Short's Hotel?"

"Damn your hotel!" cried Mr. Campbell, clutching his head. "My God! S——! One hundred miles from Dublin. I'm due to appear in Court at three o'clock this afternoon. Where are the others? Who the blazes are you, anyway?"

"I'm Paddy, the boots," said the man. "Don't be uneasy.

41

What others would you be looking for? You came in here on your own last night."

"I did?" said Mr. Campbell. "The devil I did. What time is it?"

"It's not so late," said Paddy. "Why don't you look at your watch and it there on the table beside your bed?"

"Never mind," said Mr. Campbell. "There is no point in worrying about the time just now. Get my bath ready."

Here Paddy spat out his straw and whistled.

"A bath!" he cried. "You want a bath? Now, that's a different story, and I'll tell you why it is. The bath is not properly mended yet."

"What? No bath?" cried Mr. Campbell.

"Oh! Take it easy now, sir," cried Paddy. "There is a bath and a fine one, but there was an Englishman here last week. He was a loud-spoken class of a man, travelling for a firm of jewellery men in Birmingham; my curse on him, anyway; he must have been roaring with the itch from some awful disease, for he was in and out of that bath from daylight to dark. In the heel of the hunt he broke it and I don't know is it properly mended yet. It was a spout he pulled out and he trying to get at the hot water. Oh! By the holy! You should have heard the curses of him. He was a heavy, gutty sort of a man with a bull neck. Crump was his name. Now, isn't that a funny bloody name for a man to have and he selling rings and bracelets?"

Here Paddy burst out laughing incontinently. Mr. Campbell groaned and said:

"Oh! God! I feel so awful."

"Leave that to me," said Paddy. "That's easily settled. We'll kill two birds with one stone. It would be a cold bath you'd want in your condition and the cold spout is in fine order. Now pull on that raincoat and come along with me.

42

I'll fix up your head on the way and then you'll have your bath and you'll feel fine."

He took a raincoat from the back of the door and held it towards Mr. Campbell, who looked at it doubtfully.

"I had better get dressed first," said Mr. Campbell. "I can't go around the hotel wearing nothing but my shirt and a raincoat."

"Why not?" said Paddy. "It's a nice warm summer day. We pass by the bar on the way. We'll call a halt there to fix up your head."

"What?" cried Mr. Campbell, pointing to his naked legs. "Go to the bar like this?"

"Sure, there'll be nobody there," said Paddy. "It's a nice quiet place. Hop out now, sir, and face the world."

"Well!" said Mr. Campbell. "I've got to get out somehow, I suppose."

He swung his legs onto the floor and stood erect. He was a large man, inclined to flesh, but still in his prime. His brown hair was thinning at the crown and he had heavy pouches under his pale blue eyes. His face was rather puffed. This puffiness, together with a fair moustache which he did not keep properly clipped, gave him a morose expression, even though he was by nature extremely mild. He put his arms through the raincoat sleeves and gathered the coat about his flanks. Then he peered down at his naked shins and feet. His legs were particularly hairy and the heavy brown fuzz looked repulsive to him.

"I look like a dressed-up monkey going about this way," he cried. "Suppose I'm seen by somebody I know?"

"What of it, sir?" said Paddy. "There is no sin in showing a fine pair of shanks like your own, God bless them. This way, sir."

Mr. Campbell shrugged his shoulders, took his watch off the table and looked at it. It was a little after eleven.

"Could I put through a call to Dublin?" he said, as he followed Paddy into the corridor. "My wife . . ."

"Now take it easy," interrupted Paddy. "Don't try too many jobs at once, sir. You better have your bath first and then you can telephone. You'll feel like a fighting cock when I'm done with you. It's a barrister you are, isn't it? Last night you were addressing the jury in great order and I putting you to bed. I had a great job taking off your trousers."

After going through a narrow shabby corridor, they entered a hall, at the rear of which there was a bar. A dark-haired girl was behind the counter, on which her elbows rested. Mr. Campbell started when he saw her and tried to pull his raincoat farther down over his shanks, but the girl was busy reading a magazine and never raised her eyes.

There was nobody else in the hall, nor in the passage that led by the office window to the hotel door and the street. The whole place looked very shabby and decayed. The boots led Mr. Campbell across the hall to another corridor that faced the one from which they had emerged.

"We'll see about the bath first," he said, "before I fix your head. She might be scrubbing it. It was last night the plumber was fixing the pipes. He left the place in an awful mess."

The bath tub was in a small room on the left, halfway down the second corridor. An old woman was on her knees scrubbing the floor.

"What do ye want?" she cried angrily, raising her head and pushing back her grey hair from her eyes with her naked elbow.

"This gentleman here wants a bath," said Paddy. "Will you move out of my way, until I see does the spout work?"

"This is a nice time to come foostering about this place," said the old woman. "What's the gentleman's hurry, in any case? Clear out of here, will ye, and let me finish my work."

She stooped once more and continued to scrub. Paddy shrugged his shoulders, beckoned to Mr. Campbell and turned back towards the hall.

"There's nothing doing until the ould one has finished scrubbing the place," he said. "We'll fix up your head in the meantime. Come on, sir."

As they approached the bar counter, the girl raised her eyes from the magazine, saw Mr. Campbell's naked hairy legs, uttered a cry of fright and said:

"Lord save us! Is it walking in his sleep he is?"

"He's going to have a bath," said Paddy, "but he wants a drink first. His head is bad."

"Is that so?" said the girl. "Would it be a nice fresh bottle of Bass the gentleman would have in mind?"

"I'd like to put a call through to Dublin," said Mr. Campbell.

"Don't mind the call until you have your bath," said Paddy. "Sure you couldn't talk over the telephone to a lady and you practically as naked as the day you were born. Take it easy, man."

"Very well!" said Mr. Campbell. "If the young lady doesn't object to my costume . . ."

"That doesn't matter, sir," said the barmaid. "What would you like?"

"Give him a bottle of Bass," said Paddy, "and a pint of Guinness for me. I might as well keep you company, sir, while the ould one is rinsing the dirt out of the other place. Janey! That Mr. Crump had the life tormented out of us. Now, did you ever hear of a man with a name like that before, sir?"

"What?" said Mr. Campbell. "Who are you talking about?"

"Crump," said Paddy. "An Englishman he was, from Birmingham. And now, sir, drink up and here's wishing you all the very best."

45

The barmaid had placed their drinks on the counter. Mr. Campbell forced himself to swallow the whole contents of his tumbler. The boots swallowed his pint at one draught, apparently without the slightest effort, as if it were a meagre spoonful.

"Am I to whisper the good word a second time, sir?" he said as soon as he had finished drinking. He spoke in a confidential whisper, close to Mr. Campbell's ear. "The first always feels miserable until the second arrives to keep it warm. Very well, sir. The same again, Miss Tierney."

"I really should telephone at once," Mr. Campbell thought. "I treat Molly awfully badly. I really do. I'm behaving like a cad and this little incident quite oversteps the mark. Never turned up for dinner with the McDevitts coming, never telephoned, out all night, due in court at three this afternoon and here I am at eleven in the morning, one hundred miles away, standing practically naked at a public bar. It's really too awful."

"Throw this one back after the first," said Paddy, pushing the second tumbler towards Mr. Campbell, "and then let you dare tell me, if you can, that you don't feel like a fighting cock. Throw it back, sir, and I wish you all the very best."

Mr. Campbell swallowed the second tumbler in two gulps. He felt a great deal better. He smiled and drew in a deep breath.

"Was I right or was I wrong, sir?" said Paddy. "How is the head?"

"You were right," said Mr. Campbell. "I feel almost normal again, thank you. A hair of the dog, as the saying goes."

At this moment the old woman, who had been scrubbing the floor, thrust her head around the corner of the corridor and said:

"The gentleman can have the run of the bathroom now. I have it all as scoured as can be."

46

"All right," said Paddy. "Half a moment, sir."

He emptied his pint hurriedly and continued:

"You stay here while I go and ready the water for you. You might have another drink to keep yourself occupied in the meantime. A bottle and a pint, Miss Tierney."

He went off to the bathroom. Mr. Campbell lit a cigarette, while the barmaid served the third round of drinks. Now Mr. Campbell could recall the events of the night fairly clearly, from the time he arrived at the golf club near Bray.

"Buck Flanagan met us there," he recalled, "and joined us over the first drink. That fellow is more insidious than the rankest poison. What's the odds? We'll all be dead one day. That's his invariable excuse for leading one astray. It was he who persuaded us to go on to that roadhouse on the Wicklow road. Did the American come with us? No. He went back to Dublin with his Alsatian puppy. Wise man. My God! I hope I did nothing silly at that roadhouse. That would be the limit. I think not. From there we came on to a dance at Rosslare. Remember getting to the dance and drinking some rum. Peculiar thing to drink at that hour. What? Very odd, indeed. I must have passed out after drinking the rum. I always wander away when I pass out, and that, my dear fellow, is the beginning of the end. A sure sign that a certain disease, beginning with the fourth letter of the alphabet, is on its way."

A sudden shout roused him from his reverie. He started and turned round to see Paddy beckoning to him from the corner of the corridor. Paddy's face was creased with laughter.

"For God's sake, will you come and see what's coming out of the spout?" he cried. "I never in my life saw the like."

"What is it?" said Mr. Campbell.

"Come and look at it, sir," said Paddy.

In spite of his rather gloomy reverie, Mr. Campbell was

48

beginning to feel unaccountably pleased with himself. As he crossed the hall, he thought:

"This Paddy is rather an amusing dog. Might be fun to spend a day or two in this place with him."

He followed Paddy into the bathroom. It had formerly been a bedroom and the bath, which was a cheap affair of enamelled tin, was perched on wooden trestles in one corner. The water entered from a rusty iron tank near the roof and the pipes, reaching down from the tank, were also very rusty. The enamel had worn away from nearly all the bottom of the tub, giving the impression of a small black lake, surrounded by a smooth white precipitous cliff. Into this black lake there now flowed a thin stream of black water from the cold water cock. It did not flow regularly or in volume. It would rumble in the pipe, like a man clearing his throat, a large bubble would form at the mouth of the cock, the bubble would burst, a heavy black clot would drop, followed by a dark ripple, that wound its way around the rim of the cock on emerging, sometimes making a semicircular fan, like the upshoot in a gaudy, artificial fountain.

"Did you ever see the like of that?" said Paddy.

Mr. Campbell laughed and said:

"Why is the water black?"

"The Lord alone knows," said Paddy. "It might be from the brewery. Then again, on the other hand, the plumber might have entangled this pipe with some unmentionable pipe and he fixing the broken pipe. The one that was broken by Mr. Crump."

"Pretty poor chance of my getting a bath," said Mr. Campbell.

"Oh! Don't worry," said Paddy. "We'll let it run for a while and it will soon clear itself. Let Nature take its course, as the saying goes. Sure, there's no hurry. Aren't we nice and comfortable? Don't be fretting, sir, about wasting my time, because you are very pleasant company, a well-informed gentleman like yourself, if I may say so. We'll go on back to the bar and let this black water run itself clear."

Mr. Campbell made no complaint. Instead of feeling annoyed by the delay and the foul condition of the water, he felt greatly amused. Now he was quite unconscious of being practically naked, standing there at the bar in full view of anybody who might care to come in from the public street. And Paddy was quite as amusing as the insidious Buck Flanagan. Mr. Campbell could never resist good company.

"Look here," he said to Paddy when they had returned to the bar, "what did you say about Royalty staying here once? Were you trying to pull my leg?"

"Upon my soul, I was not," said Paddy. "There was a Royal Duke that stayed here once. Ages ago, that was. He was in bad with his mother at the time and he wandering around the country, gallivanting to beat the band. His name was written in a book, but the last man that owned the hotel sold the book to an American that goes around the world buying names that are written in books. Drink up, sir, and all the very best."

Mr. Campbell took a pull at his third tumbler. Then he laughed. He was beginning to get pleasantly intoxicated once more.

"Did the Royal Duke use the bath tub?" he said.

"Oh! No," said Paddy. "The bath has only been in a few years and it's more trouble than it's worth. Except for an occasional gentleman like yourself, it's hardly ever used. What's the use of a bath, anyway? Will you tell me that now? Seems to me people got on very well without them. Take the insides of a person, saving your presence, Miss Tierney, that's a different thing entirely. The insides of a person need to get a good rinsing and scouring every day, with fine ale or

whisky; but the outsides should be let alone. Sure, isn't there
enough rain in the country tormenting us, without throwing
ourselves like suicidal lunatics into big tanks full of water?
To my mind, sir, a man lying in a bath is a helpless specimen
of humanity. Drink up, sir, and here's wishing you long life."

They both emptied their measures. Mr. Campbell was now
becoming definitely groggy.

"There is a great deal in what you say, Paddy," he said,
"but at the same time I insist on having my bath, even though
it turns me into a Negro. Just one more drink and we'll tackle
the problem of purifying the water. What did you say the
Englishman's name was?"

"Same again, Miss Tierney," said Paddy. "His name was
Crump, the Englishman from Birmingham."

"Crump," said Mr. Campbell, "is a ludicrous name.
What?"

Here they both laughed uproariously. Mr. Campbell,
ordinarily very aloof in his attitude towards workpeople,
slapped Paddy on the back. Laughter made them thirsty.
The fourth measure vanished quickly, between peals of
merry laughter and many repetitions of the idiotic name
borne by the Englishman from Birmingham. They ordered
another round. They drank that also. Mr. Campbell suddenly changed his attitude towards the boots. He became
arrogant, as he always did when fully intoxicated.

"Come along," he snapped at Paddy. "Go and look at that
bath. See is the water right yet. I can't spend the day here,
damn it. I must telephone at once. Are you aware that I'm
due in court at three o'clock this afternoon?"

"Yes, sir," said Paddy, surprised at the sudden change in
Mr. Campbell's manner. He touched his hat in a humble
fashion. "Yes, sir. I'll go right away."

He took a furtive sip at his fresh pint and then moved away

on tiptoe towards the bathroom. When he was halfway across the floor, he paused, turned his head and whispered in an insidiously gentle tone:

"I wouldn't worry about the court, sir, if I were you. A gentleman with the genius of yourself can get cartloads of people to defend and they willing to pay a shovelful of gold for the great power of oratory you gave me a sample of last night."

He moved away, raised his hands before his face and continued in a louder tone, full of admiring wonder:

"Begob, the great councillor Daniel O'Connell himself couldn't hold a candle to the flow of talk I heard last night."

The barmaid raised her eyes from her magazine, snorted contemptuously towards the boots and then moved away to the far end of the counter, to wait on two men who had just entered the bar from the street. Mr. Campbell noticed her gesture, followed her with his eyes and saw the two new customers. They were smiling, whispering to one another and staring at his naked shins surreptitiously. He heard one of them mumble something about the French Riviera. This increased his arrogance, instead of making him feel ashamed of being a public spectacle.

"Low fellows!" he growled, after sipping at his tumbler. "The country is becoming infested with vulgar louts. Bah! Democracy! Humanity is becoming one vast herd of Crumps."

Paddy came back and said that the bath water was coming on very nicely.

"It's almost a brown colour now, sir," he said. " 'Faith, you wouldn't notice it at all if you weren't particular. But sure, a gentleman like yourself has a right to be particular and small blame to you."

"Paddy," said Mr. Campbell, raising his voice, in order to

be heard by the men at the far end of the counter, "you are an unscrupulous fellow, but I like you."

"That's right, sir," said Paddy with a genial smile. "I have my points, as the saying goes."

"Drink, you ruffian," said Mr. Campbell in a louder and more arrogant tone. "Here. I drink to you. Good health."

They clinked their glasses and drained them. Then Mr. Campbell banged on the counter and ordered a fresh round.

"That's the ticket, sir," said Paddy. "Better not give the thirst a chance to get a foot in."

"Civilisation," said Mr. Campbell in the same loud tone, "is largely, one may say, the art of being graciously insincere. Your flattery, for instance, does not deceive me in the least, but I accept it with pleasure, since it is a thing well done. That is something that common people cannot understand."

Here he glared arrogantly towards the men at the far end of the counter. Then he turned back towards Paddy and continued:

"For them, successful living means being clever like precocious guttersnipes, getting together in a herd and sniggering at the caprices of their betters. My good man, you must realise that the most difficult thing in life is to learn how to be capricious without being coarse."

"Don't I know it, sir?" said Paddy. "All the very best."

They drank once more. Paddy was also getting a little intoxicated. Three more men had by now entered the bar. There was quite a little crowd at the far end, amusedly watching Mr. Campbell. Paddy decided that it was time to bring the bout to a finish. Mr. Campbell might become pugnacious at any moment. There might be a scene, or even blows; in which case Paddy's situation at the hotel might be prejudiced.

"Suppose we go in now, the two of us," he whispered in

Mr. Campbell's ear, "and fix up the bath? It must be running clear by now."

Mr. Campbell took a step away from the counter, swayed a little and then grasped Paddy roughly by the shoulder.

"Look here, my man," he cried. "Don't overstep the mark. See to the bath and report to me here at once. See is the water in proper condition. Look alive now."

"Yes, sir," said Paddy, making a humble bow.

"One moment," said Mr. Campbell, as Paddy was about to depart. "You must finish your drink first. Bottoms up."

Paddy drained his pint and smiled foolishly. Then he walked to the bathroom, rather loose and uncertain in his movements. Mr. Campbell shouted for another round. The barmaid appeared to be uncertain about the advisability of serving him, so he repeated the order.

"Yes, sir," she said. "I heard you first time."

"Impertinent wench," muttered Mr. Campbell.

Now he leaned his elbows against the counter, dropped his head and lapsed into a sadly pleasant mood of self-pity. He told himself that he was "slipping," that his conduct during recent months was attracting public attention, that the end would come soon unless he called a halt, that his wife whom he loved very dearly was being miserably unhappy owing to his laxity. Having enjoyed these gloomy thoughts for a few moments, he roused himself and reverted to his arrogant mood defiantly.

"The whole system of modern life," he cried aloud, addressing the bottles behind the bar, "is a futile bore. What people call duty and decent living are a disgusting form of middle-class hypocrisy, the barrack-room discipline of mediocrity. All this horde of guttersnipes, unable to stand on their own feet and shine out by virtue of their individual talents, band together in order to deprive the more intelligent and forceful individuals of their joy in life. Pride! They lack that glorious pride that made Lucifer contemptuous of Heaven. By Gad! I have a good mind to . . ."

He was about to address the group in an offensive manner when he heard a shout from the hotel entrance. He turned round and saw Buck Flanagan, followed by Dr. Reilly, approach hurriedly.

"Here he is, Jack," said Flanagan. "We've run him to earth at last. Alex, we've hunted all over the town for you. What do you mean by running away? Honestly, we had a dreadful job finding you. How did you get to this place?"

Flanagan seemed to think it perfectly natural that Mr. Campbell should be standing in a public bar, practically naked and obviously quite drunk. A former Rugby football international, he was a powerfully strong man, tall and well built, with a handsome, jovial face. His blue eyes seemed to be continually laughing. With the unattached manner of a big, friendly dog, he slapped Mr. Campbell on the back and then wandered around the bar, as if to sniff it and examine the contents of this new place. He opened his waistcoat as he strode about, tightened his braces, buttoned his waistcoat once more and then stood in front of a mirror to arrange his tie, while he winked at the barmaid, who was ogling him shamelessly.

Dr. Reilly, on the other hand, was completely distraught at Mr. Campbell's condition. He stared at Mr. Campbell with tears in his eyes and with quivering lips, holding his hands, palms inwards, in front of his face and rubbing each thumb against the other fingers. He was a tubby little man with secretive grey eyes. He came from the city of Cork and he was in Dublin about a lawsuit. It concerned his late uncle's will, which his aunt was contesting. The case was coming up in court at three o'clock that afternoon. Mr. Campbell held the brief for him. That was why he was distraught.

"What do you fellows want?" said Mr. Campbell. "A drink?"

"My God! Alex, do you know it's half-past twelve?" said Dr. Reilly. "My case comes on at three. For God's sake, man, why did you leave the dance? I swore I wouldn't let you get out of my sight, and here you are. It's not fair, Alex. It's not fair. A great deal depends on the verdict. A great deal. Oh! Please get dressed and come along. With a little luck we might make it. Please get dressed and hurry."

"I'll come along when I've had my bath," said Mr. Campbell. "If you are so concerned about your wretched case, why didn't you come for me sooner, you silly ass? Now, there's no hurry. Is there, Buck? You always maintain . . ."

"In this case," said Flanagan, approaching with a smile and drawling in his attractive deep voice, "there is a slight need for hurry. I've got to get back to town. I have a horse running at the Park in the three-thirty. I want to see it run. What's the number of your room?"

"He's in number twenty-seven, sir," said the barmaid. "Third door on the right down that corridor. Will I show you the way?"

"Not now," said Flanagan, winking and waving his fingers at her. "I'll find it."

"I'm not going until I have my bath," Mr. Campbell called after Flanagan. "Reilly, your uncle's will can go to the devil for all I care. Where is the boots? Paddy, you ruffian, what about the water?"

"Here I am, sir," said Paddy, coming forward and touching his hat. "I have it gathering nicely now. There is a fair depth of water in it and it would be a suspicious class of a man would say it was too brown. I often saw Mr. Crump go into darker water."

"Could you make out this gentleman's bill?" Dr. Reilly said to the barmaid.

Mr. Campbell began to laugh hysterically. Then he pointed a finger at Paddy and said:

"Let's get hold of Crump and have some fun with him. Come along?"

"What about the bath first, sir?" said Paddy.

"Certainly," said Mr. Campbell, taking Paddy confidentially by the arm and drawing him aside. "I have something very important to tell you."

He took Paddy into the corner and began to whisper with great effort into his ear. Dr. Reilly paid for all the drinks consumed by Mr. Campbell and the boots. Then he went to settle for the room. Flanagan emerged, carrying all Mr. Campbell's clothes in a bundle under his arm. One of the men at the far end of the counter came over to him and said:

"Excuse me, Mr. Flanagan, but has your mare got a chance in the three-thirty?"

"The mare said nothing to me about it," Flanagan said to the man, "but I wouldn't be surprised at anything she might do."

He laughed and strode out towards the street, while the group at the counter jeered at the questioner. He put Mr. Campbell's clothes in the back of a new and expensive car that was parked outside with the engine running. Dr. Reilly beckoned to him from the office window as he returned.

"This is a nice kettle of fish," said Dr. Reilly. "Half-past twelve and we a hundred miles from Dublin and he roaring drunk."

Flanagan pushed his hat to the back of his head, put his elbow on the window sill and grasped Dr. Reilly's shoulder.

"You don't know Alex as well as I do," he drawled. "He can only win a difficult case when he's roaring drunk. Then he's a genius. Otherwise he's too shy and mild. That's his nature, you see? I know the exact condition in which he's at the top of his form. I'll get him into it by the time we reach

Dublin. You leave it to me, Jack. We'll get back in time, because I don't want to miss that race. My bus can do eighty. Listen. We'll bundle him into the car as he is. He can dress in the car. Then I'll take down the hood and we'll blow his heavy jag off him. I'll fix up the required tonic at the bar and take it along. I've seen him go into court worse than this and perform miracles. He's one of the greatest barristers of all times. Come along."

Dr. Reilly took his change and they returned to the bar, where the barmaid made up a mixture in a small bottle and gave it to Flanagan. Flanagan marched over to Mr. Campbell, who was now making a speech to the boots, gesturing as if he were in a court of law. Flanagan seized Mr. Campbell suddenly, picked him up in his arms and hurried towards the door. Mr. Campbell struggled and shouted:

"Let me go, Buck. I'm not going until I have had my bath . . ."

"In due course," said Flanagan, striding to the door and swaying under his heavy burden. "Come along, Jack. Open the door of the car."

Mr. Campbell swung his naked legs to and fro. He tried to grab the door jamb as they passed into the street.

"My bath," he shouted. "I must have my bath."

The group of men at the bar now cheered and ran to the door to watch the departure.

"It's a disgrace," said the barmaid in a severe tone to the office girl, who had her head stuck through her window, "the way some people carry on and they supposed to be gentlemen. Standing here half-naked in the presence of ladies."

Paddy took off his hat, scratched his head and moved towards the bathroom.

"After all my trouble," he muttered, "the bath was never used in the heel of the hunt."

The Touch

WHITE MARE galloped west along the strand against the fierce spring wind. Her tail was stretched out straight and motionless. Her nostrils were blood red. Flecks of foam dropped from her jaws with each outrush of her breath. Hailstones, carried slantwise at a great speed by the wind's power, struck with a loud noise against the canvas of her straddle. The two empty baskets, that hung on either side, swayed with her uneven gait, the halters whining as they shifted round the smooth pegs of the wooden yoke. A horse-hair rope trailed from the holed bottom of each basket.

The wind tore wisps from the loose rye straw that cushioned the mare's back against the rough canvas. They were maintained in the air by the fierce gale. They sailed away to the east, one after the other, gambolling like butterflies at dance.

Kate Hernon was riding on the mare's haunches, gripping one of the straddle pegs with her left hand and holding a can

of hot tea out in front of her with her right. Her head was
bent forward over the yoke for shelter. Her flannel skirt was
the same dark blue colour as her wild eyes. She wore raw-hide
shoes, a little head-shawl that was tied under her chin and a
short sheepskin jacket that was buttoned tightly over her
bodice. She was eighteen years old. A splendid rider, you
would swear that her body was part of the mare.

The local people had been gathering seaweed from the
surf since before dawn over at the far end of the strand. Now
the grey sand was dotted with little cocks of the red weed, all
the way up the strand from where the waves were breaking.

Most of these people stopped working when they saw the
girl approach them at such a furious pace on the white mare.

"By my lance of battle!" said one of the men. "There's a
maiden fit to please a king."

"Aye," said another man. "If I were single to-day, it's on
her finger I'd want to put my ring."

"By the blade of the lance!" said a third. "I'd rather have
a son from her womb than a fourth of land."

There was a young man named Brian O'Neill working
for Kate's father as a day labourer that spring. He got angry
when he heard the remarks of the other men. He was in love
with the girl.

"May they hear the morning screech!" he said to himself
as he came out of the surf with a load of the weed on his pitch
fork. "The bawdy devils! People like them should be thrown
down a cliff."

He looked shyly to the east along the strand as he was
throwing the weed on the cock. His cheeks reddened when
he caught sight of Kate. He went out again into the tide hurriedly, his head lowered in order that the people might not
discover his emotion.

He was perished with cold to the marrows of his bones.
His hands and feet were numb. His thighs were scalded by

the brine. Yet he felt now that there was a fire burning within him. His blood ran madly through his veins.

Kate jumped deftly to the strand when the mare halted by her father's cock of weed.

"God bless the work," she shouted gaily to the people.

"You, too," the people answered her.

Her father came over to her in a state of great agitation. He was a stooped little man. His features were crabbed and contorted by the cold. He was just turned sixty years of age. His wife had given him no sons and all his daughters, with the exception of Kate, had emigrated in search of a livelihood. That was why he was obliged to hire a day labourer that spring.

"Are you crazy?" he said, as he caught the mare by the head.

"Why so?" Kate said.

"Why did you race her, you fool?" he said.

Kate laughed merrily. She was at least a hand taller than her father, a handsome, supple girl of fine limbs and features, bubbling with the exuberance of healthy youth.

"I couldn't hold her," she said. "It must be the spring she feels in her blood. She didn't want to walk fast or to trot. She only wanted to gallop. There's no end to the spunk that's in her, a little thing like her."

"You're a greater fool than your mother," her father said. "God help me, having to deal with the two of you."

He loosened the belly band and put his hand in between the mare's back and the straw.

"Aie!" he said. "A silly girl racing this one and she falling to pieces with fat after a winter's idleness."

Kate laughed merrily once more as she walked over a big granite rock.

"That bit of a race will do her good," she cried. "It will clear her wind pipe."

The father took the tail piece from under the mare's tail. Then he pulled the loosened straddle back and forth, in order to give the sweating back a little air. He stopped when she began to shudder violently and to stamp her hind feet. He put back the tail piece and half-tightened the belly band. He put a little basket of hay to her head. Finally, he took a bunch of straw and began to rub her forelegs.

"Aie!" he cried mournfully as he rubbed. "A man without sons is a pitiful person. God was unkind to me surely."

Kate took shelter under the granite rock and unbuttoned her sheepskin jacket. Her apron was rolled up about a bundle at her waist. She put the contents of the bundle on the ground. Then she spread the apron. She set out big slices of buttered griddle cake, boiled eggs, salt, two spoons and two mugs. She untied the cloth that was keeping the can of tea hot. She poured tea into the mugs.

"Come on over now," she called to the two men. "Let ye be drinking this tea while it's hot. Hurry on over."

Brian came over to the rock at once. He squatted on his heels, took off his cap and blessed himself. Kate handed him a mug of tea.

"God increase you," he said as he took it.

"Same to you," she said to him.

They looked into one another's eyes as they spoke. They both blushed. Although what they had said were merely words of common courtesy, they felt just as shy as if they had disclosed the secret of their love to one another. Kate turned away suddenly. Brian bent his head over his food.

The father came over to the rock in a great hurry, blowing on his cupped hands as he came.

"Go over and catch hold of her head," he said to Kate. "She's terribly nervous on account of this cold. She might pull her halter."

He squatted, blessed himself and began to eat. He wolfed his food.

"Lord God!" Kate said, as she handed him his tea. "Why won't you have patience with your food?"

"Blast you!" he said. "Go on over there."

Kate ran over and began to rub the mare's forehead.

"Hurry up, man," the father said to Brian. "Poor people can't spend the whole day at their meals. We have a whole lot to do and the day is half spent already. Hurry, I tell you."

The young man said nothing. Even though he had been weak from hunger for the past two hours, he was now hardly able to eat a morsel. He had difficulty in swallowing what he put in his mouth. He had ceased to be hungry when he saw Kate looking at him as she handed the tea.

Every other time she looked at him there was a gay light of mockery in her eyes and there was a smile on her lips. Now her eyes were serious and her lips were solemn. He understood what that meant.

That was why he ceased to be hungry and why his throat got so narrow that he found it hard to swallow anything. Instead of paying attention to his food, he kept stealing glances at Kate over his shoulder.

The old man finally noticed these glances.

"A cat can look at a princess," he cried angrily. "So they say and what harm is there in it? It's a different story, though, when a blackguard that doesn't have a penny to his name looks at a decent man's daughter. Do you understand me?"

The young man got angry. His eyes flashed. He looked at the old man, but he did not speak.

"Watch out for yourself," the old man continued. "You have only a small garden by your cabin door, two goats and an ass. You have neither father, nor brother, nor sister. You have only your mother and she sick these last ten years and she depending on you in every way, just like a new-born child. Nobody of your kin ever had land or foreshore to his name. Your kin were never better than scamps and vagrants; just a lot of beggars that came to these parts at the time of the great famine."

Brian jumped to his feet. He was trembling with rage.

"You have said enough," he said. "Nobody belonging to me was ever a beggar, or dishonest. All my people were decent."

"Devil a bit I care," the old man said. "Stay clear of my daughter, I'm telling you. It's not on a girl that was born in a house with two cows that a man with two goats should lay eyes."

"You have enough said," Brian cried once more.

"Go on over now," old Hernon said, "and be loading seaweed."

Brian rushed to the mare, thrust aside one of the baskets with his shoulder and tightened the belly-band. Then he began to throw armfuls of the weed into the baskets. When they were full to overflowing, he picked up his fork and continued to load weed on to the top of the straddle yoke.

Kate's heart beat wildly as she watched the wild rhythm of the young man's strength in action. She became intoxicated with passion. She was forced to lean against the mare's shoulder with her lips parted and her eyes fixed. Although another heavy shower of hail was now falling and beating sharply against her cheek, she was unconscious of the impact. Now she was indifferent to all but her desire for the young man.

The old man took note of her preoccupation as he approached from the rock. He understood. He halted, put his back to the shower and his fingers to his chin.

"There now!" he said to himself calmly. "That scoundrel has hold of her. There now, 'faith! He has her hooked."

He looked at Brian and became possessed of a savage hatred for the young labourer. He loathed the straight back, the fair hair and the shining blue eyes that could lead a young woman's fancy astray in such a way.

"Blast him!" he whispered under his breath. "The beggar. The filthy beggar! Without a penny in his pocket! Not a single penny has he got, the dirty beggar! I'll soon put an end to his schemes. The stinking fellow!"

He went to the mare and took up position with his fork on the opposite side to Brian. They both worked fiercely, loading seaweed. Soon there was a towering pile above the straddle. It was time to throw the first rope.

"Look out for it," the old man shouted to Brian.

"Let it come," Brian said.

The old man threw the rope over the top of the load.

"Got it, you bloody fool?" the old man shouted again.

Brian did not answer. When he was taking the rope end from Kate, his fingers touched the back of her hand. He started violently and gripped her hand. She started with equal violence and looked at him. Their faces were aflame. They dropped the rope end and grasped one another fiercely by both hands. They rushed together and stood bosom to bosom. They were trembling from head to foot.

They stood thus for several seconds. Then the old man shouted again. "What devilment are you up to now, you blackguard?"

Brian started. He loosed his hold of Kate's hands and picked up the rope end. He took a turn round the tooth that protruded from the bottom of the basket and made it fast. Then he threw across the second rope.

"Look out for it," he shouted.

The old man fastened the second rope. Then he rushed around the mare to Brian.

"You scoundrel!" he shouted. "I know your tricks. I know what you have in mind, but it won't be any use for you. Do you hear me?"

"I don't know what you're saying, old man," Brian said.

"You know well what I'm saying, you blackguard," shouted the old man.

"You've no right to call me a blackguard," the young man cried.

"Blackguard! Blackguard!" screamed the old man. "I'll say it as often as I like. Do you hear? Do you dare try to stop me? Do you dare?"

Brian stared with flashing eyes at the old man.

"Don't say anything you might be sorry for later," he said in a low voice.

"I'll say what I please," shouted Hernon. "I'll say any bloody thing I please. I've met many of your kind and I've chastised them. I'm telling you to keep clear of my daughter from now on. Otherwise I'll horsewhip you to within an inch of your life. Do you hear me, you bloody beggar?"

The young man's face was now deathly pale with rage. Yet he merely lowered his eyes to the sand and said nothing. The old man caught him by the shoulder and shook him contemptuously.

"Do you hear me?" the old man said.

The young man nodded.

"You'll keep away from her then?" shouted Hernon.

The young man nodded again after a slight pause.

"Don't let me catch you forgetting that either," snarled Hernon as he gave the shoulder a final push. "If you do, there'll be hell to pay."

He went around the mare's tail to his own side.

"Load away now," he shouted. "We've enough time wasted."

Brian looked at Kate. She was looking at him in astonish-

ment and appeal. He understood very well what she was saying to him with her wild eyes. She was saying that she was
ready to do whatever was necessary in order to put their
love into effect. She was urging him to take her from her
father and to do with her what he pleased. Yet he was afraid.
He only answered her passionate glance of appeal with a
hang-dog look of defeat and submission.

So that she turned away and shuddered. A look of torture
came into his eyes. He quickly thrust out his hand and
touched her on the shoulder. She drew away a little farther
and shuddered violently, just as the mare had done when
she felt the touch of the old man's cold hand against her
sweating hide. She buried her face in the mare's white mane
and kept shuddering. Brian muttered a foul oath and continued to load.

The two men loaded and cast ropes until there was a tower-
shaped heap of slippery red weed atop the straddle. They
then made fast the wet red tower for transport to the field
that was being fertilised for the spring sowing of potatoes.

"Be off now," the old man said to Brian. "Hurry back
from the garden. We have ten more loads, at least."

Brian took the halter from Kate. Now she did not glance
at him. She hurried away to the rock with her eyes downcast.
He wound the halter round his wrist and gripped the load.
He picked up a sea rod and shook it before the side of the
mare's head.

"Go on!" he cried. "Twous."

The mare went forward slowly, up through the cocks of
red weed, towards the sandbank that lined the road. Her
hooves sank deep into the soft sand, under the weight of the
heavy load.

"Twous!" Brian kept shouting as he shook the rod. "Keep
on! Twous!"

Up they went on to the high bank of sand, the wet red

tower walking on long white legs and a young man guiding it.

"There now!" the old man said, as he stood with his arms folded looking after Brian. "So he thought to come into my house as son-in-law."

When the mare and the young man passed out of sight beyond the bank, a cunning smile appeared at the old man's lips.

"I'll soon put an end to his little plan," he said half-aloud. "The silly beggar! To think he would dare look at my daughter! The bloody beggar!"

He walked east along the strand to the place where Marcus Joyce was working.

"Whisper to me a minute," he said to Marcus.

Marcus was a big strong man with red hair. Hernon and he sat down behind a cock of weed and lit the pipe.

"You were talking to me a little while back," Hernon said, "about making a match."

"That's right," Marcus said. "I was thinking of my second son, Red Mike."

"A fine lad," Hernon said. "One of the best. I find no fault with him. It was with the money you were offering him that I found fault. He'll be coming into my house, if he comes. He'll be coming in to a place of two fourths and a half, with two cows and the finest girl in the parish. Yet you only offered . . ."

"I offered good money," Marcus interposed.

"Yerrah!" said Hernon. "What did you offer but two hundred and a half?"

"And what would you want?" said Marcus. "Is it the riches of the Americas you think I have?"

"Add another hundred to it," Hernon said, "and I'll spit on my fist."

"Three hundred and fifty sovereigns!" cried Marcus. "You king of devils!"

"For three hundred and fifty," said Hernon, "I'll throw into your side of the bargain that makings of a bull I have. I know you're hankering after him."

When Kate crouched under the rock and tried to collect her kit, she found that she was in a state of complete stupor. She just stared at the ground, unable to move. It was only when the sound of her father's voice, raised in loud argument with Marcus Joyce, came to her ears that she recovered from her stupor. She looked towards the cock under which the two men were sitting. She understood at once what they were discussing. She crossed herself.

"God forbid!" she prayed fervently.

Then she hurriedly made a bundle of her kit within her apron and buttoned her sheepskin jacket. She set off eastwards along the strand towards home. She passed close to the men.

"Ah! God help me!" she moaned as she passed them.

Now they had lowered their voices. They were sitting very close together. They were pushing one another with their shoulders affectionately and striking fist against palm and passing the lighted pipe after every other word. All these were signs that the bargain was already made and that only details remained to be discussed.

"Oh! Lord God!" Kate cried in agony as she walked east hurriedly. "Why did you let them sell me like a cow or a pig?"

She mounted the sandbank and then went south along a narrow road that was bound on either side by a tall stone fence. Soon another shower of hail began to fall. She took shelter against the fence.

She sat for some time, with her mind a blank, watching the hailstones patter against the wet stones of the opposite fence. Then she remembered Brian and started as if she had been struck. Her eyes widened and became fixed.

First she thought of her hands touching his hands and of his bosom touching her breasts and of the intoxication produced in her by that touch. Then the sorrow of eternal hell followed close upon that drunkening thought, as she realised that this first touch of love would be the last touch and that she was henceforth sold to a man whose touch would be a torture to her flesh.

A scream came up into her throat, but it went no farther. It remained there unuttered. Her woe was too deep for tears. She just sat looking across the narrow road in silence at the cold white stones that were beating fiercely against the cold black stones.

The Water Hen

HE STRETCHED her left leg and laid her wing along it like an open fan. The sunshine made the moist feathers look a radiant blue. Then she wheeled, stood on her left leg and preened her right wing in the sun, making it shimmer. With her wings trailing, she stood on both legs, lowered her head slightly and shook her tail feathers. She shook them frantically, like a flag signalling. Then she began to cluck in a strident tone and ran around in a half-circle, with her breast near the ground and her tail feathers distended. Now her wings were crossed above her sleek back, like a canopy, their points towards her arched tail.

One of the two cocks grazing on the bank of the lake answered her clucking with an eager cry. Without lowering her wings, she looked sideways and saw that it was the smaller cock which had answered her. The big cock was still picking with the other six water hens, apparently indifferent to her gesture. She at once lowered her wings, twirled her tail smartly and began to tidy herself.

The small cock ran down the grass slope to the water. It was very shallow out to the mud bank, where the hen was sunning herself beside a clump of reeds. He could wade all the way. Instead of wading, however, he crossed with a great flurry of wings, skimming the water in flight and paddling fiercely at the same time. He clucked triumphantly as he came. He landed on the mud bank and ran towards the hen, with his wings raised forward and his head lowered. She did not wait to receive him. Affecting to be frightened, she took wing and flew over to the grassy slope. She landed daintily near the big cock, who took no notice of her. He was still picking with great energy.

The small cock, excited by the gesture she had made on the mud bank and taking her flight for a piece of coquetry, came after her on the wing at great speed. Clucking amorously, he landed on the sward and rushed at her. Again she fled from him and ran behind the big cock for protection.

At last the big cock deigned to notice that there was something afoot. He raised his head, clucked angrily and shook his right leg. Then he looked at the little cock and jerked his head several times. Finally, he prodded his breast with his beak, shook himself and resumed his picking.

During this time the little cock had stood still, with his body braced to receive an attack. When the big cock resumed picking, he clucked defiantly and again charged the hen, coming at her in a half-circle. She ran around the cock with her head lowered meekly and her wings trailing slightly, coming closer. The little cock kept following her at a run, leaning over as he ran, in a wide curve, like a boat careening from the wind. Now all the other hens took notice. They raised their heads and made angry noises.

Suddenly the big cock stopped picking and charged the

72

other without warning. The little one was almost caught by the charge, but he wheeled just in time and rushed to escape through the flock of hens, which scattered in confusion. He made for the water, racing down the slope at top speed. The big cock turned and followed him. As soon as the small cock reached the water, he spread his wings and scurried over the surface in the direction of the reeds. The big cock was much faster. He reached the little one some distance from the reeds and forced him to wheel out into the lake. The big cock followed closely, straining to reach him.

Like hare and hound, they curved and doubled, skimming the smooth water, leaving a labyrinth of interlacing eddies in their tracks. They moved farther and farther away, until the big cock finally gave up the chase and returned. The little cock took refuge on a small island.

The hen came forward to receive her protector as he stepped proudly up the slope, prodding his breast feathers and shrugging himself. With her lowered head turned to one side and her wings loose, she offered herself to him humbly. He went past her without taking any notice. Then she ran forward a little and again offered herself still more humbly, with her wings trailing. She stood right in his path. He turned aside, passed her once more and began to pick. She followed him with her eyes, as if spellbound, as she slowly raised herself to her full height, gathering up her wings. Then she turned away and walked a few steps towards the edge of the lake. With lowered head, she stood there brooding for a long time without movement.

Then she heard a plaintive cry far out in the lake and raised her head. It came from the small island on which the other cock had taken refuge. Presently she saw him take wing from the island, flying in the direction of the reeds. He flew only a part of the distance and then he landed on the water. He cried again, while resting on the water and then took

73

wing once more. He flew quietly now, making no sound, still afraid of an attack from the other cock. Finally, he landed among the reeds and began to edge slowly round to the mud bank, uttering sharp, low cries. The hen became excited.

The sun was now at its full height. Its warmth was full of the fever and the violence of spring. The hen felt it on her body. All morning she had felt it, since she found a spot among the reeds where she wanted to lay her eggs. It was when she lay down on some broken reeds and gathered more with her beak around her breast and sides that she felt it. Their harsh dryness against her body started the fever. Now it was much more intense, making reaction automatic and indifferent. She was no longer aware of the big cock. She was only aware of the spot among the reeds, where it was exciting to lie down upon the broken dry reeds and turn about and feel their harshness against her. She wanted to abandon herself.

She began to cluck almost inaudibly as she walked slowly along the edge of the lake towards the mud bank. She walked drunkenly, pausing frequently and blinking her eyes. She kept stretching out her neck and bobbing her head, as if she were trying to swallow something big that had stuck in her throat. She raised her wings and fanned her back with them. Her tail feathers moved spasmodically. When she came to the water's edge to wade across the narrow passage to the mud bank, she halted and stared at the water, as if afraid of it. Then she suddenly plunged into it and rolled herself from side to side, lying on her belly and fluttering her wings. She ran a little way and rolled herself once more. Then she ran around in a circle, dipping her neck and lashing the water with her wings. Now both cocks watched her excitedly.

The little cock had come forward to the middle of the bank, where he kept running back and forth in a frenzy, afraid to come nearer, his little feet making delicate patterns on the dry mud. The big cock came stepping arrogantly down to the edge of the lake, clucking angrily. He paused now and again on one leg, thrust out his breast and shook his comb. He paid no attention to the hen that was madly thrashing about in the water. He was warning the little cock not to approach. The latter, however, did not heed these threats. He was made bold by the distance and by the hen's mating dance in the water. He called to her frantically.

Then she stood up in the water, tidied herself and waded hurriedly to the bank, with her head lowered meekly. Losing all fear of his rival, the little cock ran into the water to meet her. This time she did not turn from him. She kept moving at the same pace until she reached the bank, while he danced about her, exactly as she herself had done. The big cock now uttered a shrill cry and came scurrying across the water towards them. The little cock, roused to valour by his apparent conquest, abandoned the hen and turned to meet the enemy. He set himself and charged head foremost before the big cock could steady himself. The big cock fell and the little one leaped on him, striking him with beak, wings and feet. The hen, as if nothing were happening, walked on quickly until she came to the reeds. She went in among them and lay down in the rough nest she had gathered that morning. Then she raised her neck, turned her head to one side and listened to the noise of the battle. She shuddered with delight.

It was cool here among the tall reeds. As the cocks cried and their wings swished in the charge, she felt the rough dry reeds press against her and the fever mounted into ecstasy. Suddenly there was no more sound and she started anxiously, half-raising herself. She listened in agony for some seconds. Then she heard a strident clucking at a distance. It was repeated several times, growing more distant. Then it faded away completely and there was silence. Unable to bear the torture of waiting, she got fully to her feet and strained her neck. She heard a faint, angry cluck near by and she sat down suddenly. Now she trembled and closed her eyes, with her neck drawn down into her back, pretending to hide. The clucking approached, short and sharp. He was calling her. She made no answer. Now there was the sound of feet and the light brushing of a body passing through the reeds.

She could contain her curiosity no longer. She raised herself, turned her head and saw that it was the big cock which was coming for her. His head was bleeding and some of his feathers were hanging loose. She stood up fully and uttered a cry of pretended fear. He saw her, arched his wings and rushed towards her, clucking amorously. She pretended to run from him, farther into the reeds. But she only went a little way and then lowered her head and waited for him.

In a moment he was upon her and she lay down in a swoon.

The Flute-Player

A FIERCE BLAST of icy wind rushed into the tavern room as the door flew open. A newspaper was swept from a man's hand by the near end of the counter and thrust with violence against the legs of another man, who stood farther down with a pint of porter held to his upraised mouth. Hailstones entered with the wind. They rattled against a small partition that jutted from the wall in front of the door. A paraffin lamp, hanging from the tall ceiling by a chain, flickered and almost went out. Then a cloud of black smoke billowed upwards through the narrow chimney.

"Shut that bloody door before we perish," a drunken man shouted from the far end of the room.

Colonel Matt Lynam, who owned the big house down by the lake in the glen, entered through the gale of wind. He was a large man, with a fat face that was completely red. He wore a heavy brown overcoat, a tweed cap and field boots that were splashed with mud right up to his knees. He carried a gun and a game bag slung over his shoulders.

"Come on, Jack," he shouted through the open door.

Dr. Jack O'Brien, a Dublin physician staying with the colonel at Kilcolman House for a week's shooting, ran head first into the room.

"Here I come," he gasped. "All that's left of me."

He was a thin little man with a sickly face, dressed almost exactly like the colonel. He looked exhausted.

"Put your shoulder to this door with me, Jack," the colonel said.

The two men had to lean with their whole weight against the re-closed door before they could set the latch. Then they put their gear by the wall and walked up to the counter, slapping their gloved hands under their armpits.

"Wild night, gentlemen," said Josey Hynes, the tavern-keeper.

"That's no lie," the colonel said. "Give us a couple of stiff ones."

"Wild?" Dr. O'Brien said. "Man alive! It would perish the Danes."

The drunken man at the far end of the room again shouted in an insolent tone.

"Strike it up there, Jones," he cried. "Give us a hearty one."

He was addressing a ragged flute-player that stood by the rear wall of the room, near a grate in which a large turf fire was burning.

"Give us 'The Bard of Armagh,' Jones," shouted another customer.

Several men asked for "The Bard of Armagh" to be played.

"Very well, then," the flute-player said in a dignified tone.

He glanced towards Colonel Lynam. Then he rubbed his

palms together, shrugged his shoulders in the manner of the habitual drunkard and put his flute to his lips. He began to play with great skill and delicacy.

"That's the boy, Jones," the drunken man shouted. "You take the sway from all the greatest flute-players in the world. More power to you."

The flute-player was tall and slender. He had a finely shaped head and long, tapering limbs that gave his whole body an air of good breeding. He was about forty years of age. In spite of the intense cold, he wore hardly any clothes worth the name. His feet were bare, except for the quantity of mud that had dried on them. His trousers were just a succession of ragged patches. They only reached halfway down his shins. They were held at the waist by means of a rude cord. His jacket was just as ragged as his trousers. It was too small for him and there was only one button in front. He wore nothing beneath it. His bare skin was visible above and below the straining button.

"There he is playing over there," the colonel whispered to Dr. O'Brien after they had finished their first round of drinks and ordered another one. "I can hardly bear to look at him."

The doctor stared in silence at the flute-player for a little while.

"He looks pretty far gone," he said at length.

"He plays as well as ever," the colonel said. "The man is a genius."

"I wasn't referring to his music," the doctor said. "He looks a complete wreck."

"Never mind his appearance," the colonel said. "If he could only put that woman out of his head, he'd recover in no time at all."

"You really think so?" O'Brien said. "To me he looks like a confirmed drunkard."

79

"Not at all," said the colonel. "He's in love. That's his trouble."

A look of rapture spread over the colonel's fat face as he listened to the music for a few moments, with his head turned a little to one side. Then he looked again at the doctor.

"What a tragedy!" he said. "He can make that flute speak. Ah! You should have heard him play for me at Kilcolman. It was paradise while I had him there playing for me. Especially during the long winter evenings."

He glanced at the flute-player and his face clouded with anger.

"The damn fool!" he muttered.

"Poor devil!" the doctor said. "How does he manage to keep alive in weather like this? He's almost naked."

"Love keeps him alive," the colonel said in a sombre tone.

"How do you mean?" said the doctor.

"Love drove him out of his mind," said the colonel. "It drove him from Kilcolman House up to this wild mountain tavern. It made him sleep in a miserable stone hut that is practically wide open to the sky, out there in a rocky field by the road-side, with no more clothes on him than a wild animal. Love made a drunkard of him, too. Yet it now keeps him alive. It holds him prisoner and it has him doomed to death. It only keeps him alive to torture him slowly. Oh! man alive, love is a terrible and deadly disease."

Dr. O'Brien looked at the colonel with suspicion.

"Really?" he said. "You believe that, Colonel?"

"The madness of love," said the colonel with deep conviction in his voice, "gives miraculous power to its victims, even while it is destroying them."

He shrugged his shoulders, picked up the fresh drink that had been put before him on the counter and swore under his breath. He clinked glasses with O'Brien and tossed back the whisky.

"I'll have another shot at him, in any case," he added. "I'll try for the last time to bring him home with me."

"Unless I'm mistaken," the doctor said, "he won't listen to you."

"No harm in trying," the colonel said.

"You'll be wasting your breath," the doctor said. "Whether it's love or drink, that man is too far gone."

The flute-player finished his tune and bowed politely to the few cheers of applause. Then he took a small bag from the pocket of his miserable jacket and went round collecting money from the customers. Nearly everybody gave him a few coppers. He hesitated a moment when he came near the colonel. Then he put the half-filled bag behind his back, drew himself to his full height and bowed slightly.

"Good evening, sir," he said respectfully.

"Good evening, Jones," the colonel said. "How are you?"

"Can't complain, sir," the flute-player said.

Dr. O'Brien brought a shilling from his pocket and offered to put it in the bag. A hard look came into the sunken grey eyes of the flute-player. He stared at the doctor and then took a short step to the rear. The doctor put the shilling back into his own pocket.

"Come here a moment," the colonel said gruffly to the flute-player. "I want to have a word with you."

The flute-player's eyes became still harder as he looked at the colonel. Yet he moved forward as requested and stood very erect, with his dirty naked feet close together. His free hand rested against the centre of his thigh, in the posture of a soldier standing to attention before a superior. The other hand clutched the little bag against the small of his back.

"I want to have a final word with you, Jones," the colonel said in a tone of entreaty. "I came here again to-night hoping you might listen to reason. Will you come back with me to Kilcolman?"

The flute-player's glance became very arrogant. His delicate nostrils widened. In spite of his extreme shabbiness, he was clean-shaven and his close-cropped black hair was carefully brushed. His emaciated pale face still retained the smoothness of texture that comes from constant care and refined surroundings.

"I'm sorry, Colonel Lynam," he said in a solemn tone. "I've given you my answer several times already. I can't come back to Kilcolman with you. I must stay here."

"Good heavens!" said the colonel. "Don't you understand how all this is going to end?"

"I know that very well," the flute-player said.

"You'll be found dead in that miserable hut some morning," the colonel continued. "Or else you'll go raving mad and be carried off to the lunatic asylum."

"It makes no difference, sir," the flute-player said.

"I wouldn't mind so much," the colonel said, "if the woman were in the least interested. On the contrary, she is just laughing . . ."

The flute-player's eyes became so angry that the colonel interrupted himself.

"Very well!" he said after a short pause. "Devil take it! If that is what you want . . ."

"That is what I want, Colonel Lynam," the flute-player said. "Good evening."

He bowed, turned away slowly and walked down the room with great dignity, still holding the little bag clutched against the small of his back. Now it was obvious from his carriage that he had once been a butler. Anger had roused in him the pompous arrogance of his former calling.

As he neared the far end of the counter, however, his manner changed. His shoulders sagged. He looked furtively from side to side. Then he crouched over the board and poured out the copper coins from the bag. He counted them eagerly.

He began to mutter as he rapped on the counter with his open palm.

"What's going on here?" the tavern-keeper said, as he came down behind the counter at a leisurely pace. "Are you at it again, Jones?"

The flute-player's sunken eyes glared with hatred at Hynes.

"I want a glass of rum," he said. "Be quick with it."

Hynes put a glass on the counter and stared for a little while in silence at the flute-player. He was tall and thin, with disorderly fair hair and furtive blue eyes. He had a large mouth and decayed teeth.

It was obvious from the intense way in which the two men stared at one another that their mutual hatred was fixed and unchangeable.

"I advise you to keep a civil tongue in your head, Jones," the tavern-keeper said at length. "Otherwise, I might . . ."

"Arrah! Leave the man alone," the drunken man interrupted in an arrogant tone. "Why are you always picking on him? Haven't you done him enough harm, you and your wife? Especially your wife."

There was a roar of laughter from the other customers. Hynes got red in the face.

"Another word out of you, Bartly Spillane," he said, "and you'll go out on top of your head."

The drunken man laughed derisively.

"Who'll put me out, Josey?" he cried. "You and how many more? Give Jones his drink and stop talking."

"Is that so?" Hynes said. "A bloody man going around in his bare feet, playing his bloody flute!"

"He's as good as you any day," the drunken man said, "and a damn sight better. What's more, people come here for miles around to hear him play."

"Aye! That's the truth," a number of men cried. "He's a darling player, so he is."

"I'd have him thrown out of here," the tavern-keeper grumbled, as he poured out the rum, "only for I'm too good-natured. There's a law against people like him. On top of it all, he gives me ould guff."

The flute-player swallowed his rum hurriedly, paid for it and put the remaining coins back into his little bag. Then he returned to his position by the fire. Now he shuddered spasmodically in reaction to the violence of the rum.

"Play something real hearty for us now, Jones," the drunken man shouted.

"That's the ticket," said another man. "Give us 'Kelly the Boy from Killane'."

"Very well," the flute-player said respectfully.

As he put the instrument to his lips, his tall body reassumed the tragic dignity of its carriage. His long fingers began to gesticulate lovingly above the holed pipe. Then he turned his head to one side, laid his lips delicately against the flute's mouth and began to make sweet music.

"That's the boy, Jones," the drunken man shouted.

The colonel sipped the third large measure of whisky and put his hand on the doctor's shoulder.

"He was with me five years," he said. "I was never as happy in my life. I got him from a rich American named Hefferman, who rented Sir George Blake's house for a season's hunting and imported an enormous staff of servants from England. Hefferman kept open house for the whole district. Nothing like it was seen in these parts since the turn of the century. Place was like a big railway station while it lasted, with people coming and going the whole time, day and night. Lashings of the best for everybody. Then Hefferman suddenly got bored. He dashed off to Palm Beach while the festivities were at their height, leaving his secretary to dispose of the staff. Jones came over to see me at Kilcolman and asked me to employ him. 'I heard you were interested in flute music,' he said. 'Would you care to hear me play?' I said I would. He whipped out his flute and played for me. I was enchanted. 'Look here,' I said. 'I'm an old bachelor. I live more or less alone here. I'm not a rich man. Far from it. I couldn't possibly afford to pay the wages to which you are accustomed. We really live from hand to mouth here at Kilcolman.' He told me he wasn't interested in money. He was a Welshman by birth, he said, although brought up in England. He had become so fascinated by the Irish scene, during the weeks he had spent at Feakle Castle, that he wanted to live here for the rest of his life. 'It's like my native Wales,' he said, 'only more enchanted. You see, I am really a musician, although I work as a butler for a living. This place is melancholy and enchanted like music. I am quite willing to work and play here without any payment at all.' So I engaged him. As I said before, from that moment I entered Paradise."

The colonel drank the remainder of the whisky in his glass. The heat of the room after the cold air outside, the acrid smell of the turf and his roused emotions all combined to make it quickly take effect on him. He was already fully intoxicated. There were tears in his eyes and his upper lip trembled.

"Sooner or later," he said in a sentimental tone, "an Eve comes into every Paradise and the devil always follows Eve. About twelve months ago, I took him shooting with me. I had reached the stage when I couldn't bear to have him out of my sight. I wanted him to play for me whenever the mood possessed him. We came here on our way home. He saw her. It was the oddest thing. He stood there like a rabbit in the presence of a weasel, while she marched up and down behind the counter with her queer smile always on her lips. I knew it was all up with him. He never spoke all the way home in the car. He refused to play for me next morning when I asked him. He moped all day. It was the same thing when I asked him to play that evening. That went on for a whole week. Then I lost my temper with him. That finished it. He took his flute and left the house. He came straight up here."

"It's a strange tale," the doctor said.

"It's a tragedy," the colonel said. "For me, especially, it's a tragedy, even more than it is for him. I'm a lonely man. I have nobody left in the world and music is the only thing I really love. It's a terrible thing to see beauty come into the house and to enjoy its strange presence for a long time and then to see it walk out again without warning. His tragedy is less than mine, for he still has his music. He has it there inside him, as good as it ever was."

"A strange tale, surely," the doctor said.

The flute-player finished his tune and again made the rounds of the tavern with his little bag. This time he avoided the colonel. When he counted the coins, he discovered to his chagrin that there were not enough of them to buy a glass of rum. He walked back to his position by the fire with downcast head.

"Come on, Jones," the drunken man shouted. "Don't be downhearted, man. I have the price on me. Let me buy you a glass."

The flute-player shook his head and said:

"Thank you, but I would rather not."

Then he began to play another tune. Now he played hurriedly and without passion. He kept his eyes on the interior of the house, to the rear of the counter, while he played. He was obviously waiting for someone to appear.

"See him refuse the drink?" said the colonel. "That shows you he's not a drunkard. Yet he drinks out of sheer misery. He drinks every penny he gets for his music. He never buys anything but rum. God knows how he lives. No one sees him taste a morsel."

"This woman must really be a witch," Dr. O'Brien said. "Or else she's a great beauty. Who is she?"

"Nobody knows," the colonel said. "When Hynes came back from America and bought this place, he had her with him. He married her over there. She belongs to a strange race. There's no doubt about that. She is certainly not the type you'd expect to find . . . Hush! Here she comes now."

A woman entered the bar from the interior of the house. She paused for a few moments to look around her solemnly at the customers. Then she folded her arms on her bosom and marched haughtily down behind the counter, with a fixed smile on her lips.

"Good God!" said Dr. O'Brien. "What a strange creature!"

Her tall slender body was so lithe that it seemed to quiver as she walked, like a sapling willow that bends a thousand ways in answer to the gentlest wind. Her small, shining eyes and her hair were black as sloes. The skin of her face was as tawny as that of a mulatto. Against this darkness, the two little rows of perfectly matched teeth that showed between her parted lips looked dazzling white. Two long ear-rings reached down almost to her collar bones. They were white and shining like her teeth in the smoky lamp light. Her dress was uniformly black. It fitted her body like a male dancer's tights.

The flute-player stopped playing as soon as she appeared. He stood very erect, with his head thrown back. His sunken eyes were fixed upon her. His lips were parted. The customers also stared at her in silence, watching her progress. Her husband was the only one in the room who did not look at her. He washed glasses furiously, with bowed head, obviously in the throes of jealousy.

When she reached the far end of the counter, she halted and looked at the flute-player. She inclined her head slightly towards him. Her smile became vivacious and intimate for a brief moment. Then she took a short step to the rear and leaned her shoulder against the cash register. Her smile again became fixed, remote and indifferent.

The flute-player bowed solemnly to her. He put his instrument slowly to his lips and began to play with his sunken eyes fixed on her face. After the first few notes, there was a wild cry of applause.

"Hurrah!" cried the drunken man, waving his pint measure above his head. "Now we have it. Now we have music equal to any in the world."

"Hurrah!" cried the others. "More power! May your heart never stop beating!"

The flute-player was now putting his whole soul into his music. The notes that came from his flute were like cries of agony coming from a wounded bird, asking for succour. He reached out with all his power to the indifferent woman, struggling to touch her heart with the beauty of his music.

She turned away from him after he had played a little. She marched up to her husband, leaned towards him and began to whisper something in his ear. Then she continued to parade back and forth behind the counter, with her arms folded on her bosom, smiling fixedly and without recognition at the customers.

Now completely intoxicated, Colonel Lynam seized Dr. O'Brien violently by the coat lapels and shouted:

"Can you imagine? I had that music living in my house for years. For years, I tell you. Then it was snatched from me . . ."

The flute-player was now reaching forward almost on his toes, with his sunken eyes fixed madly on the woman, as he struggled to make his music touch her indifferent heart.

Life

THE MOTHER lay flat on her back, with her eyes closed and her arms stretched out to their full length above the bedclothes. Her hands kept turning back and forth in endless movement. Her whole body was exhausted after the great labour of giving birth.

Then the infant cried. She opened her eyes as soon as she heard the faint voice. She seized the bedclothes fiercely between her fingers. She raised her head and looked wildly towards the grandmother, who was tending the new-born child over by the fireplace.

The old woman noticed the mother's savage look. She burst out laughing.

"For the love of God," she said to the two neighbouring women that were helping her, "look at herself and she as frightened as a young girl on her wedding night. You'd think this is her first child instead of her last."

She took the infant by the feet, raised him up high and smacked him quite hard on the rump with her open palm.

"Shout now, in God's name," she said, "and put the devil out of your carcass."

The child started violently under the impact of the blow. He screamed again. Now there was power in his voice.

"Upon my soul!" said one of the neighbouring women. "I don't blame her at all for being conceited about a young fellow like that."

She spat upon the infant's naked stomach.

"I never laid eyes on a finer new-born son than this one, 'faith," she said in a tone of deep conviction.

"A fine lad, God bless him," said the other woman as she made the sign of the Cross over the child. "Begob, he has the makings of a hero in him, by all appearances."

"He has, indeed," said the grandmother. "He has the makings of a man in him, all right."

A deep sadness fell upon the mother when she heard the old woman say that this child would be the last to come from her womb. She was now forty-three. The years had already brought silver to her hair. She knew very well that she would never again bring life, by the miraculous power of God, from the substance of her body. She had done that fourteen times already. Except for the first time, when the intoxication of love was still strong in her blood, she got little comfort from giving birth. As the holy seed of life multiplied under her roof, so also did misfortune and hunger multiply. It was so hard for a poor couple like her husband and herself, with only a few acres of stony land, to feed and care for so many little bodies and souls.

Yet she now felt miserably sad at the thought that her womb would henceforth be without fruit. She closed her eyes once more, crossed her hands on her bosom and began a

ran from one. That was the class of a man I was, a man that could stand his ground without fear or favour . . ."

The old woman had to take hold of him and carry him out of the room.

"Come on down out of this," she said, "and don't be bothering the people with your foolish talk."

"Ah! God help me!" said one of the neighbouring women. "The longest journey from the womb to the grave is only a short one after all."

When the baby took up residence in his cradle by the kitchen hearth, he was like a king in the house. The whole family waited on him. It was thankless work. The new-born was entirely unaware that the slightest favour was being conferred on him. He was completely unaware of all but the solitary instinct that he had brought with him from the womb. That was to maintain and strengthen the life that was in him.

When he awoke, he screamed savagely until he was given hold of his mother's breast. Then he became silent at once. His toothless jaws closed firmly on the swollen teat. His little body shivered with voluptuous pleasure when he felt the first stream of warm milk pouring on to his tongue. He sucked until he was replete. Then again he fell asleep. When he felt unwell, from stomach-ache or some other trivial complaint, he yelled outrageously. He went on yelling in most barbarous fashion until they began to rock the cradle. They had to keep rocking until his pain had gone.

They sang to him while they rocked.

"Oh! My darling! My darling! My darling!" they sang to him. "Oh! My darling, you're the love of my heart."

Far different was their conduct towards the old man. There was little respect for him. When they waited on him, it was through charity and not because it gave them pleasure.

95

They begrudged him the smallest favour that they conferred on him.

"Look at that old devil," they used to say. "Neither God nor man can get any good out of him and he sitting there in the chimney corner from morning till night. You'd be better off begging your bread than waiting on him."

True enough, it was hard to blame them for complaining. It was very unpleasant work having to wait upon the poor old man. They had to take him from his sleeping place each morning. They had to clean and dress him and put him seated on a little stool in the chimney corner. They had to tie a horse-hair rope around his waist, lest he might fall into the fire. At mealtimes, they had to mash his food and put it in his mouth with a spoon.

He was dependent on them in every way exactly like the infant.

"Aie! The filthy thing!" they used to say. "It would be a great kindness to the people of this house if God would call him."

The grandfather remained tied in his chimney corner all day, between sleep and wake, jabbering, threatening imaginary people with his stick, scolding enemies that were long since dead, making idiotic conversation with the creatures of his folly about people and places.

He only emerged from his witless state when he heard the infant cry on awaking from sleep.

"Who is this?" he would say with his ear cocked. "Who is squealing like this?"

When the mother took the baby from the cradle and gave it suck in the opposite corner, the old man's eyes would brighten and he would recognise the child.

"Ho! Ho!" he would cry in delight. "It's yourself that's in it. Ho! My lovely one! That's a pretty young man I see over opposite me and no doubt about it."

Then he would try to reach the infant. He would get angry when he failed to go farther than the length of his horse-hair rope.

"Let me at him," he would cry, struggling to leave his stool. "Let go this rope, you pack of devils. He is over there, one of my kindred. Let me at him. He is a man of my blood. Let me go to him."

His rage never lasted long. He would get overcome with delight on seeing the infant stretch and shudder voluptuously as he sucked.

"Bravo! Little one," the old man then cried as he jumped up and down on his stool. "Throw it back, my boy. Don't leave a drop of it. Ho! You are a man of my blood, all right. Drink, little one. More power to you!"

Winter was almost spent before the infant recognised anybody. Until then he only knew his mother's breasts and the warmth of his cradle by means of touch. Even though he often watched what was happening about him, there was no understanding in his big staring blue eyes. Then the day came at last when the resplendent soul shone out through his eyes.

He was lying on his belly across his mother's lap, suffering a little from stomach-ache owing to having drunk too much, when he took note of the old man's foolish gestures in the opposite corner. He smiled at first. Then he began to clap hands and to leap exactly like the old man. He uttered a little jovial yell.

"Praised be the great God of Glory!" said the mother.

The household gathered round. They all stood looking at the infant and at the old man, who were imitating one another's foolish gestures across the hearth. Everybody laughed gaily except the grandmother. It was now she began to weep out loud.

"Aie! My Lord God!" she wailed. "The foolishness of infancy is a lovely thing to behold, but it's pitiful to see an old person that has outlived his reason."

From that day onward, the old man and the baby spent long spells playing together, clapping hands, jabbering and drivelling. It would be hard to say which of them was the more foolish. When the infant was weaned, it was with the same mash they were both fed.

According as the infant grew strong from day to day the old man weakened. He got bronchitis in spring and they thought that his end had come. He received Extreme Unction. Yet he recovered from that attack. He was soon able to leave his bed and resume his position in the hearth corner. Now he was merely a shadow of his former self. They could lift him with one hand.

A day came early in May when there was a big spring tide and the whole family went to pick carrigeen moss along the shore. The grandmother was left to take care of the house, the infant and the old man. It was a fine sunny day.

"Take me out into the yard," the old man said to his wife. "I'd like to see the sun before I die."

She did as he asked her. She put him sitting in a straw chair outside the door. She herself sat on a stool near him, with the infant on her bosom. She began to call the fowls.

"Tiuc! Tiuc!" she cried. "Fit! Fit! Beadai! Beadai! Beadai!"

They all came running to her at top speed, hens and ducks and geese. She threw them scraps of food from a big dish. The birds began to fight for the food, as they leaped and screamed and prodded one another with their beaks.

The infant took light in the tumult of the birds. He began to clap his hands and to leap, as he watched the fierce struggle of the winged creatures. He screamed with glee in answer to their harsh croaking.

"Ho! Ho! Ho!" he cried, while the spittle ran from his mouth.

The old man got equally excited and he imitated the gestures of the infant. He began to clap hands and to hop on his chair and to babble unintelligibly.

"Musha, God help the two of you!" the old woman said.

The old man became silent all of a sudden. She glanced anxiously in his direction. She saw him half erect and leaning forward. Then he fell to the ground head foremost. She rushed to him with the child under her arm. When she stooped over him, she heard the death rattle in his throat. Then there was nothing at all to be heard from him.

She stood up straight and began the lamentation for the newly dead.

"Och! Ochon!" she wailed. "It was with you I walked through the delight and sorrow of life. Now you are gone and I'll soon be following you. Och! Ochon! My love! It was you that was lovely on the day of our marriage. . . ."

When the neighbours came, the old woman sat lamenting on her stool by the corpse with the child within her arms, while the birds still leaped and fought savagely for the food in the dish.

The infant hopped up and down, shouting merrily as he struggled to touch the bright feathers of the rushing birds with his outstretched hands.

The strong young heart was unaware that the tired old heart had just delivered up the life that made it beat.

Grey Seagull

HE WHOLE DEACY FAMILY was gathered round the dining-room table at Kilfinnan House after supper, holding counsel in a state of deep depression. It was only three days to the annual point-to-point races of the Coolagh Hunt. Yet they had no rider for their five-year-old gelding, Grey Seagull, with which they hoped to win the Liosbawn Plate. The oldest son, Roger, a lad of twenty, was to have taken the mount. He now sat at the far end of the table with his right arm in splints and white bandages. He had broken it a fortnight previously while training Grey Seagull over fences.

They had tried everywhere to get a substitute for Roger, but without any success. The trouble was that the grey gelding would let nobody else stay on his back longer than two or three seconds. So that the situation looked absolutely hopeless.

"We must keep on trying," Roger said, breaking a long silence. "I tell you that Grey Seagull is not really savage.

He's just nervous and he likes very few people. If we could only find somebody he really liked to ride him, he would . . ."

"It's no use fooling yourself any longer, Roger," Mr. Deacy interrupted in a gloomy tone. "We can't find a rider for him. That's all there is to it. It's our luck. It's the Deacy luck. There's no going against it. It's been following me all my life."

"That's utter nonsense, John," Mrs. Deacy said.

"It's the truth, Dorothy," said Mr. Deacy. "You should know it is by now, after being married to me for twenty-two years."

"There is no such thing as the Deacy bad luck," Mrs. Deacy said. "I'm sick and tired of hearing it given as an excuse for incompetence, laziness and plain lunacy."

Mr. Deacy certainly looked just a little bit mad as he glared at his wife. He was a tall, raw-boned fellow of sixty-one, with a wild look in his dark eyes. There was a big scar over his right temple, due to a bad fall he got as a young man while riding in a steeplechase.

"Upon my word!" he cried. "That's a fine thing to say in front of the children at a moment like this, when I'm in the depths of misery and a kindly word of advice might help me to find a way out of my trouble. You're a fine partner for a man and no mistake. A fine partner, indeed."

"Never mind, Father," Roger said. "Pay no attention to Mother. She just likes to hear herself talk."

"I don't want to hear any more of your impertinence, Roger," Mrs. Deacy snapped. "Since you've begun to follow in your father's footsteps, gambling and race-riding, you've lost all trace of good manners and of respect for your elders. You've become a real Deacy."

"Come now, all of you," Aunt Penelope said. "Behave yourselves. You won't get a jockey by abusing one another.

If there were anything to be gained by abuse, this family would be the richest in the whole county."

Mr. Deacy struck the table with his clenched fists and swore.

"Talk about luck," he groaned. "Here I've been all my life trying to breed a good steeplechaser. I found one at last, when I'm on my last legs. He's really a good horse. There is no doubt about it. I'd give my solemn oath that he's not only good but great, even though he hasn't been yet put to the acid test of a race against first-class performers over major obstacles. If I could only bring him along in the right way I could get ten thousand pounds for him within a year."

"Ten thousand fiddlesticks!" cried Mrs. Deacy contemptuously.

"There isn't a word of a lie in it," cried Mr. Deacy excitedly. "There are crowds of hungry Englishmen coming over to Ireland now in order to eat good Irish meat. Their pockets are bursting with money. When they have a few good steaks under their belts they get so happy that they all want to buy a steeplechaser and win the Grand National. They are paying fantastic prices for old nags that aren't worth their oats."

"Ten thousand fiddlesticks!" repeated Mrs. Deacy. "If you only tilled your land, John, or even raised cattle . . ."

"He's right, Mother," Roger interrupted. "What he says is true. I know that Lord Dilisk got four thousand pounds the other day for a horse called Simpleton, that he bought from Barney Gouldrick for three hundred and fifty pounds only two months ago. Remember, father? Everybody in the place said he was mad for giving Barney the three hundred and fifty."

"That's a fact," said Mr. Deacy. "He got four thousand for Simpleton, a ten-year-old horse that never finished better than third. Smart boy, that Dilisk. Oh! I could be just as smart if I only could get a rider for Grey Seagull. If I could win the Liosbawn Plate with him and then a couple of other point-to-point races, I'd have enough money to enter him for big events. Then I could go to Punchestown with him next year, and if he won for me there, he'd be recognised as a young champion. I could get a barrel of money for him."

"Every Deacy is born a lunatic," Mrs. Deacy said, "and he dies a lunatic, without a single interval of sanity during his whole life. If you only did some honest work, instead of dreaming these impossible schemes for getting rich quickly, we wouldn't be overdrawn at the bank and we wouldn't be ashamed to show our faces in the town on account of all the money we owe."

"There's a great deal in what you say, Dorothy," Penelope said, "but I'd like to point out that your own family, the Fitz-maurices, are not exactly models of industry and thrift, either. Are they now?"

"That's enough, Penelope," Mr. Deacy said. "Don't get personal."

"For God's sake," said Brian, a red-headed lad of seventeen, "can't you old people try to think of someone else to ride Grey Seagull instead of quarrelling like tinkers?"

"I'm the most unlucky man on earth," said Mr. Deacy. "When I had abandoned hope of ever breeding a good horse, I'm given a champion by the merciful dispensation of Divine Providence. Then the champion turns out to be savage and unmanageable."

"Grey Seagull is not savage, father," cried Roger indignantly. "Why do you keep on saying that he is savage?"

"If he's not savage," said Mr. Deacy, "then I'll eat my head. That animal is the most savage creature I ever saw in my life."

"He's really very gentle with anybody he likes," said Roger, "and he has a mouth like an angel. How can he be savage when he has such a beautiful mouth?"

"When that animal sees me coming," said Mr. Deacy, "he bares his teeth and lets a roar out of him that would put the heart crosswise in a Zulu warrior."

"That's just his nerves," Roger said. "He's very sensitive. There are only a few people that he trusts."

"A few did you say?" cried Mr. Deacy. "You're the only one he lets near him and that proves he's mad. Every mad horse has a streak in him like that, letting only one person come near him. Oh! What's the use of talking? It's the bad luck of the Deacy family that keeps pursuing me."

"He lets Aunt Penelope come near him, too," Roger continued, "and that proves he's not mad. He likes her even more than he likes me. Isn't that true, Aunt Penelope?"

"So he does," said Mrs. Deacy in a spiteful tone, "but that merely goes to prove that he's very mad, indeed."

"You never miss a chance, Dorothy," Penelope said. "Do you?"

Then the youngest child, a girl of sixteen called Charlotte, made a startling suggestion.

"If he's so fond of Aunt Penelope," she said in a deep voice, "why doesn't she ride him in the race?"

Mr. Deacy and the three children all looked intently at Aunt Penelope. Mrs. Deacy snorted contemptuously and continued to knit her jumper.

"That's right," said Aunt Penelope indignantly as she pushed back her chair. "Make fun of an old woman. What next?"

She was sixty-three and strongly resembled her brother, being tall and raw-boned, with wild dark eyes that gave her red-cheeked face a slightly lunatic expression. She had a fine head of steel-grey hair. In her youth she had been a noted rider to hounds. She had also ridden with some success in point-to-point races. For the past twenty years, however, she had not ridden at all owing to defective sight. Otherwise, she was still very strong and active. She had the reputation of being the best walker in the whole district.

The three children crowded round her and protested in loud voices against her accusation that they were making fun of her.

"It's a wonderful idea," Roger shouted.

"We should have thought of it long ago," said Brian. "You are the best rider in the whole county. I heard Jack Hynes, the veterinary surgeon, say so and he should know, being a great rider himself."

"I've been thinking of it for two days, Aunt Penelope," Charlotte said in her solemn voice, "but I couldn't get a chance to speak."

Mr. Deacy struck the table and said gloomily:

"Sit down, children, and don't talk nonsense. You know very well that a woman of Penelope's age couldn't handle a savage animal like Grey Seagull in a race of that length. Man alive! When that animal gets excited . . ."

"You're wrong, Father," Roger cried in a shrill tone. "Grey Seagull is really so gentle that . . ."

"You must remember, too, Roger," Mrs. Deacy interrupted, "that Aunt Penelope is as blind as a bat."

"I'm nothing of the sort," Penelope cried indignantly. "I can see far better than you can, Dorothy. I can see quite well with my glasses. Just to prove it, I'll get up on Grey Seagull to-morrow and jump a couple of those fences out there."

The three children raised a cheer.

"Good old Aunt Penelope!" cried Roger. "I knew you had it in you."

"Easy now, children," Mr. Deacy said, as he got to his feet. "We mustn't talk nonsense. I couldn't let Penelope ride him. I'd never be able to forgive myself if anything happened to her."

"Don't be a fool, John," said Penelope haughtily. "I can

ride as well as ever. I just want to show Dorothy I'm not blind."

Mr. Deacy stroked his chin and a wild light came into his eyes as he looked at his sister. His heart began to beat much more quickly.

"All right, Penelope," he said, after swallowing his breath with difficulty. "If you really want to try him to-morrow . . ."

Next morning Penelope looked like a child when she climbed on to the back of the huge animal in her spectacles and grey sweater and riding-breeches. He was over seventeen hands and powerfully built.

"Take care now, Penelope," Mr. Deacy shouted at her from a distance.

He did not dare come any nearer, for fear of exciting the horse.

"Rubbish," Penelope said. "Let go the reins, Roger. Why are you all so nervous? One would think I'm a four-year-old girl, getting her very first lesson."

She spoke to the horse and walked him slowly down the paddock, towards the big field where Mr. Deacy had built some regulation fences to school young horses. Grey Seagull did not at all behave like a wild animal. He obeyed her in most docile fashion. After trotting around the field for a little while she shook him into a gallop and put him at one of the fences. He sailed over it beautifully. Penelope showed that she had lost none of her old skill during her long absence from the saddle. She gathered him after landing like a professional.

The children raised a great cheer as they watched the horse and the little old woman go over the jump safely. Mr. Deacy smiled broadly.

"What did I tell you, Father?" Roger shouted. "Grey Seagull is as gentle as a lamb with anyone he likes. Watch him take this next one now. He is a born jumper. He rises to them like a stag."

Penelope and the horse jumped the second fence and a third in the same faultless style. Then they returned to the paddock.

"There you are," Penelope said, after they had helped her to dismount. "That proves that I'm not blind."

Mr. Deacy grasped his sister's hand and shook it excitedly.

"You're wonderful," he said, "but do you think you could stick it out for the four miles of the Liosbawn course? It's tough going."

"Of course she could," cried Roger. "She could and she will."

"I can try," Penelope said grimly, "since there is nobody else available. I know you have your heart set on winning this race, John. I know how much it means to you. Personally, I'm just as anxious as you are to see Grey Seagull make a name for himself. I love the animal. I think he's a great horse and I want the whole world to know how really good he is."

The three children again cheered and hugged their aunt.

"That settles it," Mr. Deacy said. "We'll have a go at the race and Penelope will ride. Now we must see about getting the necessary for a good bet. With Lord Dilisk's mount a hot favourite, we should at least get five to one about Grey Seagull."

He spent the intervening days trying to raise money. That proved very difficult, for he had no credit in the district. Nobody would lend him a penny. He finally managed to collect forty-seven pounds by selling a new set of harness and some other things. To be exact, he got forty-five pounds in cash and a bottle of brandy.

"It's not much," he said to the family at breakfast on the morning of the race, "but it's a start in any case. If I can get

four or five to one, we'll have a couple of hundred pounds to
put on the next race."

At that moment Aunt Penelope threw five pounds on the
table in front of her brother, telling him to put on a bet for
herself.

"It's all I've got left," she said, "out of the legacy that my
uncle Anthony bequeathed to me eighteen years ago."

"Bravo!" cried Mr. Deacy.

"Wilful waste makes woeful want," Mrs. Deacy said
bitterly. "At this moment I don't know where I could get an
ounce of tea or a pound of beef on credit."

It was really a terrible day, with a fierce wind and inter-
mittent showers of hailstones. The cold was intense. Yet an
enormous crowd came out to Palmer's Bog, where the races
were being held, high up among the mountain peaks. Tinkers
were there in hordes from six counties. The vast number of
tents gave the impression that an army was encamped on the
wild moor. These vagrants began to make merry at an early
hour, drinking and playing their accordions and dancing. So
that there was a tremendous tumult by the time racing began.

The Deacy people delayed their arrival as long as they
could, in order to save Grey Seagull from being made entirely
unmanageable by the noise. Even so, he behaved very badly
as they led him through the crowd on the way to the saddling
enclosure. In spite of Roger's efforts to pacify him, the huge
animal kept rearing and kicking so savagely that people fled
from his path in terror.

"Is that the wild horse from Borneo you've got there, Mr.
Deacy?" a man shouted in a mocking tone.

"Is it to the zoo you're taking him?" cried another. "Janey!
It's not every zoo would admit a ruffian like that."

Mr. Deacy became almost as wild as the horse on hearing
these remarks. He shook his stick at the crowd and retorted
in a way that only incited them to further outbursts.

"You ignorant louts!" he shouted. "I'll soon show you what this horse can do. You bog-trotting apes!"

"Come along, John," his wife said to him as she seized him by the arm. "Don't be foolish."

He shouted back over his shoulder at his tormentors as she dragged him away by force. In the meantime, Penelope and Roger managed to get Grey Seagull into the saddling enclosure without mishap.

Then Lord Dilisk came forward and made a remark that caused Mr. Deacy to go into another rage.

"Got a rider yet for your horse, John?" Lord Dilisk said.

"I have," said Mr. Deacy arrogantly, "and a damn sight better one than your horse is going to have."

"Oh! Have you?" Lord Dilisk said in an insolent tone. "May I ask who it is?"

Dilisk was a tall, hard-faced man with a black moustache and cold blue eyes that seemed to look at everybody with hatred. He had a great name as a successful rider and breeder of steeplechasers. He was equally successful in selling them to visiting English people at high prices.

"My sister is going to ride for me," Mr. Deacy said.

Dilisk glanced at Penelope, who looked ever so slender and old as she stood shivering in her shabby belted raincoat and jockey cap.

"Are you serious?" he said to Mr. Deacy, raising his eyebrows.

"What do you mean?" said Mr. Deacy angrily.

Dilisk shrugged his shoulders.

"If you let her ride that untrained animal," he said, "it's really tantamount to signing her death warrant. At her age any sort of fall would most assuredly be fatal."

"Did you say my horse is untrained?" cried Mr. Deacy.

"Entirely untrained," Dilisk said. "He's quite savage and unmanageable."

"Are you being deliberately offensive?" cried Mr. Deacy.

"Not in the least," said Dilisk. "I'm just telling you for your own good that you shouldn't run the horse at all."

"Untrained? Eh?" shouted Mr. Deacy, livid with rage.

"It's common knowledge," Dilisk added, "that you couldn't get a man in the whole district to ride him. He's going to be a menace to the rest of us during the race. It's very unsporting of you to run him."

Then he turned abruptly and walked away.

"Untrained? Eh?" shouted Mr. Deacy, as he brandished his stick. "You impudent cockscomb! You damned horse-coper! You're furious because I turned down your offer to buy my horse. That's your trouble, you miserable skinflint!"

He then turned to address the crowd that had collected round him.

"The miser came to me a month ago," he shouted, "and offered me two hundred pounds for my horse. I told him I'd rather put a bullet through Grey Seagull's head than sell him at that price. Then he offered me two hundred and fifty. I ordered him off my property. I told him I'd rather starve than . . ."

The whole family had to gather round the foolish man and make frantic appeals to him before his shouting ceased. They looked pathetic standing there in a little group, with their shabby clothes and their wild faces and their wild horse; like a pack of hungry wolves surrounded by a crowd of people that taunted them.

"Never mind," Mr. Deacy said when he had regained his composure a little. "We'll see who'll be laughing after the race."

When he went to make his bet the bookmaker freely offered to lay him odds of ten to one.

"I hate to take your money, Mr. Deacy," the bookmaker said with a laugh, "but business is business."

"You won't have it long," Mr. Deacy said as he strode away.

Mr. Deacy looked so confident that the bookmaker whispered to one of his assistants.

"Go and lay off half that fifty," he said. "You might get twenties down the line. That lunatic might really have something up his sleeve. Miracles are always happening at the races. The old woman might win it."

"If she does," said the assistant as he hurried away, "I'll take the pledge for life."

When the moment came for Penelope to get on Grey Seagull's back, she asked her brother for some brandy. Mr. Deacy opened the bottle and gave it to her.

"Don't drink too much of it," he said, "or it might go to your head. You'll need to keep cool, I'm telling you. Remember now to keep behind Dilisk's horse until you're over the second last jump. Then come away."

In spite of her brother's warning, Penelope took a really long swig at the bottle. Then she secured her spectacles with tape and they hoisted her into the saddle.

"Goodbye, Penelope," Mrs. Deacy said to her. "I don't bear you any ill will. Remember that."

"You are a bitter pill, Dorothy," Penelope said. "Even at this moment you can't resist sticking your little knife into my back. You are a real Fitzmaurice, every inch of you."

"Enough of that now, Penelope," said Mr. Deacy as he clutched his sister's knee. "Remember what I told you. You don't know the course, so make sure not to get pushed into the lead before you come to the second last fence. It's a straight road from there on in to the winning post. Keep behind Dun Emer until you're over the second last. Then give him his head and come away. Of course, if Dun Emer falls before then, let some other horse lead you to the second last.

Good luck to you now and don't let Dilisk play any dirty tricks on you. That scoundrel would stop at nothing."

Oddly enough, Grey Seagull became as gentle as a lamb once Penelope got on his back. He did not even mind Mr. Deacy coming near him. He cantered down through the crowd, on the way to the post, as quietly as if he were a veteran. In spite of that, the people kept whistling and cracking jokes about Penelope.

"They've got the old woman of the sea riding the wild horse from Borneo," shouted a bookmaker. "There's a combination for you. Even money Dun Emer. Four to one Umbrella. Six to one Fighting Cock and Shaun Murphy. Ten to one Grey Seagull."

Fortified by the brandy she had drunk and the excitement of again taking part in a race after a lapse of thirty years, Penelope had no difficulty in getting Grey Seagull to line up properly at the post. She got him away with the field. Indeed, she realised at once that he was a born racehorse, one of those animals that always do their best in a competition with others. She felt thrilled at being able to govern his great power by the slightest touch of the reins.

"He's a marvel," she said to herself as they approached the first jump. "If I can only stay with him, he'll win in a canter."

The nine horses took the first fence almost in a row and maintained close order without mishap of any sort until more than a mile had been covered. Then Shaun Murphy fell at the jump leading to the ploughed field. A little farther ahead, a horse called Rowdy Tim dislodged the young woman who was riding him and bolted into the country. Umbrella then quickened his pace and soon led the field by ten lengths, with Fighting Cock and Dun Emer running level in second place. Following her brother's instructions to the letter, Penelope lay a couple of lengths behind Dun Emer.

During the first half of the race the horses ran with the wind at their backs. So that Penelope had nothing much to do but sit Grey Seagull, who was going beautifully. She was only aware of the great thrill of being in a race once more. Then the field turned for home, straight into the teeth of the fierce gale, with almost two miles still to go. The poor woman then forgot the thrill and gritted her teeth, as she felt the icy cold penetrate her frail body. She had barely enough strength to prevent herself from being dislodged by the storm.

"Good Lord!" she muttered in despair. "I'll never be able to stay with him. I'm done."

Umbrella made a bad mistake at the stone wall, cutting both his hind legs and being brought to his knees on landing. Although righted by his rider's skill, he was so shaken that he soon dropped out of contention. Fighting Cock then took a slight lead of Dun Emer, with Grey Seagull still going easily in third place a few lengths to the rear. Going up the slope to the double, Fighting Cock began to show signs of exhaustion. Although he took both obstacles under urging without making any mistake, it became obvious shortly afterwards that he had shot his bolt. He slowed down almost to a walk and joined Umbrella far to the rear of the field.

It was at this point that Lord Dilisk decided to make his effort and part company with Penelope. He suddenly shook up his mount and drew away rapidly at full speed.

"Here we go," said Penelope to herself, as she sent Grey Seagull in pursuit. "Now we begin to race."

The big horse responded readily and soon regained his former position, three lengths behind Dun Emer. There Penelope checked him, not yet wishing to take the lead. Dilisk glanced back over his shoulder and then gave his mount a few sharp cuts of the whip. Even so, Dun Emer could not quicken his pace any further. He was already going as hard as he could.

"If I don't fall out of the saddle," Penelope said to herself, "the race is won. Only for this awful cold. . . ."

Three-quarters of a mile from home a fierce shower of hailstones began to fall. The stones were almost as big as marbles. The cold was now extreme. She tried to hide her face behind her horse's head lest her spectacles might get blurred. As the horse rose to the next jump, however, a flock of the hailstones crashed against the lenses and deprived her of all sight. When Grey Seagull had landed safely she put up her left hand and tried to clear the lenses. That only made matters worse. Her fingers were completely numb. They had almost lost all power of movement. They had also become caked with wet mud during the race. Their awkward groping merely transferred some of the mud to the already dirty lenses. Then she got panic-stricken and tried to remove the spectacles. She failed to do so. She had secured them firmly about her ears with tape. Her remaining strength was insufficient to remove them. Indeed, the shock of finding herself blinded almost made her unconscious.

She rallied, however, dropping her hand back to the reins and gripping desperately with her knees in an effort to maintain herself in the saddle.

"I must hang on," she muttered through her clenched teeth. "I must."

Using the last ounce of strength in her frail old body, she clung blindly to the big horse's back as he plunged ahead through the hailstorm. Then she felt him rise to the jump, land safely and race away once more. She heard Dilisk's voice calling frantically to his mount. To her joy, she realised that the voice of her rival came from the rear and that it was rapidly becoming more remote.

"We've passed him," she said to herself. "Oh! If I can only hang on. If Grey Seagull can only find his way home."

After taking the next jump she heard the roar of the crowd straight ahead of her and she knew that the horse was still running truly. Then the thrill of victory took possession of her and she became hysterical.

"Go on, Grey Seagull," she cried shrilly, with her teeth chattering. "I knew you could do it. Go on, you beauty. It's your race now. You've won it. Go on."

The big horse galloped past the winning post more than forty lengths in front of Dun Emer, with Penelope chirping shrilly on his back like a hen bird whose nest has been robbed. He galloped through the cheering crowd, leaped a big car that stood parked in his way and then came quietly to a halt at the exact spot where Penelope had mounted him.

Penelope was still shouting hysterically when they removed her from the saddle. They wrapped her in blankets and rushed her into a tent and gave her the brandy bottle.

"He jumped the last mile on his own," she said to her brother when she had recovered a little. "I got blinded by the hailstones. I saw nothing for the last mile. He came home on his own. He is a marvel."

Mr. Deacy himself took a long swig at the brandy. Then he swung his stick and yelled.

"On to Punchestown!" he cried. "On to the Grand National!"

They carried Penelope on their shoulders, the crowd did, over to the tattered old car that belonged to the Deacy family. They wanted to lead Grey Seagull also in a triumphal procession, but the big horse would have none of their adulation. With Penelope no longer on his back, the wild animal returned to his former savage temper. He screamed and reared on his hind legs and kicked in such a frenzied fashion that the people soon fled from him. Roger had to lead him away quietly.

Then Mr. Deacy got into his old car and sat there with his arm around Penelope's shoulder and they drove away amid the frantic cheering of the people.

"Ah! Miss Penelope," the people said, "you're a great little old woman, sure enough."

Mr. Deacy kept waving his stick and shouting:

"On to Punchestown! On to the Grand National!"

The Lament

HE TIDE began to flow. The surface of the bay convulsed and then heaved its increase of water gracefully, with a sound like a deep sigh, against the low shore. Strands of yellow weed, left waterless on the sea floor by the ebb, now floated curling above the stones from which they grew. The risen water paused and then receded, leaving a dark wet flounce on the stones and on the strips of sand. The weeds strained after it, taut and straight, like fingers reaching for its touch.

For a few moments the sunlight sparkled in silence on the fringe of land that had been darkened by the sea's wetness. Then the tide rose again, covered the wetness and went farther, making a deeper flounce. Now there was power in its movement and it made a fierce murmur as it raced along the strips of sand, its surface flecked with foam.

The sound of the turning tide roused Sheila Manning from a day-dream. She was sitting on the edge of the little concrete pier that jutted out into a corner of the bay. Her father's boat was moored, high and dry on the rocks, against the side of the pier. Her father was in the bow of the boat, sewing a patch on the jib. It was afternoon towards the end of autumn, but the sun was strong. The heat of the sun and the silence of low tide had induced in her a sleepy torpor, within whose cloak she had woven a dream of passionate love.

Awakened from this dream by the sea's movement, a yearning for the reality of love gnawed at her like hunger. With the turning of the tide, a gentle breeze had risen from the land and swept out over the bay, rippling its surface. It came from the high mountains and its breath was chilly on her cheeks. Awed by its sinister murmur, she became ashamed of her foolish dream.

"Oh! God!" she thought. "I must be going crazy!" She bowed her head and muttered a prayer against improper thoughts. As she prayed, a loud sound came from behind the low range of hills that bound the shore towards the east. She stopped praying and looked in the direction of the sound. Along the Galway road, which lay behind the hills, a cloud of dust came moving rapidly. Then a large red bus appeared. It was half-concealed by the cloud of dust it had raised along the sunbaked granite road. It slowed down after coming into view and halted by the entrance to the path that led from the road to the pier. A man descended from it.

"Oh! Look, Father," she cried excitedly. "A man got off the bus. He might be a tourist for the islands."

Her father raised his head and looked towards the road.

" 'Faith, he looks like a tourist, sure enough," he said.

The bus had now continued its journey towards the west and the man was walking down the path that led to the pier.

"He has a big stick in his hand," said Sheila, "and a knapsack on his back and he's bareheaded. As sure as you are alive, he's an artist or a scholar going out to the islands."

Her speech was now thick and halting. There was a hardness in her throat that forced her to swallow her breath after each few words.

"It's late in the year for anyone to be going out to the islands," her father said. "I didn't carry one out there now for more than a fortnight."

As the stranger approached, Sheila noticed that he was handsome and her excitement increased. It was of such a man she had dreamt. He had a fine, arrogant carriage, like a soldier or someone in authority. His hair was dark and thick. The sunlight shone on its sleek, rolling surface. His faced was bronzed. His jaws were strong. When he reached the end of the pier, he addressed them in a rich, deep voice that disturbed her as the voluptuous rising of the tide had done.

"You're Bartly Manning, I'm told," he said to her father.

"That's right," said her father.

"The bus conductor told me you take people to the islands," the man continued. "I'd like to go there if you can take me."

Her father examined the man from head to foot, shrewdly measuring his capacity to pay. Then he said:

"When were you thinking of going?"

"Right away."

"That's a different story, for my boatman is gone to Galway and he won't be back before to-night."

"Oh!" said the stranger. "That's too bad. You couldn't get someone else instead of him?"

Her father shrugged his shoulders and made a stitch with his needle. With his mind on the bargain he was going to strike, the avaricious fellow wished to make the journey appear to be more difficult than it really was.

"I would have to think hard," he said gloomily, "for it's not everyone would do for the job of going with me to the islands in a boat at this time of year."

Sheila understood her father's manœuvre and felt ashamed.

"Sure any boy out of the village would do on a day like this," she said, "with the sea so calm and a breeze rising that will take you out on one tack."

Her father scowled at her. Then he spat over the side of the boat and said:

"Little you know about it. In any case, she won't swim for half an hour yet. The tide is barely licking the stones under her keel."

He straightened himself suddenly, turned towards the stranger and cried in a menacing shout:

"It will be twenty-five shillings for the trip."

The stranger smiled and said casually:

"That's all right."

Her father's attitude changed at once. He became full of energy and a fawning grin creased his furrowed face, as he hitched up his trousers and said:

"I'll go right away up to the village and find a boy to go with me. I think I know a boy that is handy. Will you wait here for me, or will you go on up to the house? The wife could make you a cup of tea."

"I think I'll wait here," the stranger said.

Her father began to climb out on to the pier, crying excitedly:

"You could do worse, 'faith. You won't have to wait long and my daughter there will keep chat with you. The boat'll swim in half an hour. It's a spring tide and the sea comes belting in very quick. We can make the islands on one tack with this fine breeze that's rising. Wait there for me now, sir."

Sheila felt terribly ashamed of her father as he clattered up the pier in his hobnailed boots, dragging his legs after him and raising his feet very high in the manner that is pe-

culiar to Connemara boatmen. His bawneen and his frieze
trousers were very ragged, but he was a fine type of his breed.
At sixty he was wiry and agile like a youth. But the poor girl,
drunk with romantic thoughts of captivating the handsome
stranger, only saw his raggedness and his uncouth avarice.
She was afraid that the stranger would despise her for having
such a father.

"My God!" the stranger cried after her father had gone.
"What air! What a scene! Lucky people that live here."

He had taken off his knapsack and thrown it on the pier.
Now he stood with his arms outstretched, breathing deeply
as he looked out over the landlocked bay. Sheila was dis-
appointed. Somehow, she had felt certain that he would turn
to her at once and pay her attention as soon as her father had
gone. But the burning passion in his deep set dark eyes was
not for her. It was for the sea.

"God! This is a lovely harbour," he cried in rapture.
"Look at the tide coming in through its narrow neck from
the ocean, tumbling in, as if it were being poured into a
half-closed bag."

"The sea is lovely, sure enough," said Sheila sharply, "but
the land is awful. I don't think it's lucky for anybody to live
here in poverty."

The stranger turned round, put his hands on his hips and
looked inland.

"You think so?" he cried, passionately. "I wish I lived here.
I love this great Connemara desert. I've walked all over it.
It's really a desert. From Oughterard and Barna you can go
west and north for scores of miles without meeting a tree.
There's only heather and stone growing out of the boggy
earth. And yet it's full of wonders, when you go walking there
alone. It's lovely to see the streeling ropes of the white water-
falls on the mountain sides and the ghostly light on the high-
up stony peaks of the mountains, when the sunlight strikes

123

them through a wandering cloud. There is something in the air that walks with you and tries to talk to you, like music in a great empty room."

But Sheila felt scorned and humiliated by this rapturous worship of the earth, while he paid no heed to herself.

"I hate it," she said fiercely. "I hate the living sight of it."

The stranger looked at her in wonder.

"You don't mean that, surely?" he said. "You are Bartly Manning's daughter, aren't you? How could you hate where you were born and bred? How could you hate the place that is part of you and it so lovely?"

"Well! I do," said Sheila, "and that's all there's to it. I hate the people, too, and I have reason to hate them."

The stranger laughed and sat down beside her on the pier. He looked up at her face sideways and said:

"Indeed, you don't hate them. You do nothing of the kind. How could you? Connemara is written all over your face. Look at the lovely Connemara beauty in your blue eyes. When you look cross, they are dark and fierce like the sea with the wind sweeping over it. And when you look happy they are bright like the sea with the sun kissing it. And your hair has the beauty of the Connemara earth. It is brown beneath and then there is a shiny, saffron cloak spread over it."

"You have the gift of the gab all right, whoever you are," Sheila said.

"I'm only telling you the truth," said the stranger, taking a cigarette case from his pocket. "Do you smoke?"

Her hand trembled as she accepted the cigarette. Her irritation had vanished. Indeed, she had almost swooned listening to his flattery. In her twenty-six years of life no man had ever spoken to her like that. The poor creature's short body bulged at the waist like a sack. Her throat was swollen with goitre. Her mouth and her nose were too small. There was a rent at the hip of her cheap cotton frock. But she was aware that her eyes and her hair were beautiful. So she believed his flattery.

"Why did you say that just now?" he said to her, when their cigarettes were lit. "I bet you have a grievance. Nearly everybody in Ireland has a grievance and that's a fine thing, too. It shows the people are discontented and eager to march forward. What's your grievance?"

"You wouldn't be interested?" said Sheila.

"And why not?" said the stranger. "We journalists are interested in everything."

"Oh! Is that what you are?" said Sheila. " 'Faith, I thought you were a politician by the gift of the gab you have. And it's the same kind of gab that the politicians from Dublin have. They talk about the beauty of the bare bogs where the poor Irish-speaking people live and the beautiful Gaelic culture of the people that live in poverty. You'd think by the talk of them that Gaelic culture is something that could only thrive in a thatched cabin, with grunting pigs alongside it. It's all fine talk done by well-fed people to make the poor contented with their poverty."

"Easy now," said the stranger, waving his arm in a half-circle along the coast. "Look at all these new houses that have been built in the past twenty years. You won't find any thatched cabins with grunting pigs anywhere around here any more."

"What's the good of new houses," said Sheila, "when the spirit of the people is broken? They have new houses, but they live on the dole and, what's more, they don't believe any more in the old fairy tales."

"What old fairy tales?" said the stranger.

"Well! I'm going to tell you something," said Sheila, "since you asked for it. I'm an Irish teacher. At least, I was one until a year ago. I spent seven years teaching Irish at a place in the midlands. I was only a slip of a girl when I went there. At that time I believed in all the fairy tales. Upon my soul, at that time I wouldn't talk English, as I'm talking to you now, if you gave me a fortune. When I went away up to the midlands, I felt like a monk bringing the gospel from Ireland to the pagan people of Europe during the dark ages. Or like a nun, more likely, converting the unfortunate people of the midlands from the foreign ways of the devil. It was the Irish language and Irish dances and the Catholic religion that was going to save the world, according to me."

"Well?" said the stranger, as Sheila paused for breath. "And then what happened?"

"Oh! I haven't lost my religion, or anything like that," she continued at break-neck speed. "Far from it. Praise be to God, it's the only thing that has stood by me in my misfortune. Father John, that was the curate's name where I was teaching, he stood by me every inch of the way. When I went there first, I worked so hard day and night, for I had night classes as well, that I soon got worn out. I used to have to cycle four miles back and forth to the night classes, all alone on the winter nights. So Father John used to say I should get a boy to keep me company and take my mind off my work. He always went on to me like that, telling me to get a boy and that I should get a boy and that it wasn't right for a girl not to have a boy."

"Sensible man," said the stranger. "And did you follow his advice?"

"Indeed, I didn't," said Sheila. "Oh! Lord! At that time I wouldn't look at a boy. Although, to tell you the truth, I longed to have some boy, some nice, clean-minded boy, that I could go out with and have fun. Indeed, I longed to go to the foreign dances, too, same as everybody else was doing, seeing how they all had fun at the foreign dances and all the young people used to be courting one another at them.

But I would only go to the Irish dances, although I was getting to hate them at the bottom of my heart, with everybody sitting around, all serious, like a lot of sour people at a wake."

The stranger leaned back, slapped his thighs and burst out laughing.

"What's funny about it?" said Sheila, angrily.

"Don't be cross," said the stranger. "I wasn't laughing at you, only what you said about Gaelic League dances is the truest thing I ever heard."

Then he continued to laugh heartily. Sheila now felt that she hated him. Laughing, he showed a perfect set of teeth that looked extremely white against the tan of his cheeks. She hated these white teeth. They annoyed her particularly. She felt humiliated by his laughter and thought her humiliation was a punishment for her improper thoughts.

"It's not against the Gaelic League I have anything," she cried, "but against the people who make fun of it for a mean reason. The people in the Gaelic League are just as holy as priests and nuns, but they believe in the wrong things. If all the people in Ireland were as holy as the people in the Gaelic League there would be no sin in the country. But the Gaelic League is following the wrong road. It is based on a fairy tale, because the Catholic religion is the important thing and it's a waste of time preaching anything else. If all the people in the world spoke the same language and danced the same dances and had the same way of making nice, clean, healthy fun, it would be easier to spread the Catholic faith over the whole world and save everybody's soul. It's Catholic Action we need and not the Gaelic League."

"Now, look here," said the stranger; "don't take me up wrong. I didn't mean to annoy you. Don't be cross with me. It wasn't at you I was laughing. I didn't laugh for any mean reason."

He reached over with his left hand and touched her knee as he finished speaking. As soon as he touched her, she flew into a passion.

"Don't you dare touch me!" she cried, drawing away from him.

She stared at him with blazing eyes as if he were the devil. Indeed, the poor girl had a confused idea that he was the devil and that God had punished her for her improper daydream by sending her the devil to torment her. She put her hand over the part of her knee he had touched, just as if it had been burned.

"I'm sorry," said the stranger contritely, drawing away from her. "I seem to be putting my foot in it at every move I make."

"You're just like him!" cried Sheila. "You're the dead spit of him!"

"Like whom?" cried the stranger in astonishment. "What in the name of God are you talking about?"

"You're like the man that persecuted me!" cried Sheila passionately. "You're a pagan. I can see it by the look in your eyes and the way you tried to touch me. He hated me because I was pure and because he knew he couldn't touch me. So he persecuted me because I complained of him. He wouldn't leave the girl pupils alone. They were all grown-up girls and boys at the evening class, all of them qualifying in Irish for Government jobs. That was the only reason they were learning Irish, because it was necessary to qualify in the language for a job under the Government. He was a horrible man. He wouldn't leave any of the girls alone. Three of them got into trouble over him!"

She paused for want of breath and looked at the stranger with a peculiar expression in her eyes. Her eyes were half-closed and there was a brilliant light in the pupils. Although they were fixed on the stranger's face, they seemed to be looking beyond him, contemplating something remote, in dark rapture.

"You mean . . . ?" said the stranger. "You mean that . . . ?"

He had put his hand on the warm concrete and drawn up his right leg under him, as if preparing to rise. Now he paused, arrested by her strange expression. He was beginning to think that her mind was deranged.

"Three of them," she continued, turning away from him and looking out over the bay. "At first I didn't pay much attention to what was going on, because I was so wrapped up in my religion. I was a daily communicant, even though I had a long way to go to the chapel every morning. It was too much for me. It was ruining my health. It was Father John that noticed me first. He noticed that my lips were parched when he gave me the Sacrament in the morning. He then tried to persuade me to take a rest, go away for a holiday, or even give up being a daily communicant. But I wouldn't pay any heed to him. 'I won't give in,' I said to my-self. I noticed the way things were going and how paganism was sweeping over the country and I felt that I must carry on the struggle against it. Paganism had crept into my own class, with this man annoying all the girls. It was when I caught him with one of them going home one night that I complained. He had her up against the wall of a house in the darkness and he forcing his will on her although she was begging him to let her go. She was one of the three that got into trouble. I complained to the Civic Guards about him and the trouble began. His father was an important person in the place. He had a public-house and he was on the County Council. I fought against them, for right was on my side. I knew I was fighting against paganism and that I was doing a noble thing, even if I had to suffer for it. In the end, though, my nerves gave way and I had to resign."

Again she paused for breath and looked at the stranger. The latter did not seem to be paying any further attention to her story. He was leaning forward over the edge of the pier, looking down into the boat, which had begun to rock as the rising tide heaved up under it.

"But you," she said spitefully, "would think it's the price of me for meddling, I suppose? Ye are all alike, ye pagans. Ye stick up for one another."

The young man looked at her wearily.

"No need to get into a rage with me," he said quietly, "just because I put my hand on your knee. I didn't mean to be impudent. I was only sorry for you, because I thought . . ."

"I don't want anybody to be sorry for me," Sheila interrupted. "The people here pretend to be sorry for me since I came back a year ago. But I know they are only delighted at my misfortune. They are all pagans at heart. 'Poor Sheila,' they say, 'the poor creature, it's hard luck on her and on her people.' All that is from their tongues, but in their hearts there is paganism and all pagans hate those that fight against sin."

"I think you're all wrong," the stranger said, looking up at her.

"What do you mean?" said Sheila.

They stared at one another in silence for some time. Now it was the stranger who looked angry. The recital of her woes made Sheila feel pity for herself. Tears were coming into her eyes.

"You had bad luck," said the young man. "I'm not saying whether it was your own fault or not. All I am saying is, that nobody has a right to accuse our people of being bad. Our Irish people are good and kind people. And if they were left alone they would be gay, happy people. But they are not left alone. The iron heel of superstition is pressed down on their necks. All this damn fool nonsense about paganism, for instance, and Catholic Action. Hatred! That's all you people preach. Why not preach love for a change and see what will happen? Why not believe people are good instead of believing they are possessed by the devil? Eh? I'm certain you would be a lot happier. You would get your job back, too."

Tears began to roll down Sheila's cheeks and she covered her face with her hands. The man put his hand gently on her shoulder. Now she did not draw away from him.

"I'm sorry," he said. "It was awful of me to talk to you like that. Please forgive me."

Sheila jumped to her feet and walked hurriedly over to the slash wall at the back of the pier. The young man looked after her.

"Poor kid!" he said to himself. "It's tough on her. I shouldn't have lost my temper with her. It's sympathy she needs."

He leaned his chin on his fists and looked down into the boat that was rocking and straining against the mooring ropes. The ropes made a groaning sound as they grated over the worn timbers of the boat's side. The grumbling seemed to come from the boat itself. It seemed to be waking from sleep and to be grumbling at the sea that came lashing against its black bottom. It had lain asleep on the rocks during low tide. Now the sea was calling on it to wake up and float on its strong bosom.

"Dope merchants!" said the stranger to himself. "That's what they are. There should be a law against people who spread bigotry and superstition same as there is against people who sell cocaine. The poor girl has been corrupted by them. Even her health is ruined. God! How wonderful it will be when we free Ireland from all the repression and hatred spread by the dope merchants!"

He turned and looked towards Sheila. She was leaning

over the slash wall. He noticed how shapely her legs were beneath her short frock. Her back quivered spasmodically as if she were sobbing. The sunlight had now begun to fade and her hair no longer had a saffron cloak drawn over it. The strong breeze had loosened strands of it. They fluttered in disorder about the small crown of her head.

He got up and walked over to the slash wall.

"Well!" he said. "Do you accept my apology?"

Sheila made no reply. He leaned over the slash wall beside her and looked down at the rising tide. The wall sloped outwards into the sea, that came swaying up, advancing inevitably, inch by inch.

"You and I are young," the stranger said softly. "We belong to the new life that is dawning on our country. We shouldn't get angry with one another and quarrel. The young people, to whom the future life belongs, should unite and make plans instead of quarrelling. This is our earth and our sea and they are both lovely. It is up to us, the youth of Ireland, to be worthy of the brave people that went before us, the people who broke the power of the landlords and drove out the English garrison that oppressed us. There isn't much happiness here yet, for the enemy left us only desolation and poverty. There is a lot of work to be done. Why don't we unite to do that work instead of quarrelling? Eh?"

His voice was tender, and Sheila, listening to him, wanted to throw herself against his bosom and weep. But she could not speak or make any movement towards him. She was paralysed by shame of what she had said. She had bared her soul to this stranger. She had stood naked before him.

Then he looked up into her face and said tenderly:

"Do you still hate me? Do you still think I am a pagan?"

The tenderness in his voice made a wave of passion sweep through her body. Her shame found voice. She uttered an hysterical little laugh, turned her tear-stained face towards him and said:

"You must think I am an awful fool!"

The stranger was surprised by her sudden change of mood. He gaped at her and said:

"Indeed, I do not."

"Oh! But you must," said Sheila, speaking at breakneck speed. "I get into such a state, all by myself, brooding, that I make up stories. I have nobody to talk to around here. I'm afraid to talk to them, for fear they might pity me. I hate being pitied. Then I keep to myself and I brood and make up stories. Everything I told you is all imagination. There was no man persecuting me. It was how I got sick and now I don't seem to be able to get better. I can't sleep and I have no company. I come down here to the pier every day. I try to talk to the people that go out to the islands with my father. My father draws turf out to the islands, but he sometimes takes tourists out here. Sometimes, but only an odd time, there is a tourist that's friendly and kind. Anyway, they are all from the world outside. But I never talked to anybody the way I talked to you. I am so terribly ashamed. Honestly, I don't know what came over me. But I was so lonely to-day and I thought you might . . ."

She interrupted herself suddenly, as she recalled the passion of her day-dream. She pressed her clenched fists against her little mouth. Then she shuddered and pointed towards the mouth of the harbour.

"Look," she said in a matter-of-fact tone. "You can see the islands very clearly now. It's queer, but you can see them better in the evening, just before the sun goes down. In the broad daylight they are dim. They rise up out of the sea with the fall of evening. Evening time is lovely, isn't it?"

"Yes," said the stranger quietly as he looked towards the

islands. "It is lovely. Those islands are a lovely sight from
here, sure enough, far out there on the shining sea beyond
the narrow gateway of the land. The sun is turning red. They
look like fairyland out there, with all the colours changing
while you watch."

Sheila waited for him to say more, but he kept silent. She
glanced at him quickly. His lips were parted and his eyes
looked exalted. He was again unaware of her existence. She
shuddered and turned her eyes towards the islands.

"Oh! God!" she thought in agony. "I've driven him away
again. Why did I drive him away and I wanting him so much
to notice me? Why do I tell lies and pretend?"

The round, blue shapes of the islands, like breasts on the
glistening bosom of the sea, became blurred as a fresh flood
of tears welled up into her eyes.

Just then, however, she heard her father's voice in the
distance. With an effort, she restrained her tears and turned
round. She saw her father coming down the path that led
from the road to the pier. He was followed by a lad, who
carried a bucket from which smoke issued. Up on the road
there was a man from the village at whom her father was
shouting.

"Here's my father now," Sheila said to the stranger. "He
has found a lad."

The stranger did not answer for a little while. Then he
straightened himself suddenly, looked at her and said:

"What's that?"

Sheila pointed towards her father and the lad.

"Oh!" said the stranger. "Upon my soul, I had clean forgotten about the trip. Well! Here goes for a look at fairyland."

He laughed heartily and strode over to the boat, which
was now afloat. It was not yet quite clear of the rocks on

which it had lain. It staggered, like a person trying to walk after a long illness, as its keel grated against the rocks. It tried to run out to sea with each outgoing wave. It heaved angrily at the mooring ropes that halted it.

"Did you do any courting?" shouted Bartly Manning as he reached the pier.

He now looked gay and excited. He had celebrated his bargain by drinking two glasses of poitheen.

"Devil a bit," said the stranger. "Sure what chance would I have against the fine men of Connemara?"

"Ho!" shouted Bartly. "Little you know about it. Sure that daughter of mine wouldn't look at a man that wears a bawneen. It's men from the city she's after. She has the heart broken in me and I trying to find a man for her."

"Will you shut your mouth, you fool?" Sheila cried angrily.

But her father only laughed lustily, as he leaped on board the boat with the agility of a cat.

"It will take a man like yourself, sir," he cried, "to put a ring on her."

Sheila bit her lip and began to walk up the pier hurriedly.

"Aren't you going to wait to see us off?" the stranger called after her.

She looked back over her shoulder without stopping and said:

"I'm getting cold. I must go home. Goodbye."

"Goodbye," the stranger called after her. "And good luck to you."

Then he jumped on board the boat with his knapsack. He threw the knapsack into the empty hold and then took off his tweed jacket. The lad had climbed on board carefully with the bucket, in which a few sods of turf were burning. He removed the lid from the entrance to the cabin on the fore deck. Then he lay on his belly and let the bucket down through the square hole into the cabin. The stranger spat on his hands and went over to the mast, from whose base Bartly Manning was loosening the sail ropes.

"Let me hoist the sail," he said.

"More power to you," said Bartly. "Hoist away, while I pull her ahead and cast off."

Sheila was turning off the pier on to the path when she heard the musical sound of the sail rope creaking through the block. She halted and looked towards the boat. With one foot against the mast, the young man was heaving at the sail rope with all his might. When he crouched at the end of his pull, she could see the muscles bulging through the tight sleeves and shoulders of his grey sweater. His bent thighs were taut against their flannel covering. She was thrilled by his male strength in action.

A lump came into her throat and she said to herself in despair:

"He's going now. I'll never see him again."

The great brown sail unfurled along its rising boom. It made a deep rustling sound that mingled melodiously with the creaking of the rope through the block. As it rose and unfolded, its spreading brown canvas made a fluttering curtain against which the young man's sleek hair shone black in the changing light of evening.

"Oh! God!" thought Sheila. "His voice was like music and he said such wonderful things!"

Her father was out on the end of the pier hauling on the mooring rope. The boat came forward slowly. The lad was unfurling the jib sail on the foredeck. The mainsail had now reached its full height and its boom swayed slowly from side to side. The breeze roared through the flapping belly of the sail. Then the boat passed the end of the pier. Her father cast the coiled end of the mooring rope on board and then leaped into the stern as the boat passed him. He put his back to the rudder and threw out the boom with his foot. The

mainsail filled with wind. The boat careened and swung towards the mouth of the harbour in answer to the helm.

The young man waved to her from the stern and shouted: "Goodbye, now!"

Sheila waved her arm and answered:

"Goodbye!"

Then he disappeared from view, as the hulk of the boat passed behind the pier. Now only the top of the mainsail was visible. She wanted to continue on her way home, but was unable to resist the desire to have another look at him. She hurried back to the slash wall and leaned over it. Now the hull of the black boat was towards her, as it sailed swiftly, careening, towards the narrow mouth of the harbour. The stranger was sitting beside her father in the stern. She heard her father laugh raucously.

"Oh! God!" she whispered as she put her chin in her hands. "It's always like this. I dream of something lovely and then I wake up to hear the people laughing at me and they pointing the finger of scorn!"

Her father began to sing at the helm. The stranger joined in the song. His young voice came rich and voluptuous over the water. She listened to his singing voice in sad rapture, as it grew faint over the lengthening water.

Tears flowed from her eyes and she felt utterly forlorn. She had a horrid feeling that this was the turning-point in her life, that she had missed her last chance of happiness and that the future was going to be barren.

The sound of his voice died as the boat passed out through the harbour's mouth, bound for the distant isles. Now there was no sound but the heavy, powerful murmur of the rising tide.

Light

T HERE WAS total darkness. The tropic air was motionless. There was no sound but the gentle murmur of the waves that rolled across the beach. The smell of the sea was drowned in the heavy perfume of the jungle.

Then the dawn wind came whispering from the east. It swept through the level forest of tall cypress trees, through the mangrove swamps and through the belt of drooping palms that fringed the shore.

The trunks of the cypress swayed before the impact of the breeze. Their topmost branches brushed against each other. The mangroves shook their pendent roots and dipped them towards the earth, as if in homage. The sedge grass leaned over, rustling like silken dresses in a dance. Dead twigs snapped and fell.

The pointed leaves of the palm trees trembled on either side of their spear-shaped blades, like a myriad oars feathering in frenzied haste about a fleet of galleys.

The confused symphony that the wind wrought within the darkness was the earth's long sigh of awakening. Light began to come at once. Land, sea and sky took on a robe of uniform grey. Dim shapes came swimming in ghoulish silence from behind the torn veil of night. The air turned cool. The wind died down. All became still, as at the beginning of the world, except for the drowsy murmur of the waves.

Then the sun rose above the tops of the giant cypress trees and sent a fiery blaze across the eastern sky. Its rays spread everywhere with magic speed, painting the earth with colours of divine loveliness. There was tumult in the forest, as life sprang into action at the urging of the voluptuous heat. Now the symphony was triumphant, as the myriads of risen creatures gave voice.

For a little while the beach remained still. Then a flock of sand-larks came running by the edge of the surf, their long grey legs like swiftly moving matchsticks under their motionless oval trunks. Their hungry eyes searched the curving rim of the tide, on which gaily painted shells and pieces of sponge were rolling to the shore. Sea-gulls came after the sand-larks, running sideways and scavenging on the dead fish that protruded from the shells.

Black vultures swooped from the clouds in groups of two and three. They dropped on to the sand near the carcass of a shark that they had picked clean on the previous day. They waddled to and fro around the skeleton, hungrily searching the white bones for another morsel. Then they stood close together in a half-circle. They leaned back and held up their half-opened wings to the increasing heat of the sun. The pale flesh on their naked heads and throats looked obscene, as they stood blinking and swaying like drunkards with their raised wings half spread.

Pelicans came in pursuit of the fish that leaped from the waters by the shore. They flew low, barely moving their giant wings and with their cunning eyes downcast. Now and again one of them dived at great speed, seized his prey and flopped on to the water with a loud splash. Then he raised his head and shook the capacious bag of his gullet violently to engulf the fish.

White herons rose from the marshes, flying with dream-like elegance. Their long black legs trailed like stiff pieces of string from their bellies. They alighted on the mangrove trees that faced the shore. Soon the whole shimmering green surface of the mangroves was speckled with spots of dazzling white.

A black sow, followed by six tiny black piglets and by a black boar, came from the jungle in a row. They walked along the sand, high up, where there were banks of withered shells. Now and again the boar halted to rummage with his snout among the shells. Then he ran smartly to rejoin the others.

The pigs halted when they came abreast of the white tent that was pitched under a cluster of palm trees, by the edge of a narrow creek where a boat was moored. They grunted and stood close together in a row. They came closer and began to sniff. Then they raised their snouts and listened attentively as a noise came from within the tent. Presently the door was opened and a girl walked out on to the sand. She was naked except for a large white towel that she carried around her neck. The pigs took fright, turned and ran grunting to the jungle. They halted and looked back at her when they reached its edge. Then they turned once more and went crashing through the underbrush.

The girl walked slowly towards the sea. Her short golden hair shimmered in the sunlight. The rest of her body was the colour of bronze. She spread the towel on the sand near the water. Then she raised her hands above her head, stretched herself and ran shouting through the tide.

A young man came from the tent just as the girl reached deep water. He shouted to her as he ran down the sand. She turned, waved to him and then plunged. She began to swim, with her short hair floating behind her on the surface. The man plunged and swam after her. He soon reached her side and they swam far out together. The man's hair was black and his skin was the colour of old oak. They landed far up the beach.

The girl began to run as soon as they touched shore. The man ran after her. He caught her, put his palm against the small of her back and raised her high above his head. There she lay, with her limbs and her wet hair dangling, laughing at the top of her voice.

He ran with her limp body raised that way above his head, back towards the towel, by the edge of the surf. The muscles of his small hard buttocks rose and fell as he ran. The girl kept laughing at the top of her voice.

He laid her down gently on the towel. Then she stopped laughing and encircled his neck with her hands. She drew him down to her. The sun's heat was now so strong that it had already dried the sea-water on their bodies, over which the light passed, rippling with each movement of their limbs.

A flock of scarlet birds flew out from the jungle and crossed the beach. They became afraid when they found themselves above the sea. They turned with a loud swish of wings and flew back into the jungle at full speed, passing over the lovers like a vast red undulating shawl.

The Tide

HAT MORNING when the sea was full, a small grey bird with scarlet legs ran north along the beach in search of food. The tide was then so high that its foam-laced edge came to the exposed roots of the palm trees that lined the shore. The little bird was forced to dodge in and out among the trees as he followed the rim of the surf, with his head turned sideways, ready to pounce on the least morsel. He found nothing. He never once paused to feed before he went out of sight behind the rocky bluff at the northern end.

The surf was immaculate. There was nothing but clear blue water in the never-ending waves that made soft music breaking on the yellow sand. The whole sea was immaculate, as it lay shimmering in the morning light, away to the far horizon in the west.

The tide began to ebb. The sea flowed back into its own bosom, laying bare a wide strip of ground that sloped down gently to the dark ocean bed outside the bar. Brine drops and flecks of foam sparkled like diamonds for a little while on the brown sand that had just been uncovered. Then the heat of the tropical sun came in the wake of the retreating sea and drew all moisture from the surface. As when a shadow passes slowly from a carpet, the brown sand became golden.

When the tide approached its lowest ebb, the beach looked radiantly beautiful from end to end. The sand was without blemish. The waves in going forth had packed its fine grains close together and smoothed out all roughness in its texture and given it minute frills and undulations that were now warm, like passionate bosoms under the sun's wild heat. It lay between the green wood and the turquoise sea like a golden belt, in majestic stillness. Yet its curving beauty made it seem to sway before the eye in dancing rhythm.

Then people came. The first car halted shortly before noon at the end of the road behind the trees. Two small boys leaped from it at once and ran screaming into the tide. An old Negress came after them with blankets and a big green umbrella. A fat man with a bald head brought a wicker lunch basket. A red-haired woman in a leopard-skin bathing suit came with pillows and the Sunday edition of a newspaper. They hoisted the umbrella midway down the beach and spread the blankets in its shade. The Negress took a spirit stove from the basket, lit it and began to cook lunch. The white woman sat on a blanket and oiled the naked parts of her body. Then she stretched out on her back and put a pillow under her head. She undid her shoulder straps and oiled her breasts out to the nipples. Her husband lay beside her on his stomach. He lit a cigar and read the comic section of the paper. The two little boys came out of the water and scraped holes in the sand. They barked like dogs as they threw it rapidly back between their spread legs.

A shabby black sedan was the next car to park at the end of the road. A very thin man got out of it. He wore a white cloth cap and purple trunks that hung loosely about his flesh-less loins. An old woman in a yellow straw hat and a long white dress followed him out of the car. They walked very slowly side by side down to the tide. The old man carried a fishing pole and a spade. The old woman had a sieve and a small pail. When he was near the water, the old man began to dig up the sand and to throw it into the sieve. The old woman shook the sieve and sifted all the sand carefully, searching for bait. After they had found some, the old man baited his hook and went surf-fishing. The old woman then took the spade and continued to dig up the golden sand.

Two young men came in a yellow roadster. They brought a parcel of sandwiches, a dozen bottles of beer, a newspaper and a shovel down to the beach. There they dug an enormous hole in the sand, using the shovel in turns. Then they had a swim, dried themselves by walking in the sun and lay down at the bottom of their hole. Each took a section of the news-paper. They ate sandwiches and drank beer while they read.

Then a large party of rowdy men and women came in three shining black limousines. They shouted to one another as they came down the beach with their loads. Some of them gathered wood and lit a fire on the sand. Others went into the tide and gambolled, making a great tumult. An elderly woman with an enormous belly sat down on a spread news-paper, beside a radio she had brought. She took off her shoes and stockings, loosened her black silk dress and lit a cigarette. Then she turned on a broadcast of Cuban dance music. Ex-cited by the savage rhythm, she slapped her belly, shook her bosom and shouted in ecstasy. Now and again she picked up a bottle of wine by the neck and drank deeply. The bathers soon joined her and danced about the radio in couples, root-

ing up the sand with their wet feet. Then the whole party ate
sausages that had been roasted at the fire. They also ate
bread, pickles, salami, beans and apple-pie. They drank
many bottles of wine, shouted, embraced one another, played
the radio, danced and sang ribald songs. They stretched out
on the sand when they were exhausted.

Two separate bands of shabbily dressed men and women
debouched on to the beach from behind the rocky bluff at
the northern end. They carried large brown sacks. They
moved along towards the south in parallel lines, digging up
the sand in search of precious shells. When they reached the
southern end, they turned and marched north again, in two
parallel lines, still digging with great energy and throwing
shells into their sacks.

So many people came in cars and on foot that the whole
beach was littered with them at low tide. By then scores of
umbrellas had been hoisted. Seventeen radios were working
at full cry. Thirteen fires had been lit. Eight parties were
fishing and digging for bait. A great crowd of children
screamed and splashed in the surf and dug holes in the sand.
The ground was strewn with sheets of newspaper, banana
skins, pieces of cooked sausage, empty cans, egg-shells, bottles,
orange peel, cardboard boxes and empty cigarette packets.

The smooth, curving beauty of the golden beach was now
all torn and destroyed. The people lay stretched out upon
its ruins, twisting about in the heat and clawing the sand
voluptuously. Oil gleamed on their naked thighs and bellies
as they moved, like slime on the bodies of enormous white
creatures that have just been unearthed.

The tide began to flow. It rolled back up the beach, putting
the people to flight. They gathered up their luggage and went
away, leaving the rubbish behind them. The returning waves
drove the rubbish before them and took back the wounded

beach into the sea's bosom, to remould the beauty that had been torn.

At sunset, when the tide again reached the exposed roots of the palm trees, a great flock of birds feasted on the offal that was borne on the surf.

The Challenge

HE FAIR was almost over. The street-cleaners were already at work on the western end of the great square. Down there the ground looked like the surface of a flooded bog after the heavy rain that had fallen almost constantly during the forenoon. The slush rose in a thick brown wave before the massive brooms of the sweepers. There was a brisk wind blowing from the east and it was very cold for the middle of May. The cleaners had the collars of their greatcoats turned up about their ears.

Some horses still remained unsold on the high ground at the north-eastern corner of the square. There was a little circle of men around each horse and jobbers passed from group to group. A long row of red-wheeled carts stood before the taverns, from which the sound of drunken brawling issued in ever-changing volume. Women waited anxiously in the carts for their men. Here and there a man could be seen lying

149

on his back in a cart in drunken sleep, with an arm thrown limply across his face.

In the space between the horses and the carts there was a large crowd facing the gable end of the little house in which pigs were weighed. They stood in a wide half-circle, watching the antics of a tinker couple. The tinker's wife sat on an orange box against the wall of the house. She held a white hound on a leash with her left hand, while she threatened the people with a short stick that she brandished in her right. Five asses, with their heads tied together and their snouts to the ground, stood facing the gable end to her right. Now and again she struck at the nearest one with her stick. Her husband stood a short distance out from the gable end, with his legs spread wide and his clenched fists by his hips, challenging the people to fight him.

He yelled at them arrogantly in a hoarse voice.

"If there is a cocky man among you," he cried, "a boastful fellow that fancies himself, let him come out here to me. I'll soon pacify him. I'll tear the living heart out of him."

He was a handsome man, even though he was middle-aged and ravaged by debauch. He had no more belly than a greyhound. His body widened out gradually from waist to shoulder. Like a bull, it was about the upper chest and the base of the neck that he had most muscle. His jaws were heavy and square. His nose was short and thick. His complexion and what remained of his hair were dark. His small blue eyes lay far back in his skull. A piece of his right ear was missing as the result of a brawl. He wore a black jacket and grey trousers. Both garments were in tatters. The jacket had no buttons in front. He wore only a flimsy cotton shirt beneath it. The shirt was also in rags. It was pulled up from the trousers in front. The thick black hair was visible on his chest between the strips of blue cotton. The peak of his grey cap was turned to the rear.

"What ails the lot of you?" he yelled as he stamped with one foot and then with the other. "Has none of you got any courage? Does the very sight of me strike fear into you?"

The people watched him with amused interest, just as if he were putting on a spectacle for their entertainment. Nobody spoke.

"Come on, you pack of cowards," he cried as he made a pretence of throwing off his jacket. "Come on out here, one of you. Come out, so I can wipe one of you off the face of the earth."

His wife jumped to her feet, threw her grey shawl off her shoulders, struck the ground with her right foot and swung the stick about her head.

"I could lick the whole fair," she cried. "I could lick every man Jack here present for one lousy shilling."

She was very tall and slender. She had scarcely any breasts. Her thin, bony face was without colour. She had large green eyes like a cat. Her brown hair hung down about her cheeks in disorder. She was much younger than her husband. Her blue skirt, her grey bodice and her heavy Kashmir shawl of blue and orange colour were all new. They were also spotless. Only her shoes were filthy and ragged. There were no laces in them and the tongues protruded.

"Don't waste your breath on runts like them, darling," her husband said to her. "Sure you could lick them with one hand tied behind your back."

The wife picked up her shawl, threw it about her shoulders and sat down on her orange box. She struck the nearest ass a violent blow on the side with her stick.

"I could lick the whole bloody fair," she shouted, "for one lousy shilling without any bother at all."

The husband walked around the inner rim of the half-circle, looking insolently into the eyes of the people. He now held his fists out in front of him. He did not speak until he had returned to his former position before the gable end. Then he yelled ferociously.

"There isn't a man," he cried, "from here to Ballyvaughan that I couldn't lick. I could tear the heart out of any rowdy from Castlegar. Is there a Connemara gouger here that would dare face me? Have the pampootie men from the Aran Islands any courage, or are they the cowardly razor-bills they are supposed to be? Come on out here, you gougers from Spiddle and Rosmuc. I'm the man to tame the lot of you."

Then he turned suddenly and struck one of the asses a mighty blow in the side with his fist.

"I'm the best man in the whole county of Galway," he shouted.

"I could lick the whole bloody fair for a shilling," his wife said.

A young man spoke in the centre of the crowd.

"Make way for me, good people," he said.

He shouldered the people to left and right, until he entered the half-circle. Then he walked arrogantly to the centre of it and stood on widespread legs with his back to the gable end. He folded his arms slowly across his chest. He was no more than a stripling of slight build, tall and very handsome. His face looked rather effeminate. His blue eyes were too large and they had a soft expression of girlish conceit. He had full, rosy cheeks. A large mop of curly black hair showed between the top of his forehead and the peak of his grey cap. He wore a new serge suit, a knitted white jumper and elegant English shoes with very pointed toes.

"It seems to me," he said to the people, with his head thrown back and to one side in conceited fashion, "that I heard some man here insulting the people of Connemara. I heard the word 'gougers' mentioned. I happen to be a Connemara man myself, so I have a mind to stand here and wait for that man to repeat the insult. I'm a quiet, well-behaved

lad. I never pick a quarrel with any man. Neither do I run
from a fight, though. That's the kind of lad I am. Where I
am, I stand."

The tinker's wife leaped from the orange box and struck
the ground with the flat of her stick.

"I could lick the whole fair for one lousy shilling," she
cried.

The tinker leaped clean off the ground and struck his buttocks with his heels while in the air. He struck the ground on
descending with both feet simultaneously. Then he yelled
mightily and threw off his ragged jacket. He took it by the
end of one sleeve and trailed it on the ground behind him.
Then he walked slowly round the young man from Connemara.

"I dare any man stand on my coat," he cried as he walked
around slowly. "I dare and I double dare any man put a foot
on my coat."

When he returned to his position after making the round,
he threw down the jacket.

"There it is," he cried, "for anybody that has enough courage to put foot on it."

The young man thereupon took off his own jacket slowly.
He folded it carefully and laid it down on a clean spot in front
of him. Then he resumed his former posture, with his arms
folded across his chest. He looked around him at the people,
with his head thrown back conceitedly.

"There is my jacket," he said. "Let any man that's looking
for trouble put a foot on it. If anybody does put a foot on it,
there will be a devil of a fight. That's the kind of a lad I am.
I never start a fight, but I always finish one. Where I am, I
stand."

The tinker's wife ran over to the young man's jacket, with
her teeth clenched and growling in her throat. She shook the
stick at the jacket. Then she stooped, growling savagely and

shaking the stick at every part of the jacket. Although she came to within a few inches of it, she was careful not to touch it. Finally, she spat on the ground four times, all round the garment. Then she walked back to her box.

"That's what I think of the gougers from Connemara," she cried insolently.

The young man shrugged his shoulders contemptuously and said to the people:

"It's a cowardly man that sends his wife to offer a challenge."

The tinker leaped into the air once more clean off the ground and struck his buttocks with his heels. Then he rushed around in all directions shadow-boxing, with his teeth clenched and growling in his throat like a dog. Finally, he went to one of the asses and struck the animal in the side several times.

"That for the gougers of Connemara," he cried as he struck the poor beast. "I challenge the whole of Connemara from Leenane to Rosmuc."

He ran out to the young man's coat and leaped over it, back and forth, as if he were executing a sword dance. He spat on the ground at each jump. When he had finished, he raised his fists high above his head and struck them together.

"I challenge the whole of Connemara from Maam to Clifden," he yelled. "I challenge all the gougers that were ever pupped in Lettermullen, Letterfrack and Carraroe."

The young man walked over very deliberately to the tattered garment of his opponent. He leaped over it, back and forth, spitting on the ground with each jump. Then he returned to his former position and struck his clenched fists together high above his head.

"I challenge all the tinkers from here to County Wicklow," he cried. "There isn't a tinker now living that I couldn't crucify."

The tinker screamed and began to tear the strips of his cotton shirt from his bosom. His wife rushed to him and caught him by the arms.

"Give me a hand with him, neighbours," she cried in a tone of agonised entreaty. "If he isn't held, he'll murder the young lad."

Several people from the audience came to her aid. They laid hands on the tinker, who made a pretence of struggling violently to escape from their grasp.

"Let me at that gouger," roared the tinker as he struggled with mock violence. "I'll tear the living heart out of him. I'll put murder on my soul because of him."

The young man suddenly gave rein to simulated rage on his own account. He yelled with startling force and began to remove his knitted white jumper.

"I'll crucify that tinker," he shouted. "I'll make a pancake of him."

A group of people came from the crowd and seized the young man by the arms. With his jumper half-removed, he struggled to free himself from their grasp, while he continued to insult his opponent in a loud voice.

"Neighbours," he implored, "for the love and honour of God, let me at him. I'll drink that dirty man's blood before the sun goes down."

Suddenly there was an interruption. Voices were raised demanding passage for a horse.

"Make way for a horse," the voices cried. "Make way there."

The crowd parted to make way for a yellow pony that was being put through his paces. A very tall and bony man, dressed in a black frieze coat that came to his heels, led the pony by a halter. The animal was so tiny, compared to the giant size of the man that led him, that he had to trot at full speed in order to keep pace with the man's enormous strides.

The man kept yelling at the minute pony and striking him on the haunch with an ash plant as he paced him.

"Twous, you devil," the man cried. "Go on now."

The yellow trotting pony and the striding frieze-coated man went between the challengers, who were still struggling to bridge the gap of five yards that separated them. The pony and the man went to the gable end of the little house. Then they turned back and passed once more between the yelling, struggling challengers.

"Twous, twous, you devil," the frieze-coated man yelled at the pony, without even glancing at the challengers. "Go on there now."

When the man and the pony had passed, the challengers increased the pretended frenzy of their efforts to break loose. Those who held each man now joined in the challenging. They shouted insults at those opposite. The crowd pressed forward on all sides, so that it became impossible to determine who were the chief actors in the spectacle. Dogs began to bark.

Suddenly there was another interruption, at the very moment when a general encounter seemed on the point of beginning.

"The Guards!" somebody cried. "Here come the Guards."

Silence fell on the crowd almost at once, as four Civic Guards pressed forward to the centre of the throng. The people drifted away quickly to a short distance. The tinker couple and the young man from Connemara were left alone once more in the centre of the arena.

"What's going on here?" said the sergeant in charge of the Guards.

He towered over all present. He was of enormous girth. In spite of the flesh that weighed down his body on all sides, there was no doubt about his fighting abilities. He had a hard face and he protruded from the ground like a rock.

"Holy God!" said the tinker woman. "It's bloody Sergeant Heffernan himself."

"The very same," said the sergeant, glaring at the woman. "And I may tell you that he's spoiling for a fight."

The sergeant held out his two great hands in front of his chest and added:

"There's nothing Sergeant Heffernan would rather do at this present moment than take a couple of tinkers, one in each hand, like this . . ."

He pretended to pluck two tinkers out of the air with his hand, which he then struck together.

"I'll make mincemeat of the two of you," he yelled suddenly, "unless you get out of here at once. Be off now."

The tinker and his wife turned away without saying a word. They went to collect their hound and their asses.

"You run along, too, sonny," the sergeant said to the young man from Connemara. "It's time for you to go home to your mother."

The young man from Connemara had already put on his jumper and his jacket. He was standing with his arms folded on his chest and his head thrown back in conceited fashion.

"Where I am, I stay," he said insolently to the sergeant.

Without seeming effort, the sergeant took him by the back of the neck and walked off with him to the nearest cart. He carried the youth in the way a puppy dog is carried. He threw him on to the cart.

"Get out of sight," he said, "before I lose my temper with you."

The lad lay down on the bottom of the cart and said nothing.

"Move on now, the lot of you," the sergeant said as he walked back to the little house where the pigs were weighed. "I don't want any trouble with anybody. I'm not in a good humour. I wouldn't be responsible for myself if anybody crossed me."

The tinker and his wife glanced at the sergeant as they moved west along the square. The man went in front leading the five asses by a single halter. The woman brought up the rear, leading the white hound by a leash. They took courage again when they reached the western end, where the cleaners were at work with their massive brooms. They began to shout insults at the people.

"I could crucify any man in County Galway," the tinker shouted. "I'm a terrible man. I don't know my own strength."

The woman began to flog the asses on the hind quarters with her stick, while she insulted the people.

"I could lick the whole fair," she cried, "without any trouble at all and I wouldn't ask more than one lousy shilling for doing it."

The cleaners never even raised their heads to look at the passing tinkers, as they drove the mire before their massive brooms in a thick brown wave.

The Seal

T HE SEAL had his head raised high above the water as he intently watched a row boat from which a net was being cast, a short distance to the east. There were four men in the boat. One of them stood in the stern paying out the net. The other three kept rowing gently, in order to keep the boat steady against the strong current. The man in the bow noticed the seal when the net was almost cast. He cursed and shipped his oars at once. Then he picked up a gun that lay behind him in the bow, took aim at the seal's head and fired.

The seal submerged just as the shot was about to leave the muzzle of the gun. He had barely disappeared when the pellets of lead tore the surface of the sea at the exact spot where his head had been. He sank tail first for a few fathoms. Then he stretched out flat and swam at full speed under water to the base of a steep dark cliff. He surfaced there and stood in the water with his back to the rock. Now he was safe from observation. His dun body was exactly the same colour as the stone. He again began to watch the boat intently.

The men rowed away to the east after having cast their net. They soon passed out of sight behind a sandy promontory. The sound of their rowing, however, remained loud for some time. The deep rumble of the oar glambs turning round the thole pins was distinct from the swish of the blades through the water.

When the last faint echo of these sounds had died in the caverns overhead, the seal thrust forward from the rock. He swam warily towards the small inflated buoy of tarred sheep-skin that the men had left floating at the end of a rope, above their net. He submerged when he came abreast of the buoy. There lay the net before him, like a wall of black lace, sway-ing idly back and forth on the current. He greedily inspected the meshes. They were all empty.

Then a large salmon shot past him at great speed and struck the middle of the net, which bulged deeply before the impact. The head of the hapless fish went through one of the meshes as far as the gills. He shook himself fiercely and began to struggle. His beautiful body sent rays of light streaming through the dark water as he leaped in his wild efforts to escape. His violence merely made his prison more secure. Soon his tail also was enmeshed and forced up against his belly. He continued to writhe within a circle that grew ever smaller. In the end he was caparisoned from snout to tail by the meshes and so firmly held that he could struggle no longer. He swayed without resistance with the net, back and forth on the current, gasping spasmodically for breath.

The seal waited until the leaping of the imprisoned fish had ceased. Then he came forward to secure his prey. He took the salmon's head between his jaws and crushed it at one bite. Having released the carcass by cutting the meshes all round, he took it in his teeth and swam towards the surface. He was halfway when he himself was attacked by a conger eel of giant size.

The eel had come whirling straight up from the depths at lightning speed, like an enormous black screw. He threw himself at the base of the seal's neck, which he enveloped several times in the folds of his seven-foot body. While he hugged with all his strength, he drew back his head and snapped at the seal's sleek fur with his vast semi-circular jaws. His keen teeth drew blood at several points.

Stunned by the sudden attack, the seal continued slowly toward the surface for a little way. Then he began to choke within the ever-tightening embrace of his enemy. He released the salmon and turned to defend himself. The conger eel did not wait to receive the counter-attack. He released his hold, as soon as he saw that his ruse had succeeded. He pursued the dead salmon, which had continued towards the surface on being released. Then he in turn grabbed the carcass and made off with it towards the depths. At the moment he did so, however, he found himself gripped securely by the navel in the seal's jaws.

The seal came swiftly to the surface. He raised his head high above the water and began to swing his pinioned enemy from side to side, in the way a dog shakes a rat. The conger eel clung to the salmon at first, as he curved and dangled like a dancing rope about the seal's head. Then he dropped the carcass. The salmon floated away slowly on the current, with a ring of torn meshes still clinging to the centre of his body.

The seal hurled his enemy into the air after having thoroughly shaken him. The conger eel's body curved in a graceful arc as it reached the highest point in its ascent. Then it came down head first. The seal was poised to receive it. He cut the head clean from the body at one snap of his jaws.

The headless body plunged straight down through the sea several fathoms, whirling almost as swiftly as when it had been whole. Then it lost direction and momentum. Belching blood from its great wound, it began to wander aimlessly in wide arcs. The detached head remained on the surface. It continued to snap its jaws convulsively for a while as it floated with the current.

Tiny streams of blood flowed from the seal's wound as he went after the dead salmon. He bellowed in triumph as he came up with it. He took it in his jaws and swam at full speed to his cave within the bowels of the cliff.

The New Suit

EAVING THE GRANDMOTHER at home to look
after the house, the Dillon family set forth
to shear the sheep. The two oldest children,
Mary and Thomas, walked with their parents. Mary was eighteen and Thomas was
sixteen, so they had already assumed the
dignified manner of grown-up people to
whom such an event was no longer an exciting adventure.
In fact, Mary was whispering about a coming wedding in a
neighbouring village as she walked with her mother, while
Thomas brought up the rear with his father and talked in a
loud voice about the condition of the crops with the pompous arrogance of adolescence.

The other four children, however, bolted from the yard
and ran at full speed until they entered the narrow lane that
led to the uplands east of the village. Three of them were
girls, all wearing white pinafores and with coloured ribbons
tied to the ends of their plaited hair. They chattered and

sang little snatches of song in chorus as they hopped along the smooth stones of the lane on their bare feet.

The youngest child was a boy called Jimmy, now in his seventh year. He ran far in front of all the others, pausing once in a while to look back and urge the laggards to make more haste. His round face looked so solemn that it was hard to say whether he felt happy or miserable. The fact was that he had been promised a new suit from this year's wool. The promise had been made as early as last Christmas and it had been repeated several times since then by both his father and mother on his ardent insistence. Yet he still could not quite believe that he would really get the suit, and the torture of waiting was almost equal to the ecstatic pleasure of anticipation.

Hitherto he had received his clothes in fragments. One year he would get a pair of trousers and the next year he would get a jacket. So he never had the pleasure of wearing a full suit, with all the garments of the same age. The trousers would be patched by the time he got a new jacket. Then, again, the jacket would be faded and threadbare before he got a new pair of trousers. The thought of wearing a whole new suit for the first time in his life was too good to be true, in spite of all the promises. For that reason, he was determined to keep a close eye on the wool, from the moment it was cut from the sheep's back until it was cloth in the hands of the tailor.

The sheep were in a long, narrow glen, which had a tall fence all around it. They stood in a row beneath the fence when Jimmy arrived. Although the morning was not far advanced, the sun was already hot and the animals were seeking shelter from it. Now that it was summer, their heavy wool irked them. They panted with exhaustion as they pressed close to the fence with their heads lowered.

"Chown, chown," Jimmy called to them. "You'll soon be running around in your naked pelts."

The sheep raised their heads eagerly and looked at the boy. "Maa," they said expectantly.

Then they all gathered together in a group and stared at him furtively, fearing that he was accompanied by his dog, which loved to worry them. Six of them were large and white, wearing such a heavy coat of wool that their backs were quite flat. The other five were little mountain sheep with dark wool that grew short and curly. There were five lambs of that year's increase with the flock. Three of the lambs were already half-grown and they had their tails cut. They had been held over from the sale for breeding. The other two lambs were very young. They kept trying to suckle their mother.

Jimmy and his three little sisters had the sheep all herded into a corner when the others arrived. Then four of the white sheep were thrown on their backs and the shearing began. Jimmy held down the head of the animal his mother was shearing. At first the sheep kept making attempts to rise when she felt the shears against her pelt.

"You'd think she doesn't want to lose her wool," Jimmy said, "the way she keeps moving around."

"She's afraid," his mother said. "That's why she keeps trying to get up."

"Does she think we're going to kill her?" Jimmy said.

"Maybe she does," said his mother.

"But you told me a sheep is a blessed animal," Jimmy said. "You said that God gave her wool so that we could have new clothes."

"That's true," his mother said. "She is a blessed animal, not like a wicked goat that has no wool and is a thief into the bargain."

"Then why would she be afraid we're going to kill her?"

167

Jimmy said. "God must have told her about her wool and why she has it, if she is blessed."

"You hold her head and stop talking," his mother said. "Otherwise I might cut her with the shears."

"You mustn't cut her, Mother," Jimmy said. "It would be a sin to cut a blessed animal. It might put bad luck on my new suit."

"All right, then," the mother said. "You hold her and I won't cut her."

The sheep lay quite still when all the wool had been cut from around her neck and shoulders. Now the shears were cutting deep swaths in the thick wool along her back. The thin hairs, packed closely together, were as delicate as silk near the roots. They were moist with oil and they shone brightly in the sunlight.

"Did God tell people how to make clothes of sheep's wool?" Jimmy said.

"He did," said the mother.

"Who did He tell about it?" said Jimmy.

"He told a saint," said the mother.

"Did He tell him everything all at once?" said Jimmy. "How to shear and spin and weave and be a tailor, too?"

"He did," said the mother.

"What was the saint's name?" said Jimmy.

"I don't know," said the mother.

"That's a pity," Jimmy said. "I'd like to say a prayer to him and ask him to keep Neddy the tailor from drinking when he is making my new suit. But I can't say a prayer to him if I don't know his name. It's queer, though, that you wouldn't know the name of a great saint like that. He should be the most famous of all saints, if he taught people how to make clothes out of wool. Only for him the people would die of cold in winter."

"If you're a good boy," his mother said, "until Neddy the

tailor comes to make your suit, then God will keep Neddy
sober. So he won't make a botch, same as he does with clothes
when he is drinking. Otherwise he'll get drunk and your suit
will be so terrible that you'll be ashamed to wear it. You
mustn't ask me any more questions about this saint and that
saint. You must be a good boy and not ask foolish questions."

"Oh! I will, Mother," Jimmy said. "I'll do everything you
tell me, and I don't care who the saint was."

The shearing continued until all the sheep were stripped
of their wool. According as each sheep was released, she shook
herself and began to graze with great energy, pausing now
and again to murmur with satisfaction at her relief. The
mother of the youngest lambs, however, had great difficulty
in getting her offspring to recognise her nakedness. They
were startled when they saw her approach, stripped of her
wool. So they ran away from her and paid no heed to her
frantic bleating. Finally, they had to be caught and put to
her udder. Then they recognised her and suckled.

The wool was all gathered up, put into bags, and brought
home. Then the womenfolk took it in hand, to prepare it for
the weaver. Jimmy did his best to help with every operation.
When it was washed and spread out on a field to bleach, he
felt very important because he was allowed to stand guard
over it all day. Then it was teased and carded into rolls for
spinning. He also helped with the spinning. As the rolls of
thread came off the spindle, he held them while his sister
Mary wound them on to a ball. The white thread was made
into one ball and the grey thread into another one. When all
the wool was spun, the ball of white thread was of enormous
size.

Jimmy accompanied his mother to the weaver's house with
the thread. It was in another village nearly three miles distant. She put on her best clothes for the occasion and Jimmy
felt terribly ashamed of his patched trousers as he trotted

along beside her. Yet he would not stay at home on any account, for fear something.dreadful might happen to the precious thread in his absence. Furthermore, he wanted to ask the weaver the name of that famous saint to whom God had given the secret of cloth making. Then he could ask the saint in prayer every night to keep Neddy the tailor sober.

When he arrived at the weaver's house, however, he lost courage. He stood within the kitchen door and gaped in silent wonder at the loom. It was placed in a sunken room that had no partition on the side facing the kitchen, so that he could see the whole process of weaving from where he stood. The intricate movements of the shuttles and the miraculous way the thread was changed into cloth convinced the little boy that this was a mystery similar to what happened on the altar during Mass. It pertained to God and it was just as well not to pry into it for fear of making God angry. Even so, the mysterious process acted on him as a magnet. Little by little, he crept along the wall of the kitchen until he was close to the weaver.

"Well, young man," said the weaver, "do you want to learn how cloth is made?"

"Come over here, Jimmy," said his mother, who was seated by the fireplace. "Don't interfere with the work."

"He's not doing any harm," the weaver said. "Let him stay where he is."

The weaver was a small man, with black hair and very sallow skin. He had such merry eyes that Jimmy was not the least afraid of him. So the child suddenly got courage and determined to seize the opportunity.

"Do you know the name of the saint?" he said to the weaver.

"Pay no attention to him," the mother said, addressing the weaver apologetically. "He asks such strange questions."

The weaver bent close to the little boy and said: "What saint is that, comrade?"

"The saint that told people how to make clothes out of wool," said Jimmy.

"Oh, I see," said the weaver, looking very solemn all of a sudden. "Well. Now that's a long story, but I'll tell you about it. It's a sad story, as well as being a long one. For the truth is that we don't know the name of the saint that taught the people how to make clothes out of wool, no more than we know the name of the saint that taught people how to plough, or to make houses."

"Oh, that's a great pity," said Jimmy despondently. "Does nobody know, not even the priest?"

"No," said the weaver solemnly. "Not even the priest. Everybody has forgotten the names of these great saints. That's because people were pagans in the past and there were only a few good people among them. The good people were the saints. All the others were sinful and contrary. They only remembered the names of people that were wicked like themselves, kings and tyrants and landlords and generals that made war, usurers that robbed the poor and notorious criminals of every kind. And not only did they forget the names of the saints that were their benefactors, but they even persecuted them and sometimes put them to death."

"That's terrible," Jimmy said. "I thought surely you'd know the name of the saint that told people how to make cloth out of wool. I have a reason for wanting to know."

"Will you be quiet now?" Jimmy's mother said. "You have said enough."

She took Jimmy away before he could ask the weaver any more questions. The little boy wept that night in bed, terrified by the weaver's melancholy description of humanity and convinced that some disaster would happen at the last moment to ruin his chance of getting a new suit.

Then again his hopes rose to a new height when the
finished cloth came from the weaver. The thickening-trough
was brought into the kitchen. His mother and his sister Mary
sat at the ends of the long wooden trough in their bare feet.
The cloth was laid in the centre of the trough, a few yards
at a time. Sour water was poured on it, to soften it for the
thickening. Then the women kicked at it rhythmically, until
it had reached the required thickness.

The great moment had at last arrived. The cloth was ready
for the tailor. Jimmy was awake at dawn on the morning his
brother Thomas was going in the cart to fetch that important
personage. The little boy was in such an excited state that
his mother had great difficulty in getting him to eat his breakfast. After his brother had left, his agitation increased. His
mother could not move a yard around the house without having him at her apron strings. Finally, she took him to task.

"What ails you now?" she said. "Are you still afraid you
won't get your suit?"

"No, Mother," Jimmy said. "I'm afraid that Neddy has
been drinking last night and that he'll make a botch of it.
I couldn't find out the name of the saint, so I couldn't pray
and ask him to keep Neddy from drinking."

"Never mind," said his mother. "We'll soon know whether
he has been drinking last night or not. We'll know as soon
as he puts foot in the house."

"How will we know?" said Jimmy.

"That's easy," said his mother. "As soon as he comes into
the house I'm going to offer him a cup of tea. If he refuses
the tea and asks for a drink of sour milk instead of it, he has
been drinking. But if he drinks the tea and if sweat begins
to pour from his face after he drinks it, then he has been
sober last night and he'll make good clothes."

When at last the heavy cart came rumbling up the road
towards the village, Jimmy ran down to the yard gate to meet

it. There was the tailor sitting on the bottom of the cart, with his legs curled up under him and his head bent in a gloomy attitude. The boy completely lost all hope. The tailor's posture convinced him that the man had been exceptionally wicked on the previous evening. Then the cart halted in the yard. Thomas jumped down and took the tailor's gear into the house. The tailor himself, after looking about him for almost a minute in gloomy silence, also descended and limped indoors.

He was a very thin man, with a club foot and an enormous Adam's apple. His face was deadly pale and he had heavy grey eyebrows that gave his blue eyes a fierce expression. He suffered from asthma and he kept drawing in deep breaths with a hissing sound. Every time he took a deep breath, his Adam's apple rose up as large as a small potato in his throat, paused and then retreated.

"A hundred thousand welcomes to you, tailor," said Jimmy's mother. "Sit down and have a cup of tea."

Jimmy put his forefinger between his front teeth and waited for the tailor's reply.

"Thank you, ma'am," said the tailor. "I'll have a cup of tea if it's not too much trouble."

"Oh, it's no trouble at all," Jimmy said, unable to keep silent owing to the happiness that suddenly overwhelmed him. "We have it all ready to see would you drink it. We were afraid you would rather have sour milk."

The mother picked up the tongs from the fireplace and threatened Jimmy with it. The boy blushed to the roots of his hair and retired into a corner, horrified by his mistake. The tailor, however, looked at the boy seriously for a few moments and then burst out laughing.

"Tare an' ouns," he said after he had laughed his fill. "I'll make the best suit I ever made in my life, just because you made me laugh. Any boy that makes me laugh deserves the best suit that was ever made. A good laugh is worth a good suit any day. Get ready now till I measure you."

So Jimmy became happy again. The tailor's gear was laid out on a big table and when the tailor had drunk his tea Jimmy was measured. Then the tailor set to work with furious energy, pausing now and again to burst out into a peal of hearty laughter.

"Tare an' ouns," he repeated after each laugh. "That deserves a good suit if anything ever did."

He kept his promise, too, for the little suit fitted perfectly and on the following Sunday Jimmy was the envy of all the other village boys as he went to church.

The Wedding

NUALA WENT to the door and looked towards the house where the wedding was being held. It was no more than two hundred yards away, in a deep hollow on the far side of the road, yet it was indistinct owing to the heavy downpour of rain.

"Devil mend her," she said. "She stole him from me, but little good it's going to do her. Unhappy is the bride the rain falls on. She'll have no children by him. Devil a one."

Her face was like a death mask within the triangular cowl of her thin black shawl. There was no trace of blood in it. The yellowish skin seemed made of dry leather drawn clumsily over the uneven structure of bone. When she screwed up her little eyes to look at the house, which was dimmed by the rain, the leathery skin of her face wrinkled like a sheet of crushed paper. It gathered about each eye socket in a clumsy stitch.

"Any sign of the priest coming?" Aunt Peggy said to her from the couch.

Nuala leaned forward and peered around the corner of the doorway, along the road that went to the village.

"I see only a boy on an ass going the road," she said. "Lord save us! Smoke is rising out of the ass every time the boy gives him a clout of his sea rod. Oh! Lord! This rain will drown the world. She took him from me and now God is going to drown us all."

"Come in out of that," Aunt Peggy said, "and stop blaspheming. Take off your wet shawl and dry it at the fire."

Nuala turned away from the door, took a few quick steps towards the hearth and then halted to scratch the bosom of her tight frieze jacket with both hands. She kept shrugging her shoulders and grinning while she scratched. She made a hissing sound through her closed teeth, as if what she was doing gave her extreme pleasure.

"God forgive you," Aunt Peggy said. "You're delighted that rain is going to fall on poor Barbara's wedding."

"And why wouldn't I?" said Nuala. "God's curse on her; she took him from me."

"Take off your wet shawl," Aunt Peggy said, "and don't make me hate you for your wicked talk."

Nuala took off her little shawl and began to shake the rain from it, jabbering to herself. Although she was over fifty years of age, she had the figure of a girl not yet reached maturity. Her bosom was quite flat and her waist was so narrow that a large hand could almost span it. Her movements, too, were girlish and even childlike. Shaking the wet shawl, she bobbed up and down uncertainly like a child. Her body seemed to be without weight.

"Hang it up on the nail by the fire now," Aunt Peggy said. "Draw up a stool and warm yourself. Stop casting on Barbara, or it's on yourself God will put the curse."

Nuala went on tiptoe to the hearth and hung the shawl on
a nail. Then she brought a stool to the fire and sat down facing Aunt Peggy, at whom she looked meekly. She clasped her
hands on her lap. Her hands were covered with the same kind
of yellowish, leathery skin as her face. Her long fingernails
were clotted with dirt.

"Aunt Peggy," she said in a plaintive whisper, "you
shouldn't turn on me like that, and you my first cousin. We
are the same age, too. What's more, we have the same name.
You are Peggy Lavelle and I am Nuala Lavelle. 'Dirty
Nualeen' the children call me, but my right name is Nuala
Lavelle and that's a French name. Doctor Bodkin said it was
a French name and he should know, he being a gentleman.
He said a French general invaded the west with an army and
the Lavelles were left behind after the general was beaten
by the English. They hid among the people of the land and
spread their seed, until the great famine. Then our grandfather came here, following his head before him with the
hunger. It was a poor root he took here, too, for there isn't a
man left of his seed in the parish, only women like you and
me. Seeing how it is so, Aunt Peggy, you shouldn't turn on a
poor female thing of your own bone and she foolish."

Aunt Peggy had been lying flat on her back. Now she raised
herself on one elbow and threatened Nuala with her fist.

"Honest to God," she said angrily, "if I wasn't so sick I'd
hit you. I give you bite and sup nearly every day, don't I? I
gave you that skirt you have on, didn't I?"

Nuala laughed, jumped to her feet smartly and turned
right round twice, holding out the skirt on either side. It was
of blue serge and it did not fit her. Furthermore, it was ragged and dirty.

"You did, 'faith," she said. "You did give it to me and it's
a lovely skirt, fit for a queen. I should be married in it to-day,
only for Barbara stole him from me. Ho! The lustful villain,

it's little good she'll get out of him. You did, 'faith, Aunt Peggy; you gave me this lovely dress and it should be my wedding dress only for misfortune."

She rushed over to the couch and knelt beside it. She took Aunt Peggy's hand and stroked it.

"What's the good of talking to you and you only a fool?" Aunt Peggy said.

Aunt Peggy lay back on the couch once more and closed her eyes. She was almost as slovenly as Nuala, but there was still a trace of former beauty in her ravaged face. Her long hair, which had once been golden and was now almost white, streamed down on either side of her bosom, hanging loose. Her eyebrows were still golden. There were dark smudges on her pale face, where she kept stroking it nervously with her fingers. There was a little froth about her lower lips and she was breathing with difficulty.

"That's a lovely smell of whisky from you, Aunt Peggy," Nuala said, as she stroked the hand.

"Oh! God!" said Aunt Peggy. "I wish I hadn't touched it. My head is going round. I worked so hard at the machine all night, trying to get Barbara's wedding dress finished. I was worn out. Even so, it was ten o'clock this morning before Girleen and myself had it finished. Anthony came in with a bottle at nine o'clock. He was worried for fear I wouldn't have the wedding dress finished for Barbara."

Nuala dropped the hand, shuddered and said:

"My curse on the same Anthony."

"He made me take a big sup out of the bottle when the dress was finished," Aunt Peggy said. "I had a pain in my side and he was anxious for me to go to the wedding house, so he made me take a big sup. But I was so tired and Girleen put me lying here on the couch for a rest, while she and Anthony went off with the finished dress. Anthony left me the bottle and I took one sup after another, trying to cure the pain in my side and drive off the weariness. It's awful to be lying here and I not able to go to Barbara's wedding. She's my third cousin on the mother's side."

Nuala jumped to her feet, spat on the floor and said viciously:

"The curse of God on the two of them."

Aunt Peggy sat upright on the couch suddenly and shouted:

"Stop that now, or I'll drive you out of the house."

Nuala began to blubber and wrung her hands. She knelt again by the couch and said:

"I didn't mean a word of it, Aunt Peggy. I didn't, darling. Is there a sup left in the bottle for me?"

"If there was itself," said Aunt Peggy, arranging a quilt over her on the couch, "it's not to you I'd give it. If I gave you a sup, you'd run out mad along the road, and have at the first man you saw."

"Just a little weeshy sup," Nuala implored her.

"Be off with you and let me rest," Aunt Peggy said. "Stir up the fire under that oven of potatoes. Girleen will be back from the wedding house any minute now to give little Julia her dinner."

Nuala put her hand out timidly and stroked Aunt Peggy's hair.

"You used to have lovely golden hair, Aunt Peggy," she said. "It was like a fire on your head. That's what made the young men run after you. They used to follow you in a crowd along the road and lie in wait for you in the lanes with the fall of night. Then you went to America and came back with Girleen. You lost the gold out of your hair out there and sorrow a much gold you had in your pocket-book either, for all the loveliness that you lost out there. Here you are in this poor cottage, working your fingers like a cobbler, crouching night and day over a sewing machine, making dresses for peo-

ple. And your hair is white. Devil a bit of gold is left in it.
Oh! If I had golden hair like you, it's a lovely rich man I'd
have married."

"Stir up the fire," Aunt Peggy said wearily as she closed
her eyes.

"I will," said Nuala. "I'll do what you say."

She went to the hearth and put a few sods of turf under the
oven of potatoes that was hanging from pot-hooks. Then she
grinned and said:

"My hair isn't white yet. Is it, Aunt Peggy?"

Aunt Peggy did not answer. Nuala undid the rough knot
that bound her hair at the nape of her neck. Her hair was of
a light chestnut colour and showed no signs of changing with
age. However, it was very dirty and bedraggled. When she
cast it loose from the knot and shook her head, it stood out
like a miserable bunch of withered sea grass that has been
bitten here and there by a stray donkey. It had not been
washed or combed for years.

"Look at my hair, Aunt Peggy," she whispered, coming
over to the couch. "It's not white like yours, although we are
the same age."

As the other woman paid no heed to her, she went on tiptoe to a mirror that hung on the wall near the door. She
stared into the mirror for a little while without moving. In
repose, her countenance lost its expression of insanity and
was no longer ghoulish. It became apparent that her features
had been moulded by Nature with remarkable delicacy and
in perfect proportion. Her delicate nostrils and the fine line
of her mouth showed breeding.

Then she giggled suddenly and began to preen herself,
arranging her hair clumsily in different ways.

"I could fix it up with a bit of ribbon to make it look
lovely," she said. "Then he'd notice me. It would be a white
ribbon I'd wear in it for the wedding."

She held out her skirt on either side and looked down at her feet. Then she burst out laughing and turned towards Aunt Peggy.

"Look at that," she said, pointing to her feet. "I forgot to lace my boots. How could I get married without my boots laced?"

"Ah! God help you," said Aunt Peggy. "There's no use being angry with you."

Nuala went back to her stool and began to lace her boots. They were not of a pair, as she had picked them up separately from refuse heaps in the village. She laced them with pieces of grey twine, talking to herself as she did so.

"They are wet at the soles," she said, "and the water in them makes a whisper when I move, but there is dust on the uppers of them. There is dust on the flounce of my skirt as well. In the early morning when I left home there was a lovely dust on the road. It was as thick and soft as snow. It was lovely walking through it. You could make hearts and crosses on the dust with the toe of your boot, same as on the strand at low tide. Crosses mean kisses and hearts mean sweethearts. He is going to marry her because she brought a portion back from America with her, but I love him all the same and I made hearts and crosses in the dust for him with the toe of my boot. Then the rain began to pour down. It made a lovely sound when it began to fall on the thick dust, like milk squirting out of a cow's teat into a can that is nearly full of milky froth. I was glad when it began to fall. I stood in the middle of the road until I got wet, praising God for putting a curse on her wedding."

"Lord save us!" Aunt Peggy said, opening her eyes and turning over on her side to look out the door. "The rain is getting worse. The priest is going to get drenched."

"Maybe he won't come at all," said Nuala, "and then she couldn't get married."

With one shoe still unlaced, she ran to the door, slapping her hands in delight. The rainfall was now so heavy that it clattered like hail on the slate roof of the cottage. Large drops bounced off the concrete square in front of the door. In the little garden that reached from the house to the road, the rain made a rumbling sound like distant thunder on the staggering leaves of the cabbage and potato plants. A thick steam rose from the road and the grey walls that bound it had turned black. There was a clamour of rushing streams from all sides.

"Girleen is coming," Nuala said.

Shielding her eyes with her cupped hand, she was looking towards the wedding house, whence three girls had emerged running. All three of them were trying to take shelter under a single raincoat, which they carried loose over their heads. In spite of the rain, there was a crowd of men and boys standing in the yard before the house. They yelled at the running girls. In the wide green lane that mounted steeply from the wedding house to the road, a number of horses were tied to the stone wall. One of them neighed and began to kick as the three girls passed running.

"I better be going now, Aunt Peggy," said Nuala, trotting back to the hearth. "Little Julia is afraid of me. I better go before she comes. Children throw stones at me and call me 'Dirty Nualeen,' although I wouldn't touch a hair of their heads. It's how I'd love to play with them."

Aunt Peggy took a pint bottle furtively from behind the couch.

"Sit down there," she said, "and don't be silly. Julia is not afraid of you. It's only your imagination. You can eat a bit of her dinner."

Nuala stared into the fire and said dreamily:

"Doctor Bodkin said I stopped growing at the age of sixteen when I got sick. I'm fond of Doctor Bodkin. He's the only person that pays heed to what I say. He says I have more sense than most people."

She started and turned round as Aunt Peggy pulled the cork out of the bottle with her teeth, making a loud sound. Aunt Peggy put the bottle to her mouth hurriedly and began to drink with her head thrown back. Nuala got very excited and came over to the couch. She held out her palms, close together and curved, like a cup. Her hands were trembling.

"For the love of God," she whispered, "put a drop of it on my hands, so I can get a smell and a lick. Just a weeshy drop."

Aunt Peggy stopped drinking when the bottle was nearly empty. She glanced furtively out the door and poured the few drops that remained into Nuala's cupped palms. Then she hid the empty bottle behind the couch and said:

"Be quick now, and not a word to Girleen when she comes."

Giggling excitedly, Nuala walked back to the hearth very carefully, holding her cupped hands out in front of her. She sat down on her stool and smelt the spirits, drawing in a deep breath through her nose.

"It's lovely," she said. "Oh! It's gorgeous."

Then she began to lick her palms greedily, like a cat. Aunt Peggy was now lying flat on her back, with her head to one side. Her lower lip twitched.

"Here they come," said Nuala, wiping her palms on her skirt.

There was a patter of feet coming up the garden path. The three girls were laughing merrily and the sound of youthful happiness seemed to push Nuala back with violence into the ghoulish world of her sickness. Her face darkened. She screwed up her eyes, wrinkling the leathery skin of her face once more into clumsy stitches. She crouched lower over the fire, gripping her elbows with her hands. She rocked herself and muttered incoherently.

Aunt Peggy's daughter, who was nicknamed Girleen, bounded into the room, dragging the wet raincoat after her. She was a tall, fully-developed girl of seventeen, with a freckled face and luxuriant reddish hair. Her breasts were large and firm. She was good-looking, except for the coarseness of her thick-lipped mouth and the smallness of her eyes. Her face, which had been bright with happy laughter as she entered the room, became sulky as she noticed her mother's condition.

"There you are," she said as she carried the raincoat across the floor to a rack by the stairs, "still lying there and not a move out of you. Aren't you going to put a foot in the wedding house? Do you want to disgrace me?"

"I don't feel well enough," said Aunt Peggy without opening her eyes. "I couldn't move a foot if you gave me a fortune."

It was apparent from her tone that she was afraid of her daughter. Girleen hung up the coat and then took the empty bottle from behind the couch.

"Empty," she said angrily. "No wonder you can't move a foot. You're a fine mother to have."

She dropped the bottle with a gesture of disgust. Nuala suddenly picked up the tongs from the hearth and threatened Girleen with it.

"Don't talk to your mother like that," she cried fiercely. "She reared you well, and a hard job it was for her, too."

"Oh! shut up," said Girleen, striding over to the hearth. "I suppose she gave you a drop out of the bottle. It's a sin to give you any. You might hurt someone. Give me that."

She grabbed the tongs from Nuala. Aunt Peggy sat upright on the couch and said in a maudlin tone:

"Can't you be quiet and have pity on your sick mother?"

"She has a wicked nature," said Nuala.

"Shut up, you lunatic," said Girleen, taking the lid off the oven.

"Go down to the fire and warm yourself, Julia," Aunt Peggy said to the child who was standing by the door with the other girl. "Girleen will get your dinner ready in a minute."

"I'm not cold, Aunt Peggy," the child said timidly.

She was twelve years old and had been sent down from the city to spend the summer holidays with her aunt. She was obviously terrified of Nuala, whom she kept watching furtively. The other girl, who was the same age as Girleen and belonged to the neighbourhood, seemed to be highly amused by everything. She kept giggling as she cracked a hard sweet between her teeth. She was a big, loutish creature with a red, pimply face.

Girleen began to lay the table for the child's dinner.

"Honestly, Nora," she said to the red-faced girl, "did you ever see such a miserable wedding in your life? It was more like a wake. They all sat there looking at one another, without music or dancing."

"I've seen lots of wakes," said the red-faced girl, "but it's so long since we had a wedding in the parish that I wouldn't know how to make a comparison. Nobody got married in this parish for the last five years."

"True for you," Girleen said, "and even now it's a couple of old people that's getting married. Anthony is forty-nine and Barbara is forty-three. Maybe that's why the wedding is miserable."

"It will be better to-night over at Anthony's house," the red-faced girl said.

"How does the dress fit her?" said Aunt Peggy as she threw her legs off the couch and began to scratch her hair with both hands.

"It fitted her like a glove," said Girleen, "after I changed two hooks at the waist. 'Faith, Anthony has a fine armful of a woman. She looks nice, Barbara does, but all the same you'd think a man would rather have a young girl."

"Young girls don't have fortunes," said Aunt Peggy.

Nuala jumped to her feet and came over to the table on which Girleen was spreading a cloth.

"Was Anthony taking much notice of her, Girleen?" she whispered excitedly. "Did you see him making up to her at all? Did he give her a pinch, or a hug, or a kiss, or anything? Tell me what way he was with her. Was he looking at her with wildness in his eyes, or was he just sitting there with his chin on his fist, like a man sad and miserable after a bad bargain?"

"Will ye listen to herself?" cried Girleen.

She and the red-faced girl burst out laughing.

"Laugh away," cried Nuala angrily. "What do ye know about love?"

Aunt Peggy stood up and went over to the wet raincoat, staggering slightly.

"Don't mind them, Nuala," she said. "They'll learn soon enough what it is to suffer."

She threw the raincoat over her shoulder and walked unsteadily towards the door. Nuala was now stamping about the floor, muttering to herself and wringing her hands. The child looked around in fright as Nuala came near her. Then she ran across the floor and climbed a little way up the stairs. There she sat down with her bare knees close together and her two little fists joined before her mouth.

"Suffer my eye!" said Girleen. "Fancy anybody suffering over a man like Anthony. He's a nice, poor fellow, but he's no Romeo. A podgy little man, with his legs too short for him and a harelip. I wouldn't marry him for a million."

"Stop casting on him," said Aunt Peggy at the door.

Then she stooped and ran out under the rain, going towards the gable of the cottage.

"You pretend to be in love with him, Nuala," the red-faced girl said, "but you never spoke to him in your life, or to any other man. I'm certain you didn't. You'd die of fright if a man spoke to you."

"How do we know?" said Girleen. "Maybe she does be courting them on the quiet. She lives all alone over there in her house below the road. Maybe the men come to her in the darkness."

"God's curse on the two of ye for making fun of me," said Nuala.

She ran down to the hearth and crouched on her stool, while the two girls laughed heartily.

"Come on, Nora," Girleen said. "Give me a hand. We have to hurry."

"May I help, too?" the child said.

"Come on," said Girleen. "We'll eat up quick and then we'll be in time for the wedding at the chapel. The priest won't be long now. We have to hurry."

The child got to her feet and began to come down the stairs very slowly, with her hand on the banister, keeping her eyes fixed on Nuala.

"Come on over here," Nuala whispered to the child. "Tell me a story about the big town."

The child paused for a moment and then ran wildly across the floor. She followed Girleen and Nora into a small room, where the crockery and food were stored.

Nuala rocked herself and began to mutter:

"She's afraid of me," she said. "Oh, Lord! it's terrible to be the way I am. The little drop of whisky has made a fire inside me. I want to do wild things with him. Maybe I didn't ever speak to him. Neither did I, but I want him all the same. He's ugly like myself. God was cruel to both of us. In the middle of my youth I was struck and the loveliness was scorched on my face. But Anthony was struck before he was born. He was born with a harelip and his legs were too short for him. So the lovely girls wouldn't look at him. They went off to the big towns in England and America and he was left behind. All the lovely young people went away and Anthony was left behind with me. He was left alone and I was left alone, but I was afraid to speak to him. Oh! If he'd only speak to me and maybe come and lie with me during the lonely nights, when the wind is screeching and the wicked ghosts are roaming about. In the end he'd come to me and listen to my whisper, if Barbara didn't come back from America with her hansel. My curse on her. The rain is falling now on her wedding. It will only be a man without seed that she'll have, for his seed will be flooded out with the rain."

Aunt Peggy came hurrying into the cottage. She threw off the raincoat and shook it. Then she looked out the door and cried angrily:

"Arrah! Musha, is it any wonder the young people are flying from this rainy desert and refusing to get married in it?"

She waved the wet raincoat through the open doorway at the rainy world outside and continued in a tone of mounting anger:

"Why would they marry here and spend their lives watching the rain fall on the black bogland? Driven by famine and persecution the people came here, where there are only grey rocks growing out of the bog."

Nuala jumped to her feet, clapped her hands together and cried:

"That's true talk, Aunt Peggy. True for you."

Aunt Peggy staggered across the floor to the rack and hung up the coat, crying bitterly:

"My curse on the day I left America. Any day now, Girleen
will rise up and go. Then I'll be alone like you are, Nuala."

"True for you, Aunt Peggy," Nuala said, clapping her
hands. "We'll be left alone, the two of us."

"The two of ye are mad drunk," Girleen said, coming out
of the little room with some mutton on a dish. "Shut up, the
two of ye, with your silly talk."

"That's the talk, Aunt Peggy," Nuala said as Aunt Peggy
returned to the couch. "All the lovely young people go away
from the black, lonely places. They go marching east and
west looking for the big towns where there is everlasting light
and dancing and fine music. It was for the lovely young people that God made the world."

Nora and the child now sat down to the table with Girleen.

"She's well away now," Nora said to Girleen as she nodded
her head towards Nuala.

"Lord save us," Girleen said. "My mother had no right to
give her some of the whisky. Look at the state she is in."

"Stop casting on Nuala," Aunt Peggy cried from the couch.

Nuala turned around and shook her fist at Girleen.

"You have a bad breed in you," she said.

Then she tucked the quilt about Aunt Peggy and whispered:

"Let you and me pay no heed to the young things, Aunt
Peggy. Long ago, when you and I were young, there was
singing and dancing and fine music here, too. There used
to be great hugging with the fall of night. Your hair was like
a fire on your head, Aunt Peggy. But now your hair is white
and soon you'll be all alone like me, listening through the
miserable night for a sound that never comes. She took him
from me, Aunt Peggy, with her witchery, but she'll get no
good of him. The rain is falling on her wedding."

"Come on over here, bad cess to you," Girleen called out
to her.

Nuala turned around and said angrily:

"I'm not listening to you. You have a bad breed in you."

"You lunatic," Girleen said. "I was only asking you to have a bite of dinner."

"Dinner?" said Nuala excitedly.

She jumped to her feet and came over to the table, at which the three girls were now sitting. There was a jug of milk, a dish of potatoes and a plate of mutton on the board.

"Oh! Look at the lovely meat," Nuala said.

She scratched her bosom violently with both hands and drew in a deep breath through her clenched teeth.

"Are you going to give me a bit of the meat, Girleen?" she continued. "Was it from the wedding ye got the lovely meat? I hear they killed two sheep for the wedding."

"Hold up your skirt," Girleen said.

"God bless the givers," Nuala said, raising her skirt. "May God increase all you have best in the house."

She raised her skirt up high. Her body was naked underneath it. As she wore no stockings, her naked body was exposed from her ankles to the thickness of her upper thighs. And it became manifest that her ragged skirt had concealed limbs of a startling beauty. They were as shapely as those of a dancer. The unwashed skin was tawny and without blemish. Not a vein, nor a fold of sagging flesh broke its smooth surface. The sickness, which had ravaged her face and her hands and unhinged her mind, had spared this loveliness that lay hidden behind filthy rags, longing for caresses.

Girleen threw two potatoes and several strips of mutton into the lap of the skirt. Then she poured milk into a mug.

"Eat up now," she said, "and stop whinging."

"God bless you, asthore," Nuala said. "God forgive me for calling you names a minute ago. God bless you and may he give you a fine husband."

She took the food to the hearth and crouched on her stool.

She began to eat with the speed of a hungry dog, using both hands in turn to carry the food to her mouth. She did not chew the morsels, but just swallowed them whole.

"The rain must be stopping," said Aunt Peggy, lying on her back with her eyes closed. "I don't hear it any more."

With her mouth full of food, Girleen left the table and went to the doorway.

"It's nearly over," she mumbled excitedly, putting her head out the doorway.

"What's that?" Nuala cried in alarm as she began to scoop the remnants of potato from her lap on to her palm. "Don't lie to me, you wicked thing."

Girleen stretched out her arm full length into the open air. Then she swallowed the food she had in her mouth and cried in delight:

"There's hardly a drop falling now and the sky is getting bright in the east. Whist! I think I hear the priest's car. Praised be God! It's getting brighter and brighter every moment."

Nuala threw the remnants of potato into her mouth and then swallowed some milk with them. She jumped up and ran to the doorway, while Girleen returned to the table.

"Hurry up, you two, or we'll be late," Girleen said. "Eat up quick."

Nuala began to tear her ragged hair when she saw the sky, that had been dark with rain, now become brilliant with sunlight.

"Ah! Woe!" she cried. "The miracle has happened. Out comes the sun, hard on the tail of the rain. Up it rises in the sky, with its round face jeering at me like a devil. I can hear the wheels of the priest's jaunt turning on the wet road. Oh! The lustful villain! She bribed God as well with her money. Ten pounds, I hear, the priest is getting for the wedding. Musha, darling God, you were easily bought."

194

Nora and Girleen suddenly became overcome with rapture. They began to sing in unison:

"Happy is the bride the sun shines on."

They joined hands and danced around in a circle on the floor. The child became infected by their rapture, laughed merrily and joined them. All three girls whirled around in a circle on the floor, with their hands joined, singing in unison:

"Happy is the bride the sun shines on."

With her ragged hair standing on end, Nuala dodged around the circle of dancing girls and returned to the hearth. The appearance of the sun had cowed her. In the rainy darkness, her soul had taken courage and hope of victory. Now in the sunlight, with a choir of maidens chanting a hymn in praise of joyous mating, the heat of passion faded from her untouched loins. She crouched on her stool, hid her withered face behind her hands and rocked herself.

"Praised be God," Aunt Peggy said, rising from the couch. "Barbara is going to have the sun on her wedding dress."

She staggered to the doorway past the dancing girls. Now a radiant smile gave some of its former beauty to her pale, smudged face that was framed by the thick folds of her white hair. Then tears began to roll down her cheeks as she looked out the door and said:

"Ah! Listen to the larks that have risen up already and they singing. Oh! Praised be God! The black earth that looked horrid is now shining like a jewel in the sun."

The three girls stopped dancing and crowded around Aunt Peggy in the doorway. They looked out in rapture at the miracle which the sun had wrought. From the height on which the cottage stood above the road, they could see the bogland stretch away to the distant mountains, undulating, strewn with lakes, all shining in the sun. And in the green hollow below the road, the wedding house, which had been indistinct in the rain, now seemed to be within reach of their hands. Its slate roof shimmered like a diamond. The rain which had dripped from the eaves along its front wall looked like golden bars against the lime wash. A rose bush growing near the gable was tricked out with a multitude of red blossoms. And in the yard, a crowd of women dressed in gaily painted cashmere shawls had issued from the house and mingled with the tipsy men, who were singing in groups with their hands clasped. The horses were being mounted in the lane and there was a crowd of shouting boys running towards the road.

"Here comes the priest now," said Girleen.

The priest's jaunting car went past the cottage towards the chapel, drawn by a white horse in full trot. The swiftly turning wheels of the car made the muddy water rise on either side, cascading like loam before a plough. As soon as the car had passed, the bridal couple emerged from the wedding house and began to walk slowly up the green lane towards the road. The wedding procession formed behind them. When the end of the procession had left the yard, an aged woman stood on the threshold of the house, rent her hair and began to chant the wedding lamentation in a shrill voice. She was the bride's mother.

"Can Julia come with us to Anthony's house, Mother?" Girleen said.

"Please let me, Aunt Peggy," the child said.

"All right," said Aunt Peggy. "She can go for a while, Girleen, but you must bring her back home here before dark."

"Come on, then," said Girleen. "Let's hurry and get a good place near the altar."

The three girls went skipping down the garden path to the road, chanting in subdued voices:

"Happy is the bride the sun shines on."

Aunt Peggy began to whimper in the doorway as she

scraped her cheeks nervously with the tips of her fingers. Nuala came up to her and took her by the arm.

"Let you not be standing there whinging, Aunt Peggy," Nuala whispered in a meek tone. "Put on your shawl and we'll follow after the people."

"I couldn't, asthore," Aunt Peggy said. "I couldn't stir a foot along the road with the weakness. Let us stand here in the door and watch them. Oh! Look at Barbara's dress. It's lovely on her."

The bridal couple now emerged from the lane and went west along the road towards the chapel, followed closely by the procession. They were a middle-aged couple, both short and stout. The bridegroom's legs were much too short for his stout body. He walked with bowed head, with his hands clasped behind his back, picking up his feet high off the ground. The bride walked very erect, with a fierce expression on her freckled face. She looked ridiculous in her new white dress, which bulged at the waist in front. She was the only woman in the procession that wore a hat. She carried a rose-coloured parasol in her hand.

"God bless you, Barbara," Aunt Peggy whispered in a maudlin tone, snuffling after each word. "You waited a long time, poor girl, but now you have a man at last. God bless you, darling."

Nuala cursed under her breath. She had put on her shawl again, but she had not re-tied her hair in a knot at the nape of her neck. Ragged strands of her hair streamed over the wrinkled, leathery skin of her face.

She peered out the doorway and looked up at the sky on either side, watching for a sign that the sun might disappear as suddenly as it had come and give way to another fall of rain. But there was no sign of rain in the heavens. Then she spat out the door and said:

"Sun or no sun, she'll have no children by him. Devil a one."

"You poor creature," Aunt Peggy said, putting her arm about the mad woman's slender waist, "neither you nor I ever had a wedding. Come on down to the hearth and cry with me for the wedding that we never had."

"I will, asthore," Nuala said in a gentle whisper. "I'll go down to the hearth-stone and cry with you. I'll cry for the lovely gold that was in your hair, like a fire on your head."

As they walked back to the hearth, with an arm around each other's waist, Aunt Peggy began to weep aloud, but the mad woman only burst into a peal of idiotic laughter.

The Parting

~~~~~~

ICHAEL JOYCE stood beside his mother against the gable end of the storehouse, down by the head of the pier where the steamer from the mainland lay moored. He was about to leave his native island for the first time, in order to enter the diocesan seminary and study for the priesthood.

Dressed in a new suit of blue serge, with a fawn-coloured raincoat slung across his right shoulder, he looked alert and very much at ease, as if the imminent parting were of no concern to him. Although barely thirteen, he already had a finely proportioned body. He was big and strong for his age. He stood with the assurance of a full-grown man in the prime of condition, balanced lightly on the balls of his feet, with his head thrown back haughtily. His wild blue eyes looked cold and very proud, as they glanced hither and thither. His thin lips were set firmly.

Yet this brave exterior was but a mask to hide the terrible agony he suffered. Indeed, all his strength and pride were

necessary to hold back the bitter tears that kept welling up
into his throat. He wanted terribly to throw himself on his
mother's bosom and weep aloud, as he had so often done in
infancy. He longed to feel her loving arms about him, pro-
tecting him from the frightening world that was about to
make him prisoner. He craved for her soothing words of
tenderness, that had until now softened all his woes by their
magic power.

Alas! the more he suffered and wanted to surrender, the
more his pride of race forced him to remain hard and relent-
less. Now and again, when the inner struggle almost reached
the limit of his endurance and the skin began to contract
below his eyes, or about the corners of his mouth, he just
gave his head a sudden upward jerk and drew in a deep
breath. That helped him to regain control.

This struggle had made his senses painfully acute. From
where he stood he could distinctly hear the fireman put coal
in the steamer's furnace for the journey back to the mainland. The rasping sound of the shovel against the steel plates
of the stoke-hold deck caused his nostrils to twitch. It was like
drawing his finger-nails over a smooth stone. On the fore-
castle head, they were using the donkey engine to hoist cattle
on board. Every time the little engine hissed and shot out a
jet of steam, as it was about to lift another beast, he had to
grit his teeth. The rattle of the chain unfolding from the
winch, to lower the hoisted animals into the hold, made him
feel that enormous rocks were falling down upon his head.

Worst of all was the smell of burning coal. He belonged to
the most remote hamlet on the island, nine miles to the west.
His people lived there in primitive simplicity, as their ances-
tors had lived for thousands of years, using turf and cow dung
for fuel. Coal was unknown to them. So that its acrid smell
gave him a slight feeling of nausea.

His mother turned towards him, with her head concealed

within the hood of her black shawl. She was a tall, slender woman of very dignified carriage, wearing a handsome red frieze skirt that had two deep flounces of black velvet.

"Listen to me, darling," she whispered. "Do you remember what I told you about your feet?"

"What's that, Mother?" Michael said without looking at her.

He spoke to her gruffly, in spite of his love for her. Indeed, it was the intensity of his love that forced him to be gruff and almost brutal when he spoke to her. If he allowed any tenderness to creep into his voice, it would mean the collapse of his resistance.

"You must take great care not to get them wet," she insisted, raising her voice a little and bending close to him. "Or if you do happen to get them wet, no matter where you are, you must run and change your socks at once. Promise me that now."

"All right, Mother," he said.

"Oh! Darling," she said, "I'll suffer every night from now until you come back to me on holidays, for fear you might forget about your feet. You are so headstrong and you catch cold so easily. Last spring, you . . ."

"Look, Mother," Michael interrupted. "Here's our bullock coming down now. He looks wonderful."

His mother pushed her shawl back from her head to look at the bullock. Although she was over fifty, her long, pale face was still beautiful. Her hair was very fair. Her eyes were golden.

"Ah! There's our little one, sure enough," she said. "The poor little creature! Ah! God help him! The life is frightened out of him."

"He's not little at all," Michael said indignantly. "He's one of the best bullocks on the island this year. He nearly took the sway at the fair to-day."

"Ah! the poor little one!" his mother said. "He'll always be little to me, no matter how big he has grown. I'll always remember him as a little calf. Ah! God help him! He doesn't know where he is. He's mad with the fright."

The bullock looked a splendid animal. His hide was a deep red colour except for a little white star at the centre of his forehead. His hair was long and curly, of a fine rich texture. He was very fat. He was already sold and the jobber's brand was clearly visible on his massive haunch, as he came charging down the pier. He rushed hither and thither, snorting and tossing foam from his jaws, as he tried to escape from the narrowing circle of young men that shouted and tried to grapple with him. Again and again he swung his powerful head in order to dislodge the hands of some fellow that had managed to grip his horns.

Then Martin Joyce, Michael's eldest brother, got a firm hold that the bullock was unable to dislodge. He was a powerfully built man of twenty-six, wearing grey frieze trousers and a thick blue woollen sweater. Gripping the horns fiercely in his strong hands, he began to turn the beast's head sideways and to bear down on it with all his strength, while his hob-nailed boots slithered over the cobble-stones. Man and beast only came to a halt when they were within a yard of the pier's edge. There the bullock made a supreme effort to free himself. He uttered a wild bellow, tossed his head and reared on his hind legs. Martin was carried off the ground, but he maintained his grip on the horns. When he and the bullock came down again, he deftly shifted his right hand from the horn to the beast's nostrils, into which he thrust his thumb and forefinger. That tamed the bullock. He offered no further resistance. He stood stock still and allowed his head to be twisted right round, until his foaming snout was upturned. Other men then gripped him by the tail and crowded in upon him from all sides.

"Get the slings around him," Martin said to his father.

Bartly Joyce was a tall, grey-haired man of sixty, with a very red face. He looked half crazy just now, since he was a very neurotic fellow and any excitement caused him to become hysterical. He was barely able to arrange the slings around the bullock's belly, one at either end, because of his agitation. Another man fixed a long halter to the beast's horns. Then Bartly signalled to the mate on the steamer's bridge.

"Lower away there," the mate yelled to the man at the winch.

Michael shuddered as the unfolding chain began to rattle. He felt an overwhelming pity for the pinioned animal, whose fate he instinctively felt to be somewhat akin to his own. They were both being taken away from their native island to serve the ambition of others, the bullock to be eaten and the boy to become a priest.

"Ah! The poor little creature!" Mrs. Joyce said with tears in her eyes as she watched the bullock. "Look at him standing there and he half dead with fright. The poor dumb creature! How he must be suffering!"

Michael was also very near to tears as he saw his father cross the slings over the animal's back and put the iron hook of the hoist through the loop. He recalled how he had taught the beast to drink milk out of a pail, when it was being weaned from its mother's teats. He used to let it suck his fingers, after having dipped them in the milk. Then he gradually drew the snout down into the pail and kept it there, until the calf finally began to drink the milk of its own accord.

At this moment, more than two years later, the boy vividly remembered the queer, warm pressure of the calf's gums.

"Hoist away there," the mate shouted.

The engine hissed and shot out steam. The chain began to rattle once more as it rolled back on to the winch. The bullock rose into the air, with his belly forced out to a sharp point on either side by the pressure of the slings. He kept flaying the air with his forelegs and bellowing mightily.

"Get out of my way," Bartly Joyce shouted as he ran forward to the edge of the pier, holding the guide rope that was attached to the beast's horns. "Give me room, I say. God blast ye, give me room."

The excitable fellow struck at those on either side of him with his elbows. It was a simple matter to keep the bullock's head turned towards the pier and to manœuvre the animal into the correct position above the open mouth of the hold. Yet Bartly made a botch of his task. He slipped on the cobble-stones, fell down on his buttocks and lost the rope. The bullock was carried far over to port and then forwards toward the port railing of the passenger deck. There was a wild shout as the animal almost crashed against the iron railing. At the very last moment, the hoist swung back again towards the pier and Martin succeeded in getting hold of the rope. He quickly manœuvred the bullock into position.

"Lower away now," the mate yelled.

Bartly had got to his feet in the meantime. He tried to take the rope from Martin as the animal was being lowered gently into the hold.

"Keep back there," Martin said.

"Give me that rope," said Bartly. "Let me handle him."

Martin swore and pushed his father roughly with his shoulder. Bartly again lost his footing on the slippery cobble-stones. He fell down flat on his buttocks. There was a roar of laughter from those present.

"There he is again," Mrs. Joyce said indignantly as she blushed with shame of her husband. "Making a show of himself."

Michael bitterly resented the laughter. He particularly resented the laughter of some tourists and cattle-jobbers who were watching the scene from the passenger deck of the steamer. He felt they were laughing in a different way from the islanders. Indeed, he felt that these "foreigners" looked upon all islanders as savages, whose conduct must always be ludicrous. At the seminary, other "foreigners" would laugh at everything he himself did and said, because of his humble origin.

"I don't see how he's making a show of himself," he said angrily to his mother. "He just fell down. He's not used to wearing boots. That was why he fell. Why don't you side with him, instead of siding with other people?"

"Hush! Little treasure!" his mother said in a forlorn tone. "Don't say bitter things to me, my little pulse, at the very moment you are going to leave me."

A wave of remorse overwhelmed the boy for having given pain to his mother. This time he would undoubtedly have burst into tears if his brother had not approached. Horror of letting Martin see him cry enabled him to regain his self-control.

"You'll have a fine trip," Martin said in a solemn and casual tone, as if he were addressing a grown-up man who was a perfect stranger to him.

"It should be a fine trip, all right," Michael answered in the same tone, without looking at his brother. "The sea is dead calm."

"Whatever wind there is will be with you," Martin said, "all the way!"

"We ought to make it in three hours," Michael said.

"With God's help," Martin said, "you should make it easily in that time."

Mrs. Joyce leaned towards Martin and whispered to him.

"You shouldn't have shouldered your father like that," she said in a reproving though gentle tone. "Shame on you, treasure, for knocking him down. You made a show of him, darling one, right in front of the whole island. Shame on you, I say."

Martin turned swiftly towards her. His bronzed face was dark with anger. He looked very strong and virile in his thick blue sweater and grey frieze trousers that were fouled by the dung of animals he had seized. One of the beasts had cut his right cheek with the sharp point of a horn. A large patch of clotted blood covered the whole centre of the cheek.

"Why didn't he keep out of the way?" he cried roughly. "He's always interfering and making a mess of things."

He would get married in the following spring and take command of the homestead. He was already inclined to behave like a master and to be intolerant of his father.

"You shouldn't have shouldered him, all the same, treasure of my heart," his mother said. "It wasn't a nice thing to do in front of the neighbours."

"I tell you he wouldn't get out of my way," Martin said.

"There were strangers looking on as well," said Mrs. Joyce. "It was a scandalous thing you did, little one."

"He might have killed the bullock and myself with his fooling," said Martin. "He doesn't know what he's doing when he has the least drop taken. He gets crazy."

Michael felt very hostile towards his brother, not only for having made his father a laughing stock, but also for a far more personal reason. The boy did not fully understand his other reason. He just felt instinctively that he was chiefly being made a priest in order that he might later help to rear and educate the children that Martin would beget. He now resented the barren destiny that had been planned for him, cut off from the joys of mating and from communion with the earth as a toiler.

His father came over and glanced with hatred at Martin.

"Huh! You blackguard!" he said to his oldest son. "You are very free with your shouldering."

Martin shook hands casually with Michael and then walked away.

"That's enough now, Bartly," Mrs. Joyce said. "There's no harm done. Forget about it. It was only an accident."

Bartly's wild eyes became tender as he turned towards Michael. Yet he spoke to the boy gravely and without emotion, as to a stranger.

"You'll have a good crossing," he said.

"We should," said Michael. "The sea is calm."

"The wind is with you, too," the father said.

Then he took a paper bag out of his jacket pocket and handed it shyly to the boy. Michael looked into the bag. It contained yellow sticks of candy known as "Peggy's Leg." The boy swallowed his breath and wanted to say something tender to his father. Yet his training forbade him to do so.

"May God spare your health," he said solemnly.

The father also wanted to put his arm about his boy's shoulders and say something tender. The rigid discipline of his life prevented him.

"Well! Here you all are," cried a flashily dressed young woman who pushed her way through the crowd at that moment. "I've been looking all over the place for you. Land's sake! This pier is more crowded than Broadway right now."

She was Barbara Joyce, the oldest surviving daughter of the family. She had been thirteen years in America and was now home on holiday. Although only thirty-two, her once beautiful face had become worn and faded from hard work. She still had a good figure, which a tight red dress showed off to good advantage. A little round hat, surmounted by brightly coloured artificial flowers, was perched jauntily on the side of her head. Her boisterous gaiety was in striking contrast with the grave dignity of the other islanders.

"Hello! Mickey," she cried, tapping her young brother jocularly on the chin with her knuckles. "Keep smiling, sonny boy. Don't let it get you. Everybody feels pretty homesick leaving home first time. I know how I felt myself. It was pretty terrible, but I soon got over it. So will you. Just keep that chin up, sonny boy."

All the surviving children of the family were in America, except Martin and Michael. It was money subscribed by the children in exile and brought home by Barbara that paid Michael's way to the seminary.

Michael loved Barbara very much, because of her gaiety and tenderness. Yet he now felt ashamed of the attention she attracted by her loud voice and her somewhat rowdy manner. So he blushed and looked at the ground.

"Hello! Mary Lydon," cried Barbara, as she rushed away to greet another woman. "You look lovely in that new dress. How is your mother? Hello! Bridget. Hello! Johnny Breasail. Land's sake! The whole island is here to-day."

The steamer whistle blew suddenly. Michael almost jumped off the ground with fright. The horse reared and whinnied on a shrill note. Mrs. Joyce burst into tears.

"It's time to get on board," Bartly shouted hysterically.

He picked up Michael's suitcase and added:

"Come on now. She'll be going any minute."

Mrs. Joyce threw her arms about her son and began to kiss him frantically all over his face.

"Oh! My little darling!" she muttered as she kissed him. "My pulse! My lovely little treasure!"

"That's enough now, woman," Bartly said to her tenderly after a little while. "He has to go on board."

He gently disengaged her arms and led Michael towards the gangway. She hid her face in her shawl and continued to weep without restraint. A number of relatives and neighbours pressed forward to shake hands with the boy.

"Make way there," Bartly shouted at these people. "There is very little time now. He must go on board."

Michael felt completely bewildered by the noise as he followed his father on board. Bartly put down the suitcase, shook hands hurriedly with his son and went ashore again. Barbara came on board. She was going with Michael as far as the seminary. She stood for a little while beside him at the rails, talking in a loud voice to those on the pier. Then she joined a group of cattle-jobbers, with whom she entered into a lively conversation. The gangway was pulled ashore. A bell rang on the bridge. The engines began to turn. The mooring ropes were cast loose. The steamer drew away. People began to shout goodbye and to wave handkerchiefs.

The boy was still bewildered as he stood by the rails. Like the poor beasts down in the dark hold, the strangeness of his new environment had made his senses numb. Then the steamer made a wide circuit and headed towards the open sea, with her port bow to the pier. He hurried across to the other side of the deck. The pier was now some distance away. Only a few people stood there watching the steamer. His parents stood alone, side by side, down at the very brink. The steamer gathered speed as it passed them. They were still near enough, as he passed, for him to see the look of anguish on his mother's face.

Then his mind suddenly cleared and pain came to him again with awful bitterness, as he listened to his sister's laughter and watched his parents stand motionless by the brink of the pier wall, beyond the ever-widening white lane that the ship left on the surface of the blue water.

His bitterness was terrible because his young heart knew that dark vows would make this parting final, forever and forever.

The Eviction

MAJOR GEORGE NEWELL of Barra Castle was being carried downstairs on a stretcher. He lay on his back beneath a brown blanket that was tucked in closely about his slender body all the way up to his armpits. His head was supported by two small white pillows, neatly placed, one on top of the other. His arms were stretched out to their full length above the blanket. They were so emaciated that the sleeves of his old tweed jacket looked empty. His hands lay crossed like those of a corpse, pale and supine, over his stomach. The toes of his boots stuck up stiffly side by side, against the double fold of brown cloth at the foot of the stretcher.

Miss Winifred Newell walked beside her brother's head, giving instructions to the bearers. She was a tall, thin woman of sixty-eight, five years younger than George. She was very shabbily dressed in a black tailored suit and a small black hat with feathers. Her long pale face looked very haughty. When the leading bearer had descended two steps of the last flight, she brought him to a halt by touching him sharply on the shoulder with the ferrule of her umbrella. Then she bent down and spoke to her brother.

"Say goodbye to our mountain, George," she whispered in a tone of deep emotion. "Say goodbye to the lake, too. You always loved them best on a wild day like this."

Major Newell had a stroke six months previously. He remained speechless and almost entirely paralysed ever since. It required a great effort on his part to turn his head, in order to look through the big window that gave a full view of Beann Liath and of Barra Lake at this point.

It was a scene of strange dark loveliness. The lake stretched from the castle wall to the base of a giant grey crag that rose above it to a height of two thousand feet. The mountainside was so precipitous that its mist-enshrouded peak seemed almost within reach of an outstretched hand. April was already far advanced. Yet it looked like a day in midwinter, with hail carried on a raging wind, as if the place mourned for the departure of its lord. The surface of the lake was lashed into foaming waves by the wind and showers of hail kept passing over it at a furious pace, like charging hordes of fairy horses that punctured its black water with their tiny hooves.

The old man's face showed no emotion at first as he looked for the last time at this scene he had loved so much from infancy. The peace of death seemed to have descended on his soft brown eyes, on his bloodless cheeks and on his thin lips that were no longer used for speech. Then his eyes clouded. Tears gathered at their inner corners and began to course slowly down his withered cheeks.

Winifred also turned to look at the mountain and the lake for the last time. She stood very erect, with firmly closed lips, concealing any emotion she may have felt. It was only when she turned away from the window and saw the tears on her brother's cheeks that she allowed her haughty nature to relent a little. She blinked, swallowed her breath and gripped George's shoulder. Then she raised herself to her full height and rapped the bearer sharply on the shoulder with the ferrule of her umbrella.

"Go ahead now," she said arrogantly. "Keep a firm grip on the handles and put your feet down absolutely flat. Steady now. Don't hurry."

A local solicitor named Hurley was whispering to Superintendent Geraghty of the Civic Guards down in the hall, before another large window that gave a view of the mountain.

"To look at Beann Liath on a day like this," the solicitor said in a dramatic whisper, "you'd swear that no living thing could crawl up its sides to the top."

Geraghty stared at the huge black clouds that passed across the upper slopes of the monstrous granite crag. Thousands of rainy tendrils hung from the sagging bellies of the clouds, like torn ropes dangling from balloons that have cut adrift.

"Sure enough," he said, "you'd think it's impossible to climb it."

"You would," said Hurley. "Yet I've seen a big crowd of men walking up to the very top of it, at one another's heels, like a regiment of ants, with baskets of turf on their backs. They kept going up and down for a whole week from morning till night."

"What on earth were they doing?" said Geraghty. "Why would they be carrying turf up there?"

"It was fifty-two years ago," Hurley said, "when Major Newell came of age and his father was giving a big celebration in his honour. I was only a lad at the time, but I remember it as clearly as if it were yesterday. Ah! The major was a fine handsome lad, too, at the time. He had just got his commission in a cavalry regiment and he looked lovely in his

uniform, Begob, he did. You wouldn't see a finer man in a
day's walk. They kept carrying up the turf on their backs
until they had a pile that was fifty feet high. Then they set fire
to it with tar barrels. Man alive! The roar of the flames could
be heard miles away. It was like thunder. You'd think Beann
Liath had been turned into a volcano. There were other fires
on Beann Rua and on Cnoc Na Ron and on Cnoc Leitreach,
all along the shore of the lake. They were only small fires,
though, big and all as they were, compared to the fire on
Beann Liath. That was the fire. It was lovely to watch the
reflection of the red flames at night in the black water of the
lake below. The wind used to carry great showers of spark
far out and then the sparks came down like falling stars. Oh!
It was a gorgeous sight."

"It must have been," Geraghty said. "A royal sight it must
have been, sure enough, with all those fires."

"They kept feeding the flames for three days and nights,"
Hurley said, "while a great crowd was making merry at the
castle. There was a dance band there, all the way from Lon-
don, that played lovely waltzes. There was champagne there
by the gallon."

"The Newells must have been rich people in those days,"
said Geraghty, who had just arrived in the district and was
ignorant of local history. "They must have been a power in
the land."

"They were the richest people in the county," Hurley
said.

Then he nodded towards the brother and sister, who had
almost reached the foot of the stairs.

"Look at them now," he said gravely.

"Is that all that's left of them?" Geraghty said.

"That's all," Hurley said.

"Just these two poor creatures?" Geraghty said.

"Just these two," said Hurley. "Miss Winifred inherited

214

a small house and a few acres from a cousin, at a place called Creannach, forty miles from here. She's taking the major to live with her there. Lucky for him he had this sister. Otherwise he'd have died after getting the stroke. She came hot-foot, six months ago, when he got it. She has waited on him day and night ever since. It's a pitiful sight, sure enough."

"You can't help feeling sorry for them," Geraghty said, "even though they were awful bloody tyrants in their day of power, by all acounts."

The stretcher-bearers reached the ground floor at this moment with their load. Miss Winifred motioned them to halt by the foot of the stairs. Then she turned to a small group of elderly people that stood before a great pile of travelling bags, trunks and corded boxes.

"Has the lorry not come yet?" she said.

There were three men and a woman in the group. The woman was a great age. The men were all between sixty and seventy.

They had been servants at Barra Castle since their childhood. None of them had received any wages for the past ten years, since the collapse of the Newell family fortunes. Yet they stayed on through long habit and a sense of loyalty.

The oldest of the three men touched his cap and took a pace forward. Then he bowed awkwardly.

"It's outside, Miss Winifred," he said. "It came a little while ago."

"Then why is the luggage still here?" Miss Newell said. "I distinctly told you to begin loading as soon as the lorry came."

The man coughed and shifted his feet.

"We began to take it out," he said, "but Mr. Lynch stopped us. He said we had no . . ."

"What's that?" Miss Newell interrupted angrily. "Who did you say stopped you?"

"It was Mr. Lynch stopped us, Miss Winifred," the old man said. "He said we had no right to take anything out of the house without his permission."

"Outrageous!" said Miss Newell. "The loathsome creature!"

"We had put a few things into the lorry," the old man continued, "but he made us lower them again and take them back into the hall. He said that only personal effects could be removed from the house and that there was a picture taken from the library that must be put back. He said it was against the law to take that picture."

"Where is the fellow now?" Miss Newell said.

"He's in the library," said the old man. "He kept shouting at us. He said nothing can be removed without his permission."

Miss Newell rapped the floor with the ferrule of her umbrella.

"Fetch him at once," she said.

When the old man had trotted off in the direction of the library door, she told the stretcher bearers to place the major on a table that stood by the wall. After the two men had put down their load carefully, she tucked the blanket more closely about her brother's sides.

"You must wait here, George," she whispered tenderly, "while I speak to Lynch."

As his sister moved away, Major Newell turned his head slowly from side to side, "saying goodbye to the hall." There was no beauty here to draw tears from his eyes, as the lake and the mountain had done. Except for a fine mantelpiece that was still intact above the fireplace, the great hall was in a very drab and sordid state. The walls were broken. The furniture was battered. The floor was rotted for want of care. His melancholy eyes remained absolutely indifferent as they looked at it.

Festus Lynch came running out of the library with a legal document in his hand. He was a thin little man of sixty-two, with a pale face that was spotted with red pimples. He wore spectacles halfway down his long pointed nose. His heavy brown overcoat was far too big for him.

"Put back that picture that hung over the fireplace in the library," he shouted at Miss Newell in a shrill voice. "It belongs to me by law."

"You miserable wretch!" cried Miss Newell. "That picture is without value to anyone but my brother and myself. It's just spitefulness that makes you want to keep it."

Lynch came up close to her and waved the legal document in front of her face.

"I'm within my rights," he cried, as he hopped from one foot to another like an excited bird. "I have a good reason for wanting to keep it. You can do what you like with the other pictures."

"You can't have it," said Miss Newell. "I won't surrender it."

"We'll see about that," shouted Lynch as he tapped the document with his finger. "I have it all written down here in black and white. You'll obey the law, Miss Newell, or face the consequences."

"I'd rather burn it than let you have it," Miss Newell said.

"Hand it over now," said Lynch, "or it will be the worse for you."

"You are a despicable cur to ask for it," said Miss Newell.

"You had better watch your language," shouted Lynch. "The time is long since past when you had the power to lord it over me. Now you're no better than a beggar. That's what you are. A common beggar."

"You filthy rat!" cried Miss Newell.

She swung her umbrella and brought it down with all her force on top of Lynch's skull. It broke in the middle. The little man uttered a low cry and fell back into the arms of a Civic Guard, who had come rushing forward at that moment. Miss Newell threw the broken umbrella on the ground and pounced on the crated picture, that had been the cause of the quarrel. Two other Civic Guards came and took her by the arms.

"Hand over that picture, Miss Newell," one of the Civic Guards said to her. "You have no right to it."

Miss Newell struggled to free herself and held on grimly to the picture.

"How dare you lay hands on me in my father's house?" she cried.

Hurley came forward and tried to reason with her.

"There is nothing to be gained by violence, Miss Newell," he said to her. "Try to be reasonable and face the facts. It's really the best thing for you to do."

Miss Newell ceased struggling and looked at Hurley with contempt.

"You're just a fawning cur like the others," she said bitterly.

Geraghty took Festus Lynch by the arm and said:

"Are you badly hurt?"

The little man now stood erect. He was shaking his head like a dog that has just come out of water. Although the force of the blow had been broken by his bowler hat, he was suffering from shock and hysteria. His teeth chattered.

"Get that picture for me," he said to Geraghty.

Geraghty took the picture from a Civic Guard, who had rescued it in the meantime from Miss Newell. He gave it to two workmen, who took it into the library. Lynch followed the workmen. He trembled so much that Geraghty had to take his arm.

"Would you like a drop of brandy?" Geraghty said to him when they entered the library. "It would pull you together."

Lynch waved aside the superintendent and told the work-men to unwrap the picture.

"Hurry up," he shouted. "Hang it up where it was before."

Then he struck his palms together and looked towards the ceiling.

"I've waited forty-six years for this," he cried.

Hurley came striding into the room.

"You're a hard man, Festus," he said to Lynch in a tone of reproof. "I'm surprised at you for treating that poor woman in the way you did."

"A hard man!" shouted Lynch. "Is it me? Ask anybody that ever dealt with me if I'm hard. Ask anybody that ever worked for me. Ask the clergy. Ask the poor."

Hurley took him by the arm and protested softly:

"I know there isn't a kinder man than you in the whole county, when you are in your right mind. That's why I was so surprised at your cruelty to Miss Newell."

"Cruel to her?" cried Lynch. "In what way was I cruel?"

"Why didn't you let her keep the old picture?" said Hurley. "She and her brother have suffered enough. You should let bygones by bygones."

"That be damned for a story," cried Lynch. "I had a reason for keeping that picture. I never told it to a soul before, but I'll tell it now."

He shouted at the workmen, who had by now uncovered the picture, to hang it over the mantelpiece at once.

"Take care now," he said, "to hang it in the exact spot."

Then he turned and marched down the long room hur-riedly, with his hands clasped behind his back.

"Forty-six long years," he shouted, "I've waited for this moment. So there's no danger that I'll soften now. Devil a fear of me."

Hurley nudged Geraghty in the side and whispered:

"That blow on the head must have driven him crazy."

When Lynch reached the far end of the room, he was taken by a frenzy and began to stamp with both feet, one after the other, on the worn old mahogany boards of the floor.

"I'm master here now," he shouted hysterically. "I'm master in this house. I own every bit of it."

Then he rushed back again, glancing at the wainscotted walls on either side arrogantly.

"I'm master here," he kept shouting.

The workmen had now hurriedly put the picture back into its former place. Lynch stood in front of it on widespread legs and looked up at it with hatred in his eyes.

"I have you now where I want you," he shouted at the picture. "I'll soon take that grin off your face."

"In the name of God, Festus," said Hurley, "sit down and calm yourself, like a good man."

"Look at him up there," Lynch said, as he pointed a finger at the picture. "Look at the grin on his face. Do you see that grin?"

They all looked at the portrait of a gentleman in eighteenth century dress, with a white wig, beautiful lace ruffles and a long green coat. The haughty, well-bred face bore a striking resemblance to Miss Winifred and the major. The face of the man in the portrait, however, looked eminently satisfied with life. Its upper lip was curled slightly into a contemptuous grin.

"The first time I saw that grin," Lynch said bitterly, "was forty-six years ago, when I came into this room with my mother to beg for mercy from Major Newell. He had just come into the property, after his father's sudden death. I stood where I am standing now. My mother stood to the right of me. Major Newell sat over there to the right of the fireplace. I was sixteen years old, a student at the monastery school, studying to be a priest. My poor mother, Lord have mercy on her soul, was dead set on having me ordained. It

was the dream of her life. 'Festus,' she used to say, 'you'll hear my confession before I die.' Our farm of land was a poor one. It was hard to make a living out of it. There were seven of us in family and the rent was high. The Newells were the most notorious rack-renters in the whole of the west. To cap it all, there was the expense of sending me to the monastery. Then my father died on us, leaving us in arrears with the rent. He died shortly before Colonel Newell, the major's father. We were more than a year behind with the rent and we didn't have a red copper in the house, or any means of borrowing. So my mother took me with her to the major to beg for time. She begged for it right enough, on her bended knees, with her face to the floor, but it was little of it she got."

He shuddered and took a short pace forward. He pointed to a spot on the floor in front of his feet.

"It was there she knelt to him," he said. "There is where she lay with her face touching the floor. He just shook his head and told her that we'd have to pay the full amount on the nail or be evicted. 'All those in arrears must go,' he said, 'unless they can pay the full amounts. The only way I can save my property is to clear it of useless tenants.' I stood there looking at my mother with her face to the ground and listening to her beg for mercy. 'Have pity on my little boy,' she said, 'and he going to be a priest.' Then I looked up at the picture over the mantelpiece. I saw it grinning at me. My mother got to her feet and grabbed me by the shoulder and leaned on me, to prevent herself from falling on the way to the door. I turned back and looked at the picture again as we went out of the room. It was still grinning at me. Its eyes followed me."

He raised his glance once more to the portrait and added in a savage tone:

"It was then I swore that the day would come when I would

222

be master here and deal with that insolent grin. I swore it and I've done it. Now that grinning devil is in my power."

He struck his bosom with his fists and raised his voice.

"I had to leave the seminary when we were evicted," he cried. "My mother died of a broken heart. It was up to me, the eldest, to rear the family. With God's help, I did it; I did more. An uncle gave me the money to open a little shop. Bit by bit we rose, the little ones and myself. One thing led to another. People were kind to us. I bought here and there, this and that. I contracted in a small way. I worked hard. After a few years, I was able to contract in a big way. I bought the flour mill. Then I bought the woollen mill. I started a bacon factory. I went into this and that, all round me, shipping and transport of every kind, until I became the strongest man in the county, if not in the whole of the west. In spite of my success, though, I never lost sight of my main purpose. It wasn't money I was after, or power. Oh! No, it was nothing of the sort. I'll tell you what it was."

He looked intently from one to the other of those present. Then he stamped on the floor.

"It was revenge I was after," he cried. "I wanted to get hold of Barra Castle and evict Major Newell, same as he evicted my mother."

"I wanted above all," he shouted passionately, "to get that grinning, bloody face into my power. I'll soon take that grin off it. We'll soon see who will be the last to grin. I'll soon fix that face. It won't be grinning long. Upon my oath, that face will soon look different."

He stared in silence at the portrait for a few moments, with his under-lip protruding. Then he clasped his hands behind his back and again marched down the floor.

"This is the hour of my revenge," he shouted as he stamped on the old mahogany boards, "and let no man talk to me now, at this holy hour, about pity for the fallen. Let no man talk to me at this hour of letting bygones be bygones. Let no man ask me to forget that I saw my sick mother kneel before him, with her face touching the floor."

Hurley beckoned to Geraghty. The two men walked out of the library almost on tiptoe. They were followed by the two workmen.

"It's a shocking thing," Hurley said to Geraghty out in the hall, "to see a kind man turned into a savage by bitterness."

"It's ugly all right," Geraghty said, "but the poor man had cause."

"He had cause," said Hurley, "but it's a mean and cowardly thing to kick the fallen."

All the luggage had now been removed from the hall and put into the lorry. Miss Newell signalled to the bearers. They picked up their burden carefully from the table and walked towards the door. Miss Newell again walked stiffly by her brother's head, comforting him. She had completely regained her composure. Her haughty face looked as stern as before and as cold. The four servants walked behind, in two pairs, like a funeral cortège.

Geraghty brought his heels together and saluted smartly as the stretcher passed him by the doorway. Miss Newell acknowledged the salute with a curt nod. The old man took no notice whatsoever. His soft brown eyes now stared straight ahead, beyond all sense and feeling.

"Be careful now," Miss Newell said as the bearers began to go down the stone steps to the gravelled drive. "Take your time. Put your feet down flat."

The stretcher was put into the waiting ambulance. The four servants climbed into the lorry with the luggage. Miss Newell paused for a few moments, as she was going to climb into the ambulance, in order to take a last look at Beann Liath.

She showed no emotion as she stared at the huge black clouds that raced across its upper slopes. Then she climbed into the ambulance.

"Well! That's that," Hurley said as the two vehicles moved down the drive, watched silently by a small group of the local people. "I hate evictions. Let's say goodbye to Festus and get out of here."

When the two men entered the library, they found Lynch staring at the portrait, with his arms folded on his bosom and his under-lip protruding.

The Old Woman

AGGIE CRAMPTON was coming down the path that led to the back-yard of Julia Duggan's house. She was so stooped and feeble that she had to keep her hands on her knees as she walked. Her prone back was almost level with the tops of the low stone fences that bound the lane. She thrust her bare feet forward with the extreme slowness of a huge tortoise. She grunted every time she struck her toe against one of the loose stones that lay on the ground.

A small white bag hung from her neck by a black cord. It was quite clean, in striking contrast with the filthy condition of her ragged grey dress and of her body. It swung to and fro gently with each step, like the heavy pendulum of a big clock.

She halted when she came to the stile that led into Julia Duggan's back-yard. Grunting loudly, she straightened her back and gripped the top of the stile with both hands. There she rested for a little while, with her face turned towards the sky. Her lips moved in prayer. Strands of white hair hung down on either side of her wrinkled yellow cheeks. The colour had almost completely faded from the pupils of her eyes. She had no teeth left.

As she began to climb over the stile, a yellow dog came running around the gable end of the house. He was barking furiously, with his tail and his mane on end. He stopped barking and slowed down to a walk on catching sight of the old woman. Then he put his tail between his legs and began to whine as he approached her. He crawled right up to her and put his snout against her naked right foot. He sniffed hungrily.

The old woman sat down to rest on a stone after getting over the stile. She struck at the dog with her fist and cursed. The animal darted away a short distance. There he stood watching her intently. When she resumed her journey around the gable end of the house, he followed close at her heels, with his mane on end and his tail under his belly. Now and again, as he crawled after her, he laid his snout against her dirty flesh and shuddered violently.

Nellie Duggan, a little girl of seven, came out of the house as the old woman approached the door. She had pretty flaxen hair and blue eyes. She wore a neat white pinafore and there was an orange bow at the end of her plaited hair. Her bare feet were spotlessly clean. She ran indoors after staring in fright for a few seconds at Maggie Crampton.

"She is coming," she whispered to her mother as she crossed the floor to the chimney corner at full speed. "She is nearly at the door."

Mrs. Duggan was kneading dough for a cake on the kitchen table. She turned and looked at her daughter.

"Who is coming?" she said.

"Maggie Crampton," Nellie said as she sat down on a blue stool. "She is outside in the yard."

"I never saw such a girl," Mrs. Duggan said with a smile. "You are afraid of everybody."

Nellie put her feet close together and her hands behind her back. She kept her eyes fixed on the open doorway.

"I don't know what to do with you," Mrs. Duggan said, as she resumed her work. "You are so nervous. I'm worried about you."

Nellie almost leaped to her feet again as the old woman's grunting became audible in the kitchen.

"Here she comes," she whispered in horror. "She's at the door now."

"Stop that," Mrs. Duggan said. "You should respect old age. It's against the law of God to be afraid of a good Christian."

The old woman waddled into the kitchen and halted near the doorway.

"God save all here," she said.

"You, too," Julia Duggan said. "You are welcome in God's name. Draw down to the fire."

"I'll be all right here near the door," Maggie Crampton said.

"Don't behave like a stranger in my house," Julia Duggan said, raising her voice. "Draw down to the hearth, I tell you."

Maggie waddled down to the hearth and sat on a black stool in the corner opposite to the little girl. Then she began to fumble with the cord to which the white bag was attached.

"I want you to look at it again for me," she said to Julia. "To-day I got afraid that the moths might have got into the bag since you looked at it last time. That was in March and now we're nearly at the end of July. I'm terribly worried about it, Julia."

"I'll look at it for you and welcome," Julia said, "as soon as this cake is in the oven."

"God spare your health," Maggie said. "My hour might strike at any moment now."

"It's our Christian duty to help the old," Julia said.

"I want to be sure that everything is in proper order," Maggie said in a loud voice. "I don't want to look untidy and I laid out."

At that moment, the dog thrust his head slowly around the corner of the doorway. He looked towards Maggie with hunger in his bloodshot yellow eyes. He sniffed and began to whine on a low note.

Julia turned her head quickly on hearing him whine. Her face clouded with anger when she caught sight of him in the doorway. She spat.

"Get out of here," she shouted. "You filthy creature!"

The dog disappeared at once.

"Bah!" Julia continued. "What horrid things there are in God's world."

"Don't say that, Julia," the old woman said as she detached the little white bag from the cord. "There are only lovely things in God's world."

"There are horrid things in it, too," Julia said. "There are things in it that frighten me."

"Everything that God made has a divine purpose," the old woman said.

"I know there are ugly things," Julia said. "Many ugly things."

"How could a divine thing frighten a Christian?" Maggie said.

"I have seen many ugly things that frightened me," Julia said.

Maggie put the little bag down carefully beside her on a red stool.

"Nothing that God made could be ugly," she shouted in

an arrogant tone. "I'm telling you that now, Julia, because I know it's the truth."

"It's easy for the old to be wise," Julia said. "Their blood is nearly cold. It's only the young that suffer."

"They suffer because they are sinful," the old woman said.

"Their blood is warm," Julia shouted. "How can they be wise when their blood is warm?"

"It's only sin that's ugly," Maggie said. "It was the devil made sin."

"The old only see what pleases them," Julia said. "When the blood is hot, many ugly things are seen."

She suddenly turned her head and looked out the doorway.

"Ah! Woe!" she cried plaintively. "Why should there be such ugly things in God's world?"

The old woman took a clay pipe from the pocket of her skirt and lit the tobacco in the bowl with a sod of turf from the fire. She smoked for a little while, grunting with pleasure. Then she removed the pipe from her lips and turned towards Julia Duggan.

"There are no ugly things in God's world," she cried at the top of her voice. "I'm telling you that, Julia, because I know it's the truth. God has a reason for everything."

During the silence that followed, Nellie raised her eyes timidly and looked at Maggie Crampton's feet. She shuddered when she saw the enormous size to which they had swollen. The lower parts were quite black with dirt. The upper parts were red, with greyish patches here and there, like the scales on a rockfish. Then she raised her eyes still further and looked at the old woman's face. To her surprise, she saw that it was kindly and wise, whereas she had expected to see the horrid countenance of an ogress.

Trembling with delight, the little girl looked into the fire and her cheeks flushed crimson. She had suddenly become

infinitely happy, because she had got rid of a terror that oppressed her from infancy. Ever since then, older people had
frightened her by saying that Maggie Crampton would come
and put her in a sack and take her away to a dark cave unless
she behaved. So that the existence of the old woman had
always been, until this moment, the most horrid fact in her
consciousness. She had once gone with an older cousin to the
one-roomed hut where Maggie Crampton lived, at the northern end of the village. The two children had stood hand in
hand by the open doorway of the hut, peering into the smoky
gloom, until they heard the old woman grunt. Then they had
fled in terror. From that day, little Nellie never again dared
look at Maggie Crampton's face, until this happy moment of
deliverance.

Now it was fondness that she felt for the old woman, instead of fear. As she stared into the fire, she kept thinking
how wonderful it was not to be afraid any more.

"I have seen many things that frightened me," Julia Duggan said as she was putting the kneaded dough into the oven.
"I have seen many horrible things in God's world."

The old woman knocked the ashes out of her pipe and
said:

"Only sin is ugly. It was the devil made sin."

"There are many ugly things," Julia Duggan said. "I have
seen them and they frightened me."

"It's only now when my hour approaches," the old woman
said as she put the pipe into the pocket of her skirt, "that I
understand the loveliness of God's world. Sometimes I can
hardly bear the pain of longing for it. When I'm alone on a
lovely summer day like this in my little house, saying my
prayers, I hear the shouting of children at their play, or the
song of a bird. Then I can pray no more and I hate the
thought of death. I long for my own loveliness. I long for my

youth, when I shouted and danced and picked cowslips in the fields of May beneath the singing larks. Aye! Aye! There are times when the loveliness of God's world gives me pain."

After she had put the oven on the fire, Julia scrubbed and dried the table. Then she laid a clean white cloth over the board.

"Give me the bag now," she said to Maggie.

"Be careful with it," the old woman said nervously as Julia took the little white bag to the table. "My sight is nearly all gone now, so I can't look at it myself. I can't touch it, either, because my hands are hardly ever clean enough."

"You poor creature!" Julia said, as she opened the bag. "You are to be pitied, all alone and your hour approaching, without anybody to look after you."

"Oh! I have good neighbours," the old woman said. "They look after me. It's hard, though, to keep an old person clean. I keep groping things. So my hands get dirty. That's why I'm afraid to open the bag myself."

Julia took a dark brown burial dress from the bag and spread it on the table. It was made of cheap cotton cloth. There was a narrow lace frill around the neck and silk braiding down the front, in two parallel lines. A strip of white linen was stitched over the breast, with a red heart in the centre of the strip. A religious motto was embroidered in black on the white linen, encircling the red heart.

She also took a pair of white cotton gloves and white cotton stockings from the little bag.

"They look all right," she said, after having examined them carefully.

"Thank God," the old woman said fervently. "It would be terrible if I looked untidy when I faced God for my judgment."

"I'll touch them with the iron," Julia Duggan said.

"God spare your health," Maggie Crampton said. "You're

the only one I'd let touch them, because you have holy hands. When I had my sight, I loved watching your hands."

"You say the queerest things," Julia Duggan said as she blushed slightly.

Her touch was extremely delicate. Her long, slender fingers moved ever so daintily over the coarse fabric of the burial dress. They caressed it gently as if it were made of the most precious stuff.

Little Nellie suddenly jumped to her feet and ran out of the house. She clasped her hands over her head and skipped down the yard.

"There are only lovely things in God's world," she cried gaily as she ran. "There are no ugly things."

After having ironed the burial robes, Julia Duggan folded them neatly and put them back into the bag. Then she tied the bag and gave it to the old woman.

"God spare your health, Julia," the old woman said.

"It's only kindness that saves us from damnation," Julia said, "in a world where there are so many wicked things."

"Don't say that, Julia," the old woman said as she attached the little white bag to the black cord. "Everything has a divine purpose."

She got to her feet when the bag was attached and waddled to the doorway with her hands on her knees. There she halted and turned her face towards Julia Duggan.

"There are only lovely things in God's world," she shouted in an arrogant tone. "I'm telling you that now, Julia, because it's the truth."

Then she waddled out of the house.

"There are many wicked things," Julia Duggan shouted from the hearth in a forlorn voice. "I have seen them and they frightened me."

The old woman halted and raised her head when she was near the gable end.

"It was the devil made sin," she shouted. "Remember that now and say no more."

The yellow dog came loping cautiously through the backyard as the old woman was going up the lane. He had his tail under his belly and his mane stood on end. He climbed to the top of the stile and crouched there, sniffing the air hungrily in her direction.

"There are only lovely things in God's world," she kept muttering as she advanced slowly up the lane with her hands on her knees.

The little white bag swung gently to and fro with each step.

The Beggars

HE BLIND MAN'S EYES were white. The sightless pupils were concealed beneath the drooping upper lids. The lids were naked. He had been blind from birth, so that the lashes had withered through inaction. The rims of the lower lids were turned outwards, making a half-circle of moist rosecoloured flesh around each white eyeball.

His head was raised and poised slightly to one side, motionless, as if forever waiting for the coming of light. It looked sculpted that way, with oblong white slits, semicircled by moist red flesh, for eyes. His ears were beautiful. They had assumed the functions of sight. The faintest sounds did not escape them. Their constant warnings gave his face a tortured expression. Not only his nose and his mouth, but even the skin on his cheeks and forehead quivered at each warning.

His head looked arrogant and priestly, poised that way, motionless, as if sculpted. His cheeks were ruddy and well covered with flesh. His forehead was high and broad. He was

237

bald above the temples, but the rest of his skull bore a thick crop of grey hair, cut short and well combed. His skin was clear and fresh.

His voice, too, was arrogant like that of a rich priest, as he cried to those who passed through the gateway:

"I wish you all a happy death. None of you knows the hour, or the place, or the circumstance. So it's well to be prepared. There's no better way than by helping the afflicted. Earn the blind man's blessing. Help the blind man and he'll wish you all a happy death."

Not one of the crowd took notice of him, or of the little bag in his outstretched left hand. It was a leather bag, with a green cord laced around the mouth. His plump, clean fingers shifted around the mouth of the bag, as he shook it at those who passed. At the end of each speech, he listened for a few moments with his head poised. Then he licked his lips, shrugged his shoulders and began once more:

"I wish you all a happy death. None of you knows the hour . . ."

He sat crouched on a block of stone to one side of the gateway. A long black overcoat covered the whole of his burly figure. It had rained all night and during part of the previous day. The earth of the gateway, worn bare by the hooves of cattle, was now a mass of mud and water. The end of his overcoat was steeped in the wet mud. He had placed his bowler hat, face downwards, on the earth. It was completely covered with mud, thrown up by the plunging feet of those who passed.

The gateway was right in the centre of the racecourse. The people passed through it on their way from the road to the green-roofed stands, which crowned the rising slope beyond. The road was two fields away on the other side. There was a crowd of motor coaches and jaunting cars halted down there. And the column of people, hurrying to the race stands, were importuned by many beggars on the way. All the other beggars received coins.

In the field nearest the road, there was a thin man selling tips. He wore a peaked cap and a shabby grey belted jacket. The tips were written on slips of paper, enclosed in tiny envelopes, which he sold for threepence each. He did a brisk trade with them, for he was very active and loud-mouthed. He ran to and fro, along the column of hurrying people, like a collie dog worrying sheep, yapping and offering his envelopes.

The back stretch of the course, where the horses were to run, lay between this field and the second one. There were white wooden railings on either side of the course. As the people crossed it through two little picket gates, they halted to have a look at the jumps. There was a water jump on one side and a double ditch on the other. A youngish woman with red hair, wearing a black shawl over a ragged blue dress, stood singing on the bright green sward in the middle of the enclosed track. Her daughter, a child of ten, went among the halted people with a tin mug. There was hardly a person that resisted her piteous cry and the forlorn expression on her weazened face.

"Good luck to one and all," she chanted. "May the orphan's blessing bring ye luck."

The second field sloped sharply down from the course to the gateway by which the blind man sat. In this field, all down the slope on either side of the hurrying people, there were many beggars. Chief among them was a young man who stood on a grassy knoll playing an accordion. The young man had a handsome, girlish face, topped with luxuriant black hair. His moll did the begging for him, using his cap to collect coins. She got so many pennies that she had to empty the cap now and again into the sagging pockets of her raincoat.

The hurrying people, so generous to the other beggars,

went past the blind man in the gateway with the fixed stare of cattle stampeding in a herd. The more active of them leaped the puddle. The majority waded through it stolidly, throwing mud on his hat and on his coat with their indifferent feet. And yet he kept repeating his speech arrogantly, unmoved by their indifference.

Like a talking statue, perched on a block of stone beside the gateway, he intoned in his priestly voice:

"I wish you all a happy death. None of you knows the hour . . ."

The crowd began to thin. Up above around the stands, the bookmakers were already shouting the odds on the first race. A tall man came down the slope at a run towards the gateway. He carried his hat in one hand and a heavy blackthorn stick in the other. His grey overcoat was unbuttoned. The ends of his trousers were clamped above his ankles with cycling clips. His shoes were white with mud. His blue serge suit was spattered with it right up to his waist. A gold watch-chain crossed his slightly corpulent stomach. His brick-red face was dotted with beads of sweat. The top of his skull was bald. Thin wisps of fair hair were combed across it horizontally. They lay matted against the heated white skin. He had buck teeth.

He was halfway across the puddle when the blind man began his speech afresh. He started, looked at the blind man and slackened his pace. He halted a few yards beyond the gateway. Then he frowned and raised his stick high above his head, as if threatening the blind man with it. With his stick raised that way, he walked back and stood in the middle of the gateway, facing the beggar. His little blue eyes looked frightened and he was muttering something inaudible. The blind man finished his speech and licked his lips. Then the tall man lowered his stick, frowned, looked about him furtively and opened his mouth wide. He grinned from ear to ear. He stooped, hunched his shoulders, spat on his stick and uttered a wild yell.

"I have it," he cried exultantly. "I have it."

Startled by the yell, the blind man had half risen from the block of stone and then paused on bent thighs, listening intently. Hearing the tall man's words, he hurriedly withdrew the hand that held the little bag.

"Eh?" he cried fiercely. "What have you got, you thief? Are you robbing the blind?"

The stranger made off up the slope towards the bookmakers at a run, waving his stick and shouting at intervals:

"I have it. Blood an ouns! I have it."

In great agitation, the blind man searched the interior of his little bag. There was only one penny there, one that he had himself deposited at the beginning to encourage the charitable. He sat down once more, looking puzzled. His nose twitched and he shifted his ears hither and thither, trying to catch some sound that would explain the strange event. Then he started and groped about on the ground for his hat. He found it, picked it up and put it on his knees. He passed his fingers suspiciously over the crown. Discovering that it was fouled, his face contorted with anger.

"Let the blind man's curse fall on whoever did it," he cried.

His voice had lost its priestly arrogance. It was spiteful, guttural and indistinct. His countenance looked vicious.

"I wouldn't mind them going past without putting a red penny in my bag," he continued. "It's the price of me for coming to this sinful place, looking for charity. But he jeered at me."

He suddenly went into a frenzy of rage. He leaned forward, with his hat clutched between his knees, spat and then stamped on the ground with both feet several times in quick succession. He shook himself like a wet dog and cried in a loud voice that was hoarse with hysteria:

"He jeered at me. He threw dirt on my hat and jeered at me. He jeered at the poor blind man. My curse on him."

The last few stragglers were now passing through the gateway. They glanced at the enraged beggar without comprehension. Then they hurried up the slope, staring fixedly at the stands, around which the bookmakers were shouting frantically. The first race was about to run. The horses had already emerged from the paddock and they were cantering down the course past the stands. The other beggars, however, coming in a group to the rear of the stragglers, halted at the gateway. Having no interest in the race, they gathered about their blind colleague.

"What ails you, poor man?" the singing woman said to him. "Why are you shouting?"

The blind man ceased his tirade as soon as he was addressed. He made no answer for some time. The trembling of his body gradually subsided. His face became cunning. His sensitive ears shifted restlessly, trying to explain the voice. His forehead was furrowed.

"Who is that?" he said at length.

"Musha, you poor man," she said, "it's only a singing woman that heard you let out of you. So I'm asking you what ails you. Was it how some rascal robbed your begging bag?"

Again the blind man waited before making a reply. He was drawing in deep breaths through his nostrils, in the effort to recover his priestly dignity. He had gone into a rage when startled, just as a hedgehog raises his quills. Now that the danger had passed, he was masking his wild power. His head again became motionless like a statue, poised to one side, with oblong white slits for eyes. The only sign of his rage that remained was a slight twitching of his delicate nostrils.

"Indeed, nobody stole out of my bag," he said arrogantly,

"for there was nothing there to steal, only the penny I put there myself. It was how a man jeered at me, after throwing dirt on my hat. A wicked man. I put the curse of the blind on him."

"Arrah, sure it wasn't at you at all he shouted," said the black-haired young man with the accordion. "I saw the man doing a caper in front of you and he shouting. It was drunk he was. He did a caper in front of me, too, but he gave Dulcie a sixpenny piece. He meant no harm."

"He did, 'faith," said the musician's moll. "He put six-pence in the cap. He was grinning like a mad fellow, Lord save us."

"He jeered at me," the blind man insisted, "and he threw mud on my hat. I put my hat on the ground beside me, same as I always do. Now there's dirt all over it."

"You poor man," said the singing woman. "Give me the hat and I'll clean it for you. Ah! God help the blind."

The blind man let her take the hat and then he said:

"The blind have a great power given them by God. There's a great power in their curse."

The singing woman made the sign of the Cross on herself and began to clean the hat. The thin tipster went on one knee in front of the blind man and took the remainder of his little envelopes from the breast pocket of his jacket.

"Janey!" he said. "Sure it's no wonder there's dirt on it if you put it down in the puddle. That was a foolish thing to do. You shouldn't be sitting there at all. You were too near the stands. It's well known, at the races, that a begging man must keep away from where the bookmakers can be heard."

"Is it giving me advice you are?" cried the blind man in a tone of outraged pride. "Is it to me you are giving advice? To me, that's known all over the country?"

"Sure I meant no offence," said the tipster. "No need to be so touchy. In any case, I never saw you at the races before."

"Neither did you," said the blind man. "I never begged at races to this day. This is the first time I ever set foot in a place of this sort."

"And not a penny did you take for your trouble, poor man," said the singing woman. "That goes to show that there's truth in the old saying. Every beggar has his pitch."

"True for you," said the tipster, taking the slips of paper from the remainder of his little envelopes. "It's more likely he'd take pennies at a chapel gate than on a race-field."

"And cemeteries," said the blind man. "At a cemetery gate, on the day of a good funeral, I take a lot of money. But it's not often these days you get a good funeral, or even a middling one. Funerals are a thing of the past. Fairs used to be good, too, but they're getting worse every year. Nowadays, I'd starve only for the missions."

"The missions?" said the accordion player. "Why so?"

"I'll tell you," said the blind man. "It's the fear of death makes people help the blind. A blind man is halfway between this world and the next. So people are afraid of him, for fear he might put a curse on them. They think he knows the dark things beyond. That's why they are generous during missions. The priests that give the missions have a wonderful power of speech. There's one of them, so I'm told, that works himself into a fit. I follow him around the country wherever he goes. Oh! 'Faith, they are all good, the missioner priests. They put the fear of Hell into the people. They terrify the life out of them. The people come out of the chapel shaking with fright. There I am sitting, waiting for them. I wish them all a happy death. The poor creatures need a blessing and they in that state. They give me their last red penny. Oh! Missions are wonderful things, sure enough, praise be to God."

"Amen!" said the singing woman. "Here is your hat now. I cleaned it as well as I could."

"God bless you, woman," said the blind man.

As he took the hat from her, a great roar came from the stands.

"They're off," said the black-haired musician.

With his accordion strapped on his back, he climbed to the top of the stone wall. The tipster and several of the other beggars climbed up with him.

"What's that?" cried the blind man pettishly. "What's all the row about now?"

"The horses are running," said the singing woman. "Come on over here, Lizzie. I want you to go on an errand for me."

The child climbed down from the stone wall reluctantly and came over to her mother, who had a can in one hand and a paper parcel in the other. She handed the can to the child and said:

"Go on up to the tent there, the nearest one to you. Get that can filled with tea and hurry back. Tell them to sugar it well. Ask them to give it to you for the love of God, but if they refuse, here's the money."

She gave the child a number of coppers.

"All over the second hurdle," said the tipster on the wall. "A field of ten. All together in a bunch now. It will be a great race if they all stand up. There they go past the stands now."

The dull thunder of hooves mingled with the excited shouts of the people as the horses galloped between tall black railings past the crowded green-roofed stands. Then they disappeared into a hollow and only the bobbing caps of the jockeys were visible, as they wheeled outwards towards the back stretch. The shouting became a murmur.

"I shouldn't be here at all," said the blind man querulously.

"I was asking myself why you came," the singing woman said to him. "Will you have a slice of bread?"

She was now squatting on a stone beside him and she had

opened her parcel on her lap. There were six thick slices of griddle cake, covered with bloater paste, in the parcel. The blind man accepted the bread and thanked her.

"It was a dream I had last night," he said. "That made me come. I am staying this past year with a sister of mine that keeps a lodging-house. There were country people staying last night in the room next to mine. In town for the races they were. When I woke up out of my dream, I could hear them talking about the races and the money they were going to win at them. The wall was thin and I could hear every word they whispered to one another, about how they were going to make a lot of money. And then I remembered the dream. It was about making money as well. In the dream I was going to rise in the morning and go to a place I had never been before and I was to be given a lot of money."

Another roar from the crowd on the stands interrupted the blind man. A voice, that rose clear about the rest, shouted:

"The favourite is fallen."

"There are four of them down," said the tipster on the wall. "The race is spoiled now."

The running horses now stood out against the cloudy sky on the far side of the course. Their sleek and lordly bodies, mounted by jockeys dressed in garish silk, looked outlandish about the wild, stone-walled fields that were speckled with yellow gorse. The cold sunlight, curtained by the whitish clouds, gave an aspect of bleak winter to the April afternoon.

"So you came here on account of the dream," said the singing woman, "thinking you'd get lashin's of money."

"I could think of nowhere else I hadn't been," said the blind man. "Besides, there hasn't been a funeral or a mission for over a month. And since the end of Lent I take hardly anything at my pitch outside St. Augustine's Church. Oh! Woman dear, at this time of year, it's not of death people do

be thinking, but of joyful sin. At this time of year, woman,
lust is in people's blood."

The roar of the crowd reached its highest now as the race
came near its end. Even the beggars on the stone wall began
to shout. The singing woman jumped to her feet and waved
her arms towards a loose horse that came galloping down the
slope towards the gateway.

"Hi! Hi!" she cried. "Be off with you."

"What's that?" cried the blind man excitedly. "What's
this I hear coming?"

"It's a horse," cried the singing woman. "He'll run over
us. Be off with you."

The horse, fallen in the race, had leaped the wooden fence
that enclosed the track. Now it was galloping riderless, with
trailing reins, making for the paddock. Its neck was white
with foam on either side and there was a red gash on one of
its hind fetlocks. When it came near the gateway, it paused
for a moment and stared wildly, with its red nostrils opened
wide. Then it snorted and galloped away in the opposite direction.

"Great God!" said the blind man. "This is a terrible place.
The life is frightened out of me."

"Never mind," said the singing woman. "He's gone now."

She squatted down once more on her stone and munched
at her bread.

"Have you no one with you, poor man?" she said. "Neither
a dog, nor a child, nor anything at all but your stick? Did you
tap your way out here from the town all on your lonesome?"

"I didn't then," said the blind man. "My nephew, little
Johnny, came with me. He's up there in Flanagan's tent wash-
ing glasses. I came out on Flanagan's dray with him in the
early morning. I asked him to put me sitting in a good place.
They told me the rich people came in motor cars by the back
road around the hill and in through the main gate, but no

beggar man is allowed to pitch by the gate. So I chose this spot, seeing it is by a kind of gate as well. Little good it did me. Sure it's only jeers I got and dirt thrown at me."

"Eat up your bread," the singing woman said. "Sure you got the fresh air, anyway, and the day isn't spent yet."

The first race was now over and there was silence up above around the stands. The musician's girl jumped down from the wall and said:

"Are you coming up to the tents, Fred? You might play a few tunes before the next race."

"Devil a tune," the musician said. "My fingers are numb from playing for four hours at a stretch."

He sat down on top of the wall and took a packet of cigarettes from his pocket. He gave a cigarette to the tipster who sat down beside him on the wall.

"You're right," said the tipster. "There's no use going among the tents until the fourth or fifth race. Then the people have a good sup taken and there's money to be cadged. Let us rest awhile here. I'm hoarse with the shouting myself."

The child came running back with a can of tea.

"They gave it to me for the love of God," she said to her mother. "I cried and said I was hungry and then the man told the woman to give it to me for the love of God. Can I keep one of the pennies for sweets, mammy?"

"The blessing of God on you," said her mother. "Indeed, then, you can keep one of them. It's well to reward the clever. Give me the rest of the money."

The child gave her mother all the coppers except one. She was running back to the tents with the remaining penny when her mother recalled her and gave her a slice of the griddle cake. She took the slice and began to eat it as she ran through the gateway.

"Hurry back," the singing woman said, "and you'll get a sup of tea."

She poured some of the tea on to the lid of the can and gave it to the blind man, who was now eating his bread with relish. In the calm following the race he looked much more at ease.

"Thank you, ma'am," he said as she put the lid into his hand. "It gives a man courage to find a woman like you in such a place as this. That goes to show how wrong a person can be in his judgments. I always thought people that went to races were sinners against the Holy Ghost. But it appears they are kinder than church beggars. Now you'd think church beggars would be holy people, wouldn't you?"

" 'Faith, you would," said the singing woman, "and they perched near the house of God. And aren't they?"

"They hate the living sight of one another," said the blind man passionately. "They wouldn't lend you the heat of their breath and you frozen."

"Is that so?" said the singing woman. "Have a sup out of the can, Dulcie."

She offered the can to the musician's girl, who was sitting on the ground near by. The girl took the can and said:

"Thank you, Mary. I'll just take one hot slug to keep me going 'till we go to the tents."

"Drink away, darling," said the singing woman. "Don't spare it."

The blind man lowered his head to sip at his lid of tea. As he did so, his faintly coloured pupils became visible. Then he smacked his lips and raised his head once more. The pupils disappeared.

"I never made a friend among them," he said. "A cripple nearly killed me once with a blow of his crutch, when I butted in on his pitch outside St. Mary's Church."

The two women uttered an exclamation. The musician and the tipster leaned forward to listen on the wall. The blind man realised that he was attracting general attention.

His manner became still more arrogant and he raised his voice as he continued.

"I was within my rights," he said, "for it was during a mission and it's well known that missions are open to all beggars, big and little, like fairs and funerals. But this cripple was a ferocious man that broke all rules. He used to be a fancy man in a bad house before he became a cripple."

All the other beggars now gathered round the blind man in a half-circle. So he paused and took a sip of tea in order to heighten the dramatic interest in his story.

"He came on me all of a sudden," he continued after his pause. "He gave me a clout of his crutch right across the nape of the neck. It would have killed many a man. Then he struck me a worse blow on the side of the head. That nearly did for me. Lucky for me, though, he lost his balance and followed after the blow and I got my hands on him. That was the ruin of him, for I gave him the hug and he had to be carried away between hands when they separated us."

"Aw!" said the singing woman, deeply impressed. "There's great power in a blind man's hug."

"So I've heard," said the tipster.

The blind man put the lid on the ground and then got to his feet.

He stretched out his arms in front of him and then doubled them, with his fists clenched. His biceps rose up powerfully against the black cloth of his overcoat sleeves.

"Feel that muscle," he cried proudly. "Feel my chest as well."

He expanded his chest and then struck it two mighty blows with both fists simultaneously. The chest resounded like a big drum that is struck. Then he bent his arms once more and shook his clenched fists.

"Believe it or not," he cried, "there isn't a stronger man in the county than me. Come and feel me, good people, if ye doubt my word. Let any man among ye try to move me from my standing."

"I believe you," said the singing woman. "You have the neck and chest of a strong man. What God took with one hand he gave to you with the other."

The blind man grunted with satisfaction, sat down on his block of stone and again poised his head a little to one side like a statue. He relapsed into a dignified silence, sitting very erect, with his hat in one hand and the other hand on the crook of his yellow stick.

The other beggars began to chatter about the strength of blind men.

"They have to be blind from birth," the tipster said. "Otherwise they're not strong."

Their chatter was interrupted by the tall man who had shouted and waved his stick on the way to the stands. He was coming down between the two lines of tents that stretched along the slope from the iron rails by the stands. He was again shouting and waving his stick. His overcoat was unbuttoned and he had his hat on sideways. He held his stick by the middle in one hand. In the other hand he had a bottle. The neck of a second bottle was sticking from his overcoat pocket. People were whistling after him and laughing. A group of children ran beside him and in front. They were begging for pennies. He was grinning from ear to ear and there was froth at his lips.

The blind man cocked his ears as soon as he heard the shouting. His face contorted.

"That's the man that jeered at me," he said. "He's coming again."

The singing woman got to her feet and looked over the wall.

"Take it easy now," she said to the blind man. "He means no harm. He's just a drunken man."

"Let him watch out for himself," cried the blind man angrily.

He was beginning to tremble. He tapped the ground nervously with his stick.

"Ha! There he is," cried the tall man exultantly, as he reached the gateway. "There is my good angel. There is my darling blind man. I could kiss him with love. Hold these for me."

He handed his stick and the bottle to the singing woman.

"Who are you?" cried the blind man. "What do you want? I'm warning you now to be careful. You're dealing with a strong man. It's well for you to know that."

"Hold on there, friend," said the tall man as he opened the top buttons of his waistcoat. "Don't be afraid. It's good news I have for you. I came back to give you a present. It's a luck-penny you earned."

From the inside pocket of his waistcoat he took a large bundle of greasy notes. He wetted his thumb and removed one of the notes. He paused as he was about to remove another note.

"One moment," he said. "Is your name Barney, by any chance?"

"Indeed, it's not," said the blind man indignantly. "My name is Paddy Kerrigan. And what is it to you? Is it making a fool of me you are?"

The tall man uttered a yell of triumph, turned to the crowd of beggars and began to gesticulate.

"I knew it," he cried. "I wouldn't ask him his name, for fear it wouldn't be Barney. I turned back and went over to him, intending to ask him his first name as soon as he'd finished talking, but I changed my mind. It was enough, in any case, that he was a blind man. I never saw one before on a racecourse. So what difference did it make whether he was Paddy or Barney?"

253

Then he turned once more to the blind man and said:

"Hold out your hand now. Here's your luckpenny and may you enjoy it."

The blind man had become terribly excited on hearing the crinkling of the paper money. He held out his hand eagerly and said:

"What's this? What's happening at all?"

"One," said the tall man, putting a note into the blind man's palm. "Two, three, four, five. There's five pounds for you now. Easy come, easy go. It only happens once a year. I'm Furlong, the butcher. I have my skite once a year. Huroo!"

He yelled again and then gave a pound note to the singing woman. He gave a note to the musician and another one to the tipster. He was going to give one to the musician's girl, but the whole crowd of beggars rushed at him and he backed up to the wall, clutching his wad against his bosom.

"Will ye keep back from me?" he cried. "Keep back or I'll give ye nothing at all."

Clutching the wad of notes firmly in his left hand, he put his right hand in his trousers pocket and pulled out a great number of silver coins. He hurled them into the air. The beggars dived for the coins and began to fight, screaming at one another. Another race had now begun and there was great shouting up above, but that noise was trivial compared to the tumult of the struggling beggars. The tall man, freed from the importunity of the beggars, went on one knee and stowed his wad of notes into the inside pocket of his waistcoat.

"One, two, three . . ."

Over and over again, the blind man counted the wrinkled notes that had been put into his hand. He was trembling with joy.

"I took a hundred pounds to eight about Blind Barney," said the tall man, addressing no one in particular. "Then I came down off the stands at the last moment and took another hundred pounds to six about him. Two hundred pounds I won on an animal that didn't have the ghost of a chance only for the others falling. I had no notion of backing him either, although he belongs to a friend of mine, until I saw the blind lad at the gate. A thing like this happens only once in a lifetime. Give me that bottle."

He took the bottle from the singing woman and began to open it.

"So my dream came true after all," said the blind man in a voice that was broken with emotion.

He had rolled up the notes very small. He had opened his clothes at his chest and he was putting the rolled notes into a little bag that hung around his neck on a string.

"I declare to God," said the singing woman, "it's true. You told me about the dream you had. Little I thought there would be any truth in it."

"What dream?" said the tall man. "Here. Take a slug of this."

The blind man accepted the bottle of whisky and said with great feeling:

"May God bless you, sir. I dreamt I would meet you here and that you'd give me a lot of money. It was God sent me here, after all. It was God sent you, too. I wish you a happy death."

"Amen to that," said the singing woman.

"God bless you, sir," said the tipster.

A number of the other beggars, those who had been successful in the scrimmage, added their voices to the blessing. Those who had got nothing were still begging querulously in subdued tones.

"That be damned," said the tall man, taking the second bottle of whisky from his overcoat pocket. "This is no time for praying. Let us drink up and be merry. I'm on a skite.

This only happens once a year. I'm Furlong, the butcher. Huroo!"

The blind man put the bottle to his lips, threw back his head and drank deeply.

"Ha!" he said. "That's wonderful."

His face beamed with satisfaction. He offered the bottle to the tall man.

"Keep it all," said the latter. "You deserve it and more. Here's luck."

He put the second bottle to his lips and drank. Then he gave a drink to the musician. The black-haired young man took a long swig and passed the bottle to the tipster.

"Strike up a tune for me before I go," said the tall man. "I'm on a skite. I'm Furlong, the butcher. I go on a skite once a year. Strike up a hornpipe for me."

The musician swung his instrument around from his back, rubbed his palms together smartly and began to play a hornpipe. The tall man yelled and began to dance clumsily.

"Music!" said the blind man, tapping the ground with the balls of his feet in time with the tune. "Oh! Merciful God! Do you hear the loveliness of it? Who would think there was so much joy on the field of sin?"

The singing woman took the bottle from the tipster and drank. Then she put her fists to her hips and tripped out to dance in front of the tall man. The bottle went from mouth to mouth among the other beggars.

"Huroo!" yelled the tall man.

He danced with his head thrown back, unsteady on his feet, holding his blackthorn stick by the middle. His grey overcoat was unbuttoned. His hat was on sideways. His brick-red face perspired. His buck teeth were widely exposed in a grin.

The blind man drank again and then leaned back against the wall, breathing deeply. His face no longer bore a tortured expression. It beamed with happiness. His beautiful ears had ceased their constant vigil. They only heard the sweet notes of music and the hilarious shouts of the beggars.

"It was God sent me," he murmured. "It was my guardian angel whispered to me in my sleep, telling me to rise up and go among these good people that are carousing. Black, hungry winter is no more and the son of man is dancing on the grass. Oh! Merciful God! Give a happy death to all sinners. I take back all my curses. I forgive all that did me wrong. Let my joy be everywhere."

Once again he put the bottle to his lips and took a long drink. His lips parted. His head sagged a little. His faint pupils appeared.

"Huroo!" yelled the tall man at the end of a bar.

He stopped dancing, struck his hat a blow with his fist, raised his stick and cried:

"Three cheers for Furlong, the butcher. Hip! Hip!"

"Hurrah!" cried the beggars.

When the cheering was finished, the tall man came over, put his arms around the blind beggar's neck and kissed him on both cheeks.

"Goodbye now," he said, "and in your prayers remember Furlong, the butcher. Goodbye now. Huroo!"

Waving his stick and grinning from ear to ear, he again set off through the gateway at a run, going up the slope towards the stands. Like a pack of dogs giving chase, the crowd of beggars ran after him. Men, women and children followed close at his heels, asking God to bless him for what he had given, begging him to give more in God's name.

The blind man was again alone on his block of stone by the gateway.

For several minutes he prayed aloud for his benefactor in a maudlin tone. Then he paused for breath, put the bottle to his lips and took a sip of whisky. He shook himself after drinking and listened. The shouting of the beggars was lost in the tumult of the racecourse. The third race was about to begin. The horses had issued from the paddock and they were cantering past the stands on their way to the post. The book-makers were shouting at the top of their voices. That noise was distant. Near by there was silence.

He started on becoming aware of this silence. He sat erect on his stone, raised his head and poised it a little to one side. His face assumed an expression of priestly arrogance. Clutching the bottle by the neck, he held it towards the gateway and began to intone:

"I wish you all a happy death. None of you knows the hour . . ."

Galway Bay

HE OLD MAN raised his stick and cursed towards the islands that were becoming round and blue on the horizon. Something flashed in the sunlight, like an enormous diamond, on the island farthest to the west. The old man thought it was an eye threatening him.

"May you die without Extreme Unction," he cried. "Wink, you devil, for all the good it will do you. I have the power now."

Then he leaned on his stick and stared at the round, blue mound that was settling down into the whitish sea on the horizon, like a hen on a nest. The diamond ceased to flash as the sunlight turned yellow, throwing a broad, shimmering mantle over the rocky isles that began to fade from view.

"By Brasil!" cried a tourist dressed in brown knickerbockers. "The land of youth! The island of saints and scholars! No wonder we are a race of poets with such a galaxy of beauty. Look at that sky over the islands."

He pointed towards them with one hand as he gripped his wife's arm with the other. The old man stared at the couple of tourists with contempt. Then he walked over to them and tapped the husband on the thigh with the ferrule of his stick.

"Little you know," he said, "what goes on there. If you did, you wouldn't talk that way. There's persecution there. I'm a persecuted man."

The tourists stared at the old man, smiling timidly. He looked mad. They drew away from him.

He shook his stick once more at the western island and cried: "I have the power now, though. I escaped from ye."

Then he bent almost double, put both hands on top of his stick and stuck out his tongue at the island. Although the little steamer moved on a perfectly level keel through the calm water, he stood with legs wide apart on the deck, swaying to an imaginary heaving, after the manner of an old seaman.

He was eighty years old. Never a large man, he had almost dwindled to the size of a dwarf. It was a warm evening in early autumn, yet he wore several layers of heavy frieze clothes. His shrivelled head protruded from these layers of clothes like the head of a turtle. His fleshless hands were like claws. His face was the colour of old parchment, all except his eyes and his lips. His lips were still rose-coloured, very pale and delicate. With his lips drawn back in an angry grin, two rows of perfectly even little teeth were exposed. He had not lost a single tooth. Nor had his eyes lost any of their power. They were of a wild blue colour, without feeling, cruel, like the eyes of a captured hawk. Unwillingly, they were being captured by approaching death, while still in their prime. They had gathered into their shining globes all the wisdom and cunning of a long life. Indeed, as he crouched there on the deck, with his tongue stuck out towards the island, swaying, he was very like a disabled bird, spitting at its captors; with nothing left to defend him but his wise eyes and his lashing tongue.

"What ails you now, Tom?" said a tall, handsome man in a blue suit, striding towards him across the deck. "Why don't you quieten down?"

The old man straightened himself and looked at the newcomer. He took a little quick step to one side and then shielded his eyes with his hand, pretending to be unable to recognise the speaker. He wore a new black hat with a wide brim. The hat was attached under his chin by a cord like a schoolgirl. He walked around the other man twice, taking sudden little steps and peering from behind his hand. He moved with astonishing quickness and vigour for one of his age, especially as he was wearing heavy, hobnailed shoes that were several sizes too large for him.

"You old rascal," said the other, "you are pretending you don't know me, are you? Only for I'm a kind man and I pity your age, you'd be in the Black Hole now, instead of being on the steamer going to Galway with your cow."

The old man came to a halt and struck the deck with his stick.

"Ha!" he cried. "I'd be in the Black Hole, would I? I dare and double dare you, Sergeant Toomey."

He put his stick under his arm, spat on his palms and then squared himself to box.

"Come on now," he said, "until we see which of us will take the sway with him. You're in plain clothes now, so you haven't the law behind you. Ha! You don't want to fight? You're afraid of me? I knew you were a coward."

The sergeant put his hands behind his back and laughed uncomfortably. A little crowd gathered on the deck to watch the scene. All the people were laughing.

" 'Faith, he has you cornered now, sure enough," said a thin cattle-jobber, wearing spectacles and carrying a fawn raincoat over his shoulder. "Look out for yourself, sergeant."

The old man spat on the deck at the sergeant's feet contemptuously. Then he moved towards the people and addressed them.

"Huh!" he said. "They have fine courage when they have their uniforms on them, but it's little courage they have otherwise. What do we island men care about the Civic Guards? We didn't care about the English peelers in the old days and we care less about De Valera's Civic Guards. We are free men. All this belongs to us."

Here he stretched out his arms and waved them, back and forth, in a circle. The steamer was coming abreast of the Black Head and the great circular bastion rose majestically to starboard in terraces of grey stone that were slashed with the gold of the declining sun. Away in the boat's wake, beyond the low-lying Clare coastland, the giant cliffs of Moher stood out against the horizon, their sheer faces made purple by the distance. To the west of the cliffs, the islands now looked like a spear lying in the sea, a long, thin frontier on the horizon. To port lay the Connemara shore, flanking the smooth water of the lordly bay. Beyond the shore, the mountains ran undulating to the west, where their shapes mingled with the ocean and were lost to view. A fleet of boats with dark brown sails were crossing the bay, going towards Connemara. They glided over the sea like butterflies, seemingly without substance or weight, graceful like poems, tacking in unison, seeking the scarce wind. Now and again a black prow, rising to a puff of wind, flashed silver and shimmered in the sunlight.

"All this belongs to us," cried the old man arrogantly, "to us, true men of the west. We are a breed by ourselves. We are people of the islands and of all the land that does border on the western sea. We want no foreigners to come interfering with us, putting laws around our necks, like you put a spancel on a wicked goat. We have the spunk in us and we'll take the sway from all comers. We are a breed on our own."

He stamped on the deck with his right foot and then cracked his right thumb and forefinger in the direction of the sergeant.

"Bravo!" said the tourist in knickerbockers. "We want men of that spirit. A wonderful race! A race of poets and warriors!"

The old man now marched around in a circle, crouching, shadow-boxing, sticking out his tongue, snarling, muttering to himself; just like a disabled hawk, glaring and fluttering impotent wings at its captors.

The cattle-jobber went over to the sergeant, who was leaning against the rail.

"What ails the old devil?" the jobber said. "Is he mad?"

"Partly," said the sergeant. "But he's not mad enough to be certified. At the moment, it's how he has a drop taken and he's excited over a row he had with his daughter and his son-in-law."

"That so?" said the jobber. "I noticed some kind of a row on the pier when the cattle were being loaded. Where is he going now? A man of his age shouldn't be let canter about like that."

"It's like this," said the sergeant. "All his children went to America and then the youngest daughter came home again when his wife died last year. He had a fourth and a half of land, which he made over to the daughter on her marriage to a young man of their village. The old devil was smart enough with the agreement he made, for he didn't make over the stock with the land."

"So the row was over the stock?" said the jobber. "It's often the case. The old codger hung on to the stock?"

"He did," said the sergeant. "In any case, there was only a cow and a few sheep and the cow was a stripper. The young couple bought a heifer and they wanted to sell the cow, but the old man took her from them and drove her to the fair himself. The daughter tried to stop him. She wanted me to arrest him, but I wouldn't. The cow belongs to him by law. He's entitled to do what he likes with her."

"So he's taking her to Galway," said the jobber. "More power to him."

"Yes," said the sergeant. "You have to admire him and he eighty."

The old man had now gone into a corner by the rails and sat down on the deck. He pulled up his grey frieze trousers above his knees. He had another pair of toursers underneath, of clean white flannel, just as heavy as the outside ones. Long woollen stockings, embroidered at the tops, enclosed the legs of the white trousers, almost to the knee caps. Two pieces of twine acted as garters. He undid these garters, refastened them securely and pulled down the outer garment. Then he crossed his little legs and took off his hat, which he placed upside down on his lap. He took a plug of tobacco and a knife from his pocket. He began to pare the tobacco on to his palm over the hat.

The cattle-jobber approached and went on one knee before the old man. He doubled his raincoat over his other knee and crossed his arms on the coat. The old man stopped paring the tobacco and stared malignantly at the jobber, with his head to one side, like a suspicious bird.

"Good day to you, my good man," said the jobber. "I hear you have a cow to sell. Maybe we could make a bargain."

"You're Timoney, the jobber," said the old man. "I know you."

"I'm well known," the jobber said, "like a bad penny. I suppose I bought many a beast from you in your day. It's hard for me to remember all the faces I meet."

"You needn't trouble yourself trying to remember my

face, then," said the old man. "I never sold a beast to kedgers.
I always went to the fair green of Galway with whatever I
had to sell. Even so, if you had much of a memory, you would
have heard of old Tom, the pilot. Maybe you're not much of
a man at all, but just a thin, lanky galoot of a man that thinks
he can take a rise out of the old, in order to shorten a journey.
Be off with you, skinny face, you with your pair of spectacles."

He spat viciously on the deck, right beside the jobber's
bended knee. The latter rose to his feet smartly.

"Devil take you, then, for a bad-mannered old codger,"
he cried angrily. "I was only trying to buy your beast, bad
cess to you."

He walked away. The old man stuck his tongue out after
him. A well-dressed young man, with a beautiful body and
eyes that were as blue as the sea, now came over and sat on
his heels in front of the old man. His curly fair head was
bare.

"Don't be bringing shame on yourself and on the island,"
he said, "by talking that way to a stranger and he only making
you a civil offer. What ails you at all?"

The old man took a new pipe from his waistcoat pocket
and sucked at it. Then he stuffed the tobacco from his palm
into the bowl, while he peered in silence at the young man.
Now his eyes were soft and tender. He scraped around the
bowl of his hat, to see if any of the pared tobacco had fallen
into it.

"You're from the village next to me," he said gently, in a
low whisper, to the young man. "I know your father."

"And why wouldn't you?" said the young man. "If you
don't, it's mad you are and my father your third cousin."

The old man returned his hat to his head and put the strap
under his chin. The grey hair still grew on his head as thick
as sea moss on a rock in April. Then he put his pipe in his
mouth and asked the young man for a match.

"I know all your people," he said. "They are all good people, my treasure, except your Uncle Tony. He's only a middling man, although he can row as well as the next. But he does be seasick in rough weather. Neither is he a good man with a horse on the strand at seaweed time. It takes a good man in the icy weather to manage a horse. Your father is a good man with a horse and with the land, too. Why are you dressed like a foreigner? Are you going to America, my pulse?"

"I work in a shop in Galway," said the young man in a shame-faced tone.

"God help you!" said the old man, lighting his pipe. "That's a poor way for your father's son to be, on a neighbour's floor, at the beck and call of people that are not of your kind. Anyway, blood of my blood, come down below with me and I'll give you a glass of whisky."

He got to his feet and took a pull at his knitted waist belt. It was all the colours of the rainbow. He looked very tidy in his blue frieze over-shirt, embroidered at the throat and at the wrists, with white bone buttons down the front, and his sleeveless waistcoat, with grey and black checks in front and white at the back.

The young man now looked very much ashamed, either of his mainland clothes and the old man's consequent contempt, or of the attention which he was attracting in the old man's boisterous company.

"I'm obliged to you for the offer," he said, "but I don't drink. Anyway, I think you have taken enough yourself already. Why don't you sit quiet and not be making a show of yourself before strangers?"

The look of tenderness now faded from the old man's eyes. They again became cruel and devoid of feeling. The young man had become a stranger to him; an outcast.

"I thought as much," he said contemptuously. "They soon

took the spunk out of you in the town. Be off with you, she guts. Get a piece of sugar-stick and a rattler. Wipe your nose on your sleeve, you gelding."

He spat on his stick and walked aft towards the starboard lifeboat which lay alongside the engine-room hatch. He was very bow-legged. Owing to the size of his shoes, he had to walk as if he were pulling his feet out of a bog. There was a woman sitting in the stern of the lifeboat. He shouted to her.

"What are you doing there, Mary?" he said. "You look as if you were hatching? It's long past hatching age you are, I'm thinking."

The woman made a gesture as if she were throwing something, and laughed at the top of her voice, musically. She was about fifty, but she still looked very handsome, with a long pale face and straight light-golden hair that showed above the cowl of her grey cashmere shawl. She wore a richly dyed, picked-out red skirt, with a black velvet flounce. She was surrounded by bags of wool in the boat and she did give the impression that she was hatching.

"Bad scran to you, Tom," she said merrily. "It's you have the poisoned tongue that wouldn't say a word of praise to save the dying. Too old, am I?"

Hereupon she and the old man began a rapid interchange of pretended insults, using such natural expressions that a schoolmistress, who sat near by with her three little children, took umbrage. She rose and took her children to a distance.

"There now," said the golden-haired woman, pushing the old man's chest playfully. "You made me give scandal to that lady and her children. Shame on you."

"Huh!" said the old man. "The scandal is in their hearts. They are not of our breed, Mary. If they were, they'd know there's no scandal where there's no evil."

"Maybe you're right, Tom," said the woman. "What's

taking you to Galway in this foolish way with your cow? I'm sorry to see you fighting your daughter and she after coming from America to look after you."

At this the old man flew into a temper once more. He stamped on the deck. His eyes looked mad and he seemed to be unaware of the golden-haired woman's presence, for he proceeded to address the sea with his stick raised shoulder high.

"She didn't come from America to look after me," he cried, "but to look after the land. I don't need her to look after me. I can look after myself as long as God gives me breath. Ah! Woe! My two fine sons are dead in America and I am left only with female things of my blood. This female thing that came back to me had to bring a man into my house. Now there's a stranger tilling my sod and he trying to have the power over me. No man will have the power over me. I took my cow and I'll sell her. I'll stand on the fair green of Galway and I'll bargain, same as I always did. I gave them the use of the sod, so it wouldn't go wild without being tilled, or wither for want of manure and I not able to tend it any more, but I kept the power. I'll have sport in Galway and then I'll come back with money for my coffin and my funeral and for a Mass to be said for my soul."

"God forgive you, poor man," the golden-haired woman said, "and you struggling with the devil at your age, instead of living peaceful and forgiving, resting gently in the corner of your daughter's hearth."

"It's my hearth as long as I live," shouted the old man, stamping his feet. "Eternal misfortune on you, woman, for siding with persecution."

He walked away forward, brandishing his stick, while the golden-haired woman made the sign of the Cross to ward off his curse. A crowd of young tourists from Dublin came up the companion-way just then from the saloon, where they had been drinking. One of the tourists, a wild young woman wearing trousers and a yellow sweater, had a camera. The group rushed over to the old man and gathered round him, shouting and laughing, led by the young woman with the camera.

"I want to take your picture," she shouted to the old man. "Let you all stand near him and pretend to be listening to him telling a story, while he's pointing his stick at you. Old man, stand here and be pointing your stick at these people, just as if you were telling them a story. You look like a story-teller. I'll get the picture in the paper and send you one."

The old man snarled and rushed at her with his stick raised. She uttered a cry of fright, dashed away from him and caught the arm of a young man to whom she clung.

"Shame on you, sinful woman," shouted the old man savagely, "going around like you are, dressed in trousers, without good manners or respect for the old. If you were my daughter I'd lay a whip to your back and throw you on to the road, for there is the only life fit for you."

The mate came up and pushed the old man. He was short and bow-legged, with a hooked nose and heavy moustaches.

"Be off now, Tom," he said gaily. "Don't be annoying the passengers."

The old man stuck out his tongue at the mate and went forward muttering to himself.

"Who is he?" one of the young tourists said to the mate.

"Tom O'Donnell is his name," the mate said. "He used to be a pilot in the old days of sailing vessels. There is no man knows this bay better than he does. He is touched in the head now, though."

"I think he's a horrid old man," said the girl with the camera.

269

"Maybe you won't be good-tempered yourself when you are eighty," said the mate. "You should make allowances for the old."

"Eighty!" said the young man. "Impossible! He can be no more than seventy."

"I'm over seventy," said the mate with a laugh. "I'm from the islands. We are a different breed."

He uttered the last sentence in a loud, arrogant tone, as he ran down the short companion-way that led to the after-deck.

"Oh! God of mercy," the old man muttered as he went forward, "let me die with my strength."

Now his face looked tortured. He no longer looked like a wounded hawk. His blue eyes were mild and wandering.

"Let me die on my feet in the sunlight," he muttered. "Don't let me become a mockery for the wicked and the senseless. Leave me with my strength until I die."

He went and leaned over the forward rail and looked down into the hold through the uncovered hatchway. A dozen foals and his own cow were down there. They stood together in a compact group on the iron floor. The sun was now beginning to set. Its light poured down slantwise into the hold, gilding the rusty iron of the walls and the backs of the animals. The sun's shadows shifted with the movement of the boat, moving back and forth over the animals, as if a loving, merciful spirit were drawing a golden cloak, caressingly, over them, to cheer their captivity.

The old man was so small that his chin barely reached the top of the rail. He had to put his hands on the rail and strain his back in order to look down at the animals. He began to make inarticulate sounds, beating his tongue against the roof of his mouth. They had been standing with drooping heads, without movement, but they raised their heads and moved their ears forward on hearing the old man's voice. One of the foals whinnied. He began to tap the iron deck, stepping backwards, making sharp, wooden sounds with his unshod hooves. Suddenly, as he moved backwards, his hind hoof struck a loose iron bar that lay on the deck. He struck one end and the other end was levered into the air. It fell back again with a loud, ringing sound that re-echoed through the hold.

Immediately, the foals and the cow ran about excitedly, snorting in terror. The old man now raised his voice and spoke to them articulately.

"Don't be afraid, ye lovely things," he cried. "Preoil! Ye silken lovely things. There's no harm coming to ye. Old woman, you should have more sense than to be capering with young foals. Be sensible, old cow. Stand still there and be easy. Preoil, ye lovely darlings."

The foals grew calm once more and stood together in a compact group. The cow now stood a little in front of them, with her head thrust forward anxiously. Her flanks heaved. A long wisp of foam reached from her lower jaw to the deck. One of the foals arched his glossy black tail above his dark brown back, thrust forth his tapering graceful neck and smelt the cow's red flank. The flank shuddered. The foal hurriedly withdrew his neck and arched it stiffly, staring with distended nostrils. The cow swung her head and licked her flank savagely. The wisp of froth leaped from her jaw on to the foal's back. The foal shuddered all over his body.

"Ah! Ye lovely creatures," cried the old man tenderly. "I pity ye down there, instead of being running in the lovely little glens where the grass is sweet. Ah! They'll put a halter on ye now and make ye carry loads. Or maybe it's lovely ladies ye'll be carrying on your backs. God bless ye, anyway, for ye are lovely things. But you, my poor old woman, what in the name of God is going to become of you? You are like myself now, without home or company. God bless ye. God bless ye."

He made the sign of the Cross over the animals and turned away. The steamer was now approaching the town. On either side, the long arms of the bay drew near. The land assumed shape and colour. The dying sunlight still shone faintly on the yellow houses and the russet autumn woods of Barna. Straight ahead, the ancient town was still a grey mass, covered with a soft dreamy light, as if it lay in sleep. A multitude of dark brown sails and little black hulks, Connemara boats, dotted the white water. A giant liner lay anchored ahead, the smoke from her painted funnels making an ugly stain on the clear sky, as it surged upwards uncleanly, in billowing waves, like the foul eruption from a wound. A beautiful yacht, outward bound, went sailing by them, all in white, like a bride on her honeymoon. She rode westwards, towards the horizon, where the globe of the setting sun was growing white as it sank into the sea.

"Hey! By the book!" cried the old man, clicking his teeth. "Oh! You lovely thing!"

He danced on the deck like a child and waved both hands towards the yacht. He tipped the wide flat brim of his black hat and dropped it a curtsy. All the passengers rushed over to the port rail to watch it pass, but the old man stood apart, a rapt expression on his face, standing tiptoe on the deck and straining, in order to see it. He bobbed his head from side to side and kept swallowing his breath with excess of pleasure.

The yacht began to change sail and tack as it dropped astern. The old man rushed aft a little way and began to shout commands excitedly. He drew on imaginary sails with his hands and then leaned far over, as if he were holding the helm of a careening boat. Then he straightened himself and sighed wearily, as the yacht eased away on her new course.

He went forward again, leaning on his stick, with one hand on the small of his back. The effort had tired him.

"Do you think we'll have enough water, Tom?" the captain shouted to him from the bridge.

He halted and looked up at the captain's laughing face on the bridge, a handsome, rosy face, with merry eyes, surmounted by grey hair and a uniform cap with a yellow badge in front. The old man crouched and shook himself like a wet dog. He made no reply. He went forward to the angle of the rail and leaned over it. His eyes now had the expression of a person that is lost. His madness had left him with the sun.

They passed the liner. A flock of gulls swooped about, devouring the offal that belched from her port-holes. The old man shuddered as he looked at her. Her size and strangeness terrified him. She belonged to the new breed of men that was destroying him and his kind. He walked away and became seized by another access of angry dotage. Now he moved about, crouching with his arms crossed over his breast, muttering prayers.

On the bridge the bell kept ringing. The steamer moved slowly, winding her way towards the dock. A tender passed, carrying passengers to the great ship. A jazz band was playing on her deck under an awning. People were dancing and singing. The town loomed up close to the steamer. At the water's edge lay the tall grey houses of the old Spanish town and beyond, the new town rose, bright and arrogant, like the new breed that was conquering the old.

The old man stopped moving about. He looked once more over the rail at the animals in the hold. They were barely visible in the twilight. Not a sound came from them. They also missed the sun. Its going deprived them of part of their life. It had been a link that bound them to their island. Tears came into the old man's eyes as he looked down at them. Now he repented of having quarrelled with his daughter and taken his cow. He felt lonely unto death.

The steamer docked. The animals were hoisted to the pier. Two lads on grey mares led away the foals. They ran after the mares in a compact group, up among the towering dark warehouses at which they snorted in terror. The tapping of their naked hooves was distinct from the sharp clatter of the shod mares.

The old man came after them with his red cow. The cow was almost as thin and decrepit as himself. Exhausted by her age and the journey, she walked quietly, indifferent to her strange environment.

He walked beside her with downcast head, one hand on her high hip-bone, the other leaning heavily on his stick.